No Business Being a Cop

No Business
Being a Cop

Lillian O'Donnell

G. P. PUTNAM'S SONS
NEW YORK

ISBN: 0-399-12276-1

No Business Being a Cop

ONE

If it had been up to Katie Chave she would have called in sick that morning. When she mentioned it to her husband, Loy gave her his cool, patient look and replied in that reasonable tone she'd grown to dread.

"I think you ought to try and make it, babe, if you possibly can."

She knew he wouldn't say any more, wouldn't reason, much less argue; he'd just become cooler, more polite, and very distant. Katie couldn't stand that. She would have preferred that he yell, even hit her. She sometimes fantasized about Loy's beating her; it would have shown he cared.

Katie Chave needed to be loved.

She craved admiration and attention but had no special talent with which to attract it. She tried to buy friendship by constantly giving gifts and favors, which embarrassed the recipients and placed them under irksome obligation. Anxious to be liked by all, Katie would never espouse an unpopular cause or go against the general consensus. If, on occasion, she did have an opinion of her own, she could be easily swerved from it. Pretty enough, with her short dark brown hair, dark eyes, and fine, rosy complexion, she would have been prettier if she could have lost twenty pounds and the perpetual droop of her lower lip.

Katie Chave was a cop and she didn't like her job.

Reluctantly, because she really didn't feel well, Katie swung her legs around and sat on the side of the bed. Her husband came over and sat beside her. "'Atta girl," he encouraged. "You don't want the sergeant to think you're calling in sick to protest the negotiations. You could get suspended. After all the trouble you went through to get your job back, that would be a damn shame."

Katie didn't care whether or not she got suspended; in fact, it would have suited her just fine. If she never saw the inside of a station house again, that would have been all right, too. Not only had the glamour of police work worn off, she couldn't remember why she'd ever wanted to be a cop in the first place. True, she had been proud when she got the appointment, but she knew better now. The hours were awful; she couldn't adjust to the constantly changing schedule, and she'd been refused a "hardship" tour of regular hours because the department didn't consider she had a hardship situation. But she did. It seemed to Katie Chave that she never saw Loy. She worried about what her husband was doing while she was on duty, particularly nights. Not that she suspected Loy of playing around—he had his own gas station and he was working hours as long and more arduous than hers to make a go of it. Still, she worried. She worried so much that when they were together she couldn't enjoy it. Yet, she'd managed to get pregnant. She thought it was a solution to her problem: she expected to quit right away. Loy talked her out of it.

"As it is, we need every cent you bring in. With the baby coming . . . well, you've just got to hang in there as long as you can, sweetie," Loy urged. "Think of the expense. Think of all the things the baby's going to need. Every month, every week, every day you can keep going is putting money in the kitty for him—or her. So do your best. Okay, babe?"

They never talked about what would happen after the baby came, but Katie had made up her mind. This time everybody had ganged up to make her go back to work. Not again. No way. After the baby came, she would stay home. Nobody, but nobody, not even Loy, could make her budge.

It was a beautiful September day—sun hot, breeze cool, sky vibrant blue seldom visible through city smog. There was a festive feeling in the air, Katie thought, as though people knew that this was one of summer's last dividends and they had better enjoy it before the long, cold winter closed in. It was just noon as she and her partner, Officer Guy Felcher, made their swing past the fountain at the Plaza Hotel. Office and store workers were seated along its wedding-cake tiers, eating, chatting, listening to the string trio of student musicians playing something classical. Some just raised their faces to the sun, eyes closed, smiling. Katie smiled, too. Her nausea had passed; the sector was quiet; she was almost beginning to enjoy being out.

The call came at 12:11 P.M.; bomb alarm at Gimbels East. Instantly Felcher activated the siren and swung the car east on Fifty-seventh Street, scattering shoppers, then went uptown on Park Avenue. By the time they turned again on Eighty-sixth traffic was being cleared from the area around the uptown branch of the famous department store; the street barricades were going up, and the evacuation was in full swing. They joined the line of patrol cars at the curb and reported to the sergeant. He sent them to the top floor to assist in rounding up stragglers.

On the fourth floor Officer Chave was dispatched to check out the dressing rooms of the lingerie department.

There were two sections—one near the elevators, the other on the far side of the floor, near the fire stairs. Katie checked the first section quickly; the curtains of each cubicle were pulled back and it took only a glance to see there was no one there. In the second section some of the curtains were closed. Katie called out, but no one answered. Nevertheless, she marched down the narrow aisle peering right and left into each tiny room. Her back was beginning to ache and her legs to grow heavy, but she kept on—whatever her faults, however she felt about the job, Katherine Chave was conscientious. She thought she'd come to the end of the section when she saw that the aisle bent like an L, and, turning that corner, she immediately spotted a figure standing just at the edge of the very last cubicle. The woman had on a pink negiligee and she appeared to be looking at herself in the mirror.

Katie frowned. How come she hadn't left with the others? "Ma'am?" Katie called out. "I'm a police officer, ma'am. Everybody has to get out of the store." She'd been warned not to mention the bomb in order to avoid panic but not to let anyone loiter, either. "There's no time to get dressed," she advised. "Just grab your coat and your pocketbook and come on."

The woman didn't respond. Was she deaf or something? Katie started down the aisle to get her.

The bomb exploded at 12:42 P.M.

* * *

There was a low moan from the crowd across the street as windows on the fourth floor were blown out and smoke—black smoke—billowed forth. They cringed, huddling together for protection. But nobody left.

Ray Verdeschi, riding the bomb wagon, heard the blast all the way over on Madison. "Damn," he muttered under his breath. "Wouldn't you know this would be the one that was for real?" A pulse twitched at his right temple. They'd wasted all morning on two other alarms—one at Macy's and the other at Korvette's. Both had turned out to be false, but they couldn't have known that, could they? Both stores had had to be evacuated and searched. While they were searching, the third warning had been phoned in to 911. What the hell! They couldn't be in three places at once, could they? Two, okay—not three. They didn't have the manpower. Go talk to the mayor about the cutbacks in police personnel; go talk to the commissioner; go talk to that joker up in the Bronx who said the department could use another ten percent of fat trimmed off!

Seeing the smoke spiraling out, Ray could only hope the store had been cleared. There'd been a rash of these department-store bombings in the last month. A couple of the devices had been found in time and transported up to Rodman's Neck for disarming; a couple had gone off, but they'd been of minor force— nobody got hurt: nuisances. This one was not in the nuisance class. Verdeschi's thin, sallow face broke into a series of violent twitches. He turned aside till he could pull his face together, till he could stop his hands from trembling. If there should be a second bomb inside, if they should have disarm it, that face and those hands would not betray Ray by the slightest tremor. However, the effort at control cost more each time, and each time the reaction took a heavier toll. Ray Verdeschi was twenty-three; he didn't need the scrawny mustache to make him look older.

Frank Quinn's job was to keep people moving. Amazing how once they got outside the door they stopped in their tracks, blocking those behind. Even when he managed to get them over to the other side of the street and behind the barricades, they loitered.

To watch the show. Quinn's small, neat mouth pursed in disapproval. Typical. Crowds always gathered at scenes of crimes and disasters, major and minor, waiting with ghoulish patience. What attracted them? Quinn had often asked himself. Didn't they have anything better to do with their time? God knew he wouldn't be standing around if he weren't paid for it. And where the hell was the bomb squad? Not that it mattered anymore. Now that the damn thing had gone off it would be up to the Arson guys to investigate. And where the hell were they?

"Sergeant?"

"What?" Quinn scowled. He didn't know the man; he wasn't on his squad.

"I can't find my partner. She ought to be back at the car. She isn't."

At first glance Quinn, with his tousled red hair, pudgy, freckled face, was a typical smiling Irishman—except that you'd have to wait a long time to get a smile from him. Francis Xavier Quinn believed in "facing facts." In other words, he saw the dark side of everything. He was twenty-eight years old, but his shoulders were already rounded by self-assumed burdens, and even the freckles which nature had intended to be cheerful, seemed like the scars of a long-ago illness. Occasionally, sharing a few beers with the guys in a tavern, Quinn might laugh at the jokes and even tell a few himself. Then his protuberant amber eyes would glow like an animal's in the dark. There was no light in them at this moment.

"Where did you see her last?"

Felcher swallowed. "Inside." As this did not satisfy the sergeant, Felcher was forced to be more specific. "On the fourth floor."

Quinn turned his back on the man without a word and stalked into the empty store.

He'd entered evacuated areas before and was no longer haunted by the eerie sense of men's creations continuing to function, to lead independent lives, after their masters had fled. There was nothing here that was unusual: the lights burned, somewhere a phone was ringing, the escalators slithered silently up and down Quinn headed for the elevators—all down on the main floor, doors open, apparently functional. He stepped into the nearest one, making no comment when Felcher jumped in after him as the doors started to close.

As the doors opened on the destruction of the fourth floor, the two men knew what had happened before they even stepped out. A single, confirming look passed between them. Then, together, Frank Quinn and Guy Felcher began to pick their way through the debris, past smashed counters, fallen beams, skirting shattered glass, as they moved toward the area of greatest damage, looking for the source of the explosion. Finally they reached the far side of the department, where the second section of dressing rooms had been. The dressing rooms were not there anymore. The flimsy wall-board separation was gone, the partitions demolished. Even a heavy metal fire door had been literally ripped out of a retaining wall by the force of the blast.

Quinn was the first to see the legs. They were sticking out from under the fire door—nylon-clad legs, feet without shoes. He didn't call to Felcher for help in lifting the heavy door. There was no use. Those legs would not move again. They were severed below the knees. He was standing in a pool of blood.

"Call Homicide," Quinn ordered.

He'd spotted a woman's handbag and for a long moment he stood staring at it. It could have been anybody's, a customer's dropped in panic as she fled, but somehow Quinn knew it was the victim's. At last he forced himself to walk over, stoop, and pick it up. Inside was the familiar police ID wallet. He opened it. Relief left him weak and the sweat trickled down his legs. It couldn't have been Mairead's. Mairead was on duty. Even if she hadn't been, she never shopped at Gimbels. He knew that, yet for one terrible moment he'd allowed himself to imagine . . .

Another elevator was coming up. The Bomb Squad for sure. Better late than never? Not this time. Not for . . . He looked for the name under the photograph: Officer Katherine Chave. It didn't ring a bell.

Sergeant Norah Mulcahaney slapped what her husband called the gumball machine to the roof of her Pinto and streaked across Central Park to the East Side. Nobody was going to claim credit for this one, Norah Mulcahaney thought grimly. Bombs had been popping all over town during the past weeks, and every nut and every terrorist organization had been falling all over each other to claim credit, to get the newspaper headlines and the TV coverage. Shortcut to notoriety. Free propaganda. Easy, no-risk, no-sweat way to make points with the public, with the big shots in government, and sometimes with their own leaders. Not this time, Norah thought, jaws clenched. Even the real bomber wouldn't want to be connected with this one, not when the lousy bomb had killed a police officer, and not just a police officer, but a woman. Though Norah hated to use the official designation, she did so now: police officer—female.

Once out of the park, with Eighty-sixth cleared of all traffic, Norah made it to the scene in minutes. With the bomb squad, fire and police departments on hand, it had turned into a super-spectacle. From the way the firemen were standing around, though, Norah judged the bomb had not been incendiary and they'd be leaving soon. The crowd, which by now included not merely the shoppers who had been evacuated but just about everybody in the neighborhood, had been contained. Official cars were pulling up singly and in groups, and when the word spread that a police officer had been killed, there would be a lot more. Men and women of every rank, on duty and off, from every precinct and every borough, would be arriving to offer help.

She parked, jumped out of the car, and—adjusting her handbag, which was weighed down by the .38 S and W inside—bounded across the sidewalk to the store's main entrance.

Tall as a fashion model but far from gaunt, Norah Mulcahaney Capretto was thirty-five and at her peak—in energy, confidence, skill, and looks. Though she never had considered herself pretty, and never would, Norah had learned how to set herself off to best advantage. Today she was wearing a well-tailored, light gray flannel pants suit, its severity flattering to her figure, the soft bow on the white blouse easing the blunt squareness of her chin. After wearing her dark hair short for a couple of years, Norah had let it grow back to shoulder length and she had it tied up with a turquoise scarf that emphasized the blue of her eyes. It didn't hurt to look good; it needn't interfere with efficiency. So Norah selected her clothes with care, put them on, and forgot about them. She paused for a moment so the guard could examine her ID.

"Okay, Sergeant. They just gave the all clear. She's on the fourth floor."

It took no more than a split second to note the nameplate under the man's shield. "Thanks, Officer Yates."

He responded. "Lousy shame it had to happen, Sergeant. I'm real sorry."

The death of a fellow officer touched them all, but Yates offered condolence as though the victim were a member of Norah's own family. And she was, Norah thought; she was a sister. She was also the first woman in the NYPD to be killed in the line of duty. Norah's blue eyes misted, but her jaw tightened.

Quinn scowled when he saw her get off the elevator. He'd never met Sergeant Mulcahaney, but he recognized her from her pictures—they'd been in the papers often enough. He'd also seen her at meetings of the Sergeants' Benevolent Association. There were only thirteen female sergeants in the entire department, so you could hardly miss them. Even if he hadn't recognized Mulcahaney, Quinn would have spotted her as a pro. For starters, a civilian would never have got into the building, but the main thing was that she looked as though she belonged. It was in her coolness as she surveyed the scene.

Quinn was also familiar with Sergeant Mulcahaney's record. She was one of the few police officers, barring the top brass, naturally, who had gained recognition outside the department. Not that she didn't deserve it. She'd come up fast and she'd come up by merit. She'd also had the breaks in a string of sensational cases. The public took note of her because the newspapers played up her exploits. And they played up her accomplishments, put her picture in the paper and all that, because she was a woman. He didn't hold the publicity against her; she didn't actively seek it. But she got it and she did profit by it and that wasn't fair. It only put women into competition with men, which as wrong, but gave women the edge. Mulcahaney was also married to a cop, a lieutenant, which didn't hurt, either. It all served to reinforce Quinn's belief that whether by reason of physical weakness or emotional instability or favoritism, women had no place on the force.

He was also aware that it was a matter of chance which detective sitting in a squad room caught a particular squeal; it was nevertheless unfortunate that a woman had caught this one. He wondered if Sergeant Mulcahaney had any idea what was in store for her.

"Hello, Sergeant Quinn." Norah greeted him with a friendly nod but without smiling. She looked around. "Where is she?"

Mollified because she knew his name, and also responding to his inbred instinct that a woman should be protected, Quinn stepped into her way. "Ah . . . a metal door fell right on top of the body, Sergeant. We're waiting for the photographers and the ME before we lift it."

"Right." She made to go past him.

"They ought to be here any minute." He blocked her again.

Norah was as tall as he; she could look him straight in the eye. "That bad?"

"Yeah."

He was trying to spare her and he meant well, Norah knew. She took a deep breath, exhaled slowly, then deliberately moved around Quinn.

"Sergeant . . ." Quinn called.

"Yes?"

What the Hell! he thought. If she had the stomach for it . . He shrugged. "It's up to you, Sergeant."

"No, Sergeant. It's part of the job."

He didn't like the answer and, Norah suddenly realized, he didn't like her, either. It pulled her up for a moment. Policewomen had not gained the acceptance in the department that the public thought they had. Discrimination was still practiced subtly and sometimes not so subtly. However, Norah felt she personally had established her own credentials as a detective and, particularly since she'd made sergeant, rarely ran into resistance anymore. When she did, as now, she ignored it; she'd learned it was the best way. So now, without further discussion, Norah strode past Quinn toward where she thought she would find the victim.

As she had no particular expertise regarding bombs, the devastation appeared to her to be pretty general. She did know that explosions were capricious, that they imitated the forces of nature, which could, for example, uproot a fifty-year-old tree and leave the rosebush beside it with petals untouched. She'd seen the aftermath of other explosions, but she'd never seen the victim of one. So, though she'd presented a calm exterior to Sergeant Quinn, she had qualms as she approached what she judged to be the epicenter of the blast. When she spotted the legs, it was all she could do to keep from crying out.

She'd read that the victims of explosions were often blown right out of their shoes, but at the actual sight of the stockinged feet and the shoes—black, low-heeled, sensible oxfords over to one side . . . Norah's eyes filled. She didn't care who saw—and that included Sergeant Quinn.

"Stand aside, lady. Make way for the experts."

Norah jumped, then recognized the voice of Pete Zizmor. Nobody else in the medical examiner's office brought that kind of irreverent exuberance to the scene. Forensic medicine was not only Peter Zizmor's job, it was his hobby. He considered that the ME's purview was not limited to performing autopsies but comprised scientific analysis and evaluation of the entire crime scene. He wanted police officers trained to gather scientific evidence, or at least to know enough not to disturb it. Zizmor gave talks to any group who invited him, illustrating his remarks with color slides that sent the queasy running out of the hall to the lavatory—though Zizmor continued to consider the slides absolutely innocuous. It was the assistant chief medical examiner's way of demonstrating that there was more to violence and death than appeared on the most lurid of TV shows and movies.

Even Zizmor's ebullience was tempered by what he now had to deal with. "Damned insensate bastards," he muttered as he got to work.

Flashbulbs popped as the photographers who had arrived with the assistant chief ME took shots from every angle. Then it was time to lift the metal door. Norah didn't turn aside, though she would have liked to. She stayed where she was and she looked. She didn't look long, but she looked thoroughly, fixing the image in her mind, making sure she didn't miss any detail, because she didn't want to have to look a second time.

"Any ID?" she asked when she could turn away. Frank Quinn handed her the policewoman's handbag and the ID wallet.

Norah skimmed over the particulars, then studied the photograph. Young, not particularly pretty, though you couldn't tell from these official photos—in her own, Norah looked as though she'd just been fished out of the river.

"Where's her partner?"

Quinn looked around. "Felcher?"

A big, beefy patrolman, six feet two and over two hundred pounds, a large part of it on his hips, waddled over.

"Sergeant Mulcahaney is from Homicide," Quinn informed Felcher, then pointedly removed himself.

"Yes, ma'am?" Felcher's blue uniform pants were shiny and bagging in the seat from thousands of hours of riding. His face, pale and sweaty, suggested more than ordinary nerves at having to make a report, even allowing for the present stress.

"You rode with Katherine Chave?" Norah asked.

"No, ma'am. I mean, yes, ma'am. What I mean is, we were riding together today, but she's not, she wasn't, my regular partner. He called in sick." Guy Felcher looked down.

"I see." They both knew there had been a rash of sick calls that morning and that they were a protest against the stalled contract negotiations.

Raising his eyes, Felcher pleaded his absent partner's cause. "He's gonna feel lousy when he finds out about this. Just lousy."

"Sick?"

Felcher looked sick himself.

"Okay. So when did you learn that Officer Chave would be riding with you today?"

"When I reported in. The duty sergeant told me."

"Not before?"

"No, ma'am."

"Had Officer Chave gone with you on other occasions?"

"No, ma'am."

Norah took a breath. He wouldn't lie about it; it was too easy to check. So it appeared that neither Felcher nor his regular partner could have known that Katherine Chave would be given the duty. Nor, apparently, could the bomber.

"Was your car specifically ordered to respond to the alarm?"

"No, ma'am. It was a general call."

So the bomber could not have known that Chave would be on patrol or that she would be responding.

"Who sent Chave up here?"

"The sergeant sent the two of us to join the team rounding up stragglers. We started at the top and worked down."

"How come she was left behind on the fourth floor?"

Felcher grimaced. The whole two hundred pounds of him quivered. "I sent Katie to check the dressing rooms. I figured . . . if there were any ladies still in there . . . without their clothes on . . . it would be better for Katie to look in. Otherwise, I would have gone myself. I wish I had." His eyes begged Norah to absolve him.

Matron duty, Norah thought, that's what it amounted to. Would the women ever shake loose of it? Under the circumstances, Felcher couldn't be faulted; he'd done the natural thing. She sighed. Terrible, the thing was terrible. To be killed in, say, a shoot-out would be tragic, but to go like this—without any reason, by blind mischance! Norah saw no way that the bomb could have been set in advance with the express purpose of murdering Katherine Chave. What was eating Felcher?

"Where were you when the bomb exploded?" she asked, groping.

"I kept calling Katie and telling her to hurry up. I kept yelling for her to come on. She called back 'Okay,' that she was just about through."

Now Norah caught an underlying current. "Exactly where were you when the bomb went off?"

He gulped. "On the fire stairs. There were so many people on the stairs you have no idea, Sergeant. A couple of the women were hysterical. They refused to budge. They stood on the landing screeching and blocking everybody behind them. I had my hands full. I had to get them moving. I thought Katie was right behind me."

"Where were you when the bomb went off?"

Every pore of the two hundred pounds oozed shame. "Just going out the side door to Lexington Avenue."

Norah said nothing.

"I thought she was right behind me. I swear I did. She started over. I saw her. But she must have gone back. She must have gone back for something."

"What?"

"I don't know." He groaned. "I have no idea."

According to Felcher, Katherine Chave had plenty of time to get away. If he was telling the truth, and at the moment Norah could see no reason for him to lie, then what had happened? Up to now the death appeared to be a tragic accident, the result of a string of coincidences, a matter of being in the wrong place at the wrong time. Certainly, Chave's luck had run out, for if she'd been even a few feet to the right—there, where the dummy in the pink negligee stood—the metal door would not have struck her.

A draft of air coming from one of the air-conditioning ducts ruffled the filmy folds of the negligee. The dummy looked so real —blond hair, soft and loose, dressed in that silky, fluttery pink gown, one arm extended to show off the butterfly cut of the sleeve. With the air current stirring the fabric, she seemed to be actually moving the arm, beckoning.

Norah gasped. Was that what Katherine Chave had seen and what she'd gone back for—the dummy?

Norah broke the news to the husband in person. Loy Chave was preoccupied with his own guilt. All he could talk about was that morning—how his wife hadn't wanted to go to work and how he'd insisted.

"I figured if she called in sick they might think it was part of the protest over the contract negotiations. I was afraid she might get suspended. She didn't have much more time before she'd have to stop working anyway and we needed every cent." At Norah's inquiring look, he added, "Katie was pregnant."

It was the first Norah had heard of it.

"She . . . we . . . decided she should keep on working as long as she could before putting in for maternity leave."

Norah sighed inwardly. The department was very generous with maternity leave, allowing a woman up to eighteen months—without pay.

"She wanted to stay home this morning, but I wouldn't let her," he moaned. "I sent her out to be killed. For a few lousy bucks."

Fate had put its hand on Katie Chave's shoulder and refused to let go, Norah thought. She would have liked to comfort Loy Chave, to tell him that his pregnant wife had used her life to save another. She couldn't. But she was not about to tell him that Katherine Chave had gone back for a department-store dummy, either. Right then, Norah decided it wasn't going into her report. It was only a guess, after all. Wasn't it more likely, in view of her condition, that Officer Chave had become ill during her search of the fourth floor and had taken a few moments to rest? Perhaps she had even fainted.

It would add to the burden of guilt that Loy Chave already carried, but from what Norah could sense, he owed her.

More than three thousand officers joined the mayor and the cardinal in paying last respects to Officer Katherine Chave, killed in the line of duty. Of that number four hundred were women and constituted nearly the entire female contingent of police, which numbered four hundred and thirteen. Over the weekend every one of them had visited the Astoria funeral home where the body reposed. Afterward, each one had contacted either the Policewomen's Endowment Association or Sergeant Norah Mulcahaney to offer help in tracking down the perpetrator. That included not only the rank-and-file women officers but the twelve sergeants, three lieutenants, one captain, and even the one deputy chief.

Unfortunately, there was nothing to be done. The bomb had been a crude affair made up of dynamite sticks tied together and hooked to an unsophisticated timing device. Arson detectives had canvassed the various sources for dynamite and had come up empty. Whatever other clues there might have been had been destroyed in the explosion. Officially, the case would be open until the bomber was apprehended. For all practical purposes, it was closed.

TWO

It was airless and hot down in the Central Park Zoo. The little old lady leaned on the railing around the pool in the center and watched the seals slither in and out of the water. Swathed in a couple of shaggy sweaters of different lengths, a baggy tweed skirt, black stockings wrinkled around her ankles, and a head scarf pulled down nearly to her eyebrows, she nevertheless seemed cold, but old people's bones take a good deal of warming up.

It was the nicest day they'd had in a spell of damp, gray days, the woman thought, and the sun had certainly brought out the crowd. The crowd, in turn, had brought out the vendors of hot dogs, bagels, peanuts, balloons, and along with them the muggers and the sneak thieves. The old lady would have liked to sit on the grass, peel off a couple of the sweaters, remove her head scarf, and raise her face to the sun. Instead she hunched over a little more and clutched the ratty shopping bag closer to her side, all the while darting quick, furtive looks around her, looks that proclaimed to anybody who happened to be watching that there was something valuable inside that old shopping bag. Old ladies hid their purses inside shopping bags, and every mugger on the streets knew it.

Which was exactly what Officer Pilar Nieves was counting on.

Officer Nieves and her backup team were part of the Anticrime Unit working Central Park in direct response to a rash of assaults that had been taking place there within the past three weeks. If she was successful, Officer Nieves would that day experience her thirty-ninth mugging. But it wouldn't happen unless she moved around. Under the layers of old clothes there was a pretty, energetic, twenty-six-year-old, but she let go of the railing as though reluctant to lose its support; she shuffled uncertainly away from the seal pond, across the cobblestones, and around the ugly red administration building toward the flight of stairs leading up to Fifth Avenue.

She knew she was being followed. She didn't have to turn around; a prickling of the skin warned her. Excitement coursed through her. Keeping the same slow pace, she reached the foot of the stairs. She'd let him catch up about halfway. The way her backup was deployed—Ferdi at the top covering the street, Ross Gabig and Eddie Prentiss below and behind her—it was the ideal spot to make the collar. She started up the steps, slowing somewhat as though the stairs were too much for her. Every instinct told her he was behind her, yet she had nearly reached the top and he hadn't approached.

"Don't scream. Don't make a move or you're dead."

His voice was low, so low it was barely a hiss, and so near that his breath brushed her cheek.

Out of the corner of her eye, Pilar Nieves caught the metal gleam of a gun barrel. For the first time in her thirty-nine muggings and unnumbered false alarms, she was frightened.

"I'm a police officer," she told him, raising her head and looking him full in the face while at the same time she slid her free hand under the top cardigan and reached for the gun in the shoulder holster. "You're under arrest . . ."

At least that was what she started to say, but the breath was knocked out of her before she could form the words. It felt like getting punched in the stomach, Pilar Nieves thought, knowing that she'd been shot and relieved that it didn't hurt that much after all. She went down to her knees, puzzling over how quickly and inconspicuously the whole thing had been managed. A silencer, he'd used a silencer! Her final reaction was one of mild surprise.

Ferdi Arenas had his eye on her; he was positioned precisely for that purpose. If she should provoke an attack he would be able to cut off the perpetrator's escape by way of the street, while Gabig and Prentiss could cut him off down below from either of the zoo's exits. Plainclothes cop Fernando Arenas had been doing this kind of work for three years and he had a good eye for a potential mugger. He'd spotted the guy before Pilar had even moved away from the seal pond. For a second he thought she didn't know he was on her, but the way she was dragging herself up those steps reassured Ferdi that she was actually leading the suspect up toward the best place for the collar. Arenas grinned; smart girl, but a real ham—he'd have to tell her later that she'd overplayed the part. He watched as the suspect closed in, waited for him to grab the shopping bag.

They were talking, Pilar and the suspect. What the hell was going on?

He saw Pilar straighten up. He saw her slide her hand under the coat sweater. *Dios mío!* She was going for the gun! He started to run toward the stairs.

Children spilled out in front of him. They tumbled boisterously across his path.

It wasn't till later that Ferdi Arenas realized precisely what had happened—a line of bright yellow school buses had drawn up at the curb, disgorging over a hundred excited youngsters. At the moment, all he knew was that squealing, squalling kids swarmed between him and Pilar. He couldn't get through. He couldn't use his gun. With a terrible sense of impending disaster, Ferdi Arenas also realized that the two men covering Pilar from below were equally helpless. The teachers had made no attempt to line up their charges in any kind of order before descending into the zoo. They'd simply let them run free and they were everywhere—on the sidewalk and all over the stairs. Gabig and Prentiss couldn't shoot into the children any more than he could.

Anyhow, it was too late. A shrill scream, a woman's, though not Pilar's, told him so. He watched as Pilar slowly sank to her knees, toppled sideways, and rolled over and over down the stairs to the bottom, a shapeless heap of old clothes.

"Pilar!" he yelled.

The children didn't know what was happening, but they sensed it was something bad and they stopped their joyous roughhousing, uncertain how to react. For a moment everything stopped, all action ceased, a single frame out of a film sequence frozen: the mugger used that moment for his escape. He vaulted over the stair railing to the soft slope of earth and headed for the Sixty-fifth Street transverse, With a running leap, he cleared the low wall but didn't make the tactical error of fleeing through the transverse itself, which was as restrictive as a tunnel. Instead he darted through the row of parked buses into the middle of Fifth Avenue. The blare of horns told Arenas that his prey was dodging traffic and the progression of sound indicated he was heading uptown. Ferdi followed him into the street, but his man was nowhere to be seen. Ferdi crossed to the other side. Gone. Ducked down one of the side streets, obviously. But which one?

Heart pounding, not from the chase but from dread of what he would find when he got back, Ferdi Arenas returned to the scene. If anything, there was more confusion than before. Some of the children, the little ones, were crying, though they didn't know why; teachers were trying frantically to round them up and get them back into the buses. Now there was no problem making his way through. Below, Gabig and Prentiss stood guard over Pilar's motionless form, but there was no need to hold the crowd back; it kept its own respectful distance. The crowd's awed silence told the story. Arenas ran at full tilt to kneel beside the body.

Dazed and confused, Prentiss tried to explain to himself as much as to Arenas. "It looked like he was going to make the grab. I caught Ross's eye and we were all set to close in and then . . . I don't know, he started to talk to her. I figured we'd made a mistake, that he was asking directions . . . or something."

"That's what I thought" Gabig groaned.

"I can't believe this. I can't believe it," Prentiss repeated. "He killed her right in front of our eyes."

Ferdi was crying openly. The tears filled his eyes, but his vision was clear. He saw, not the heap of tattered old clothes, but the young, lithe body they camouflaged; not the heavy crayon lines and shadows painted on her face, but the smooth, soft, dusky skin; not the dingy head scarf, but the lustrous hair underneath; and in the vacant eyes he remembered flashing intelligence and humor and that very special look that had been for him alone. He leaned over and kissed the dead woman full on the lips.

Norah sat on the edge of the bed, watching her husband pack.

"Have you got enough shirts?"

"Plenty."

"Don't forget your alarm clock."

"Got it."

"I think you ought to take your bathing suit. It's still hot over there."

"I'm not going to be anywhere near a beach."

"There's probably a pool. At the hotel."

"In Grosseto?"

"You told me it's a big tourist stopover on the way to Rome."

Joe Capretto folded the last of the three lightweight suits he was taking, closed that half of his suitcase, and went over to his wife, placing a hand on each shoulder and looking deep into her eyes. "*Carissima*, I am not going to waste time hanging around beaches and pools. I am going over there to do a job and when I get that job done, I am coming right back home to you."

"Your mother's not going to come hurrying home," Norah pointed out as she had many times before. "She's going to want to stay awhile and visit. That's to be expected."

"Absolutely," Joe agreed, as he also had before, many times. "She can stay as long as she wants. When I've got all the red tape of the inheritance straightened out, she's on her own." He bent over and kissed Norah. "I'll be coming home." His dark, handsome face creased into a teasing smile. "Having given you plenty of advance warning, of course."

"Ah . . ." Norah sighed. "I'm going to miss you. I miss you already and you haven't even left. But I don't want you to rush back. I want you to stay and spend some time with your relatives. You're going to be meeting them for the first time. You're going to see where your mother and father came from. It's going to be wonderful. Besides, I don't think you should let your mother travel alone."

"As far as that goes, Mamma can look after herself, and we both know it."

Signora Emilia, as Norah always privately thought of her, could have dealt with the entire situation on her own. She didn't need Joe to go along with her. Signora Emilia Capretto spoke the language better than she spoke English, certainly better than her son did, and was more familiar with Italian customs and legalities. She was more than a match for any lawyers or officials who might try to cheat her.

Joe's mother had been named in the will of a recently deceased brother. There were questions regarding the disposition of property jointly bequeathed and rules regarding the moneys that might be taken out of the country by a foreigner, which Mrs. Capretto now was. Signora Emilia had seven daughters. The eldest, Elena, was married to an accountant, who logically should have been the one to accompany and assist her. He had offered to do so, but the *signora* had wanted Joe. Joe was her only son. Joseph Antony Capretto at forty-four was a fine figure—tall, dark, with the classic Roman profile. He was also a detective lieutenant in the New York City Police Department. The *signora* was proud of him and wanted to show him off. Norah couldn't blame her.

"You stay as long as she wants you to."

"I wish you were coming, *cara*. It won't mean as much without you."

They'd discussed that, too, at length. Joe was taking a month, but there was no telling how much of that time the business of Ernesto Bustello's will would consume. Would it be worthwhile for Norah to take her vacation and go along? They had always planned to go to Italy together, to see Rome, Capri, the lakes. If she went with Joe now, would they get the chance? In addition to straightening out matters pertaining to the legacy, there would be family obligations. Joe's people in Grosseto would not understand if Norah and Joe went off on their own; they might be offended. Norah loved Joe's family over here, but seven sisters meant seven husbands, over a dozen nieces and nephews, uncounted uncles and aunts, cousins and in-laws. Since her own family was small— her dad living across town and two brothers, whom she seldom saw, settled out West—Norah sometimes felt swamped. Over there, in Italy, not understanding the language, it would be even worse. They had decided to make the trip another time—just the two of them.

"I'll be thinking of you every minute." Norah raised her lips to him. The kiss was long, sweet, growing in intensity. . . .

The phone rang. They broke off with a sigh.

"That can't be for me," Joe said, but eyed the telephone anxiously.

"No, of course not." Joe was head of the Fourth Homicide Division detectives, an important job, but he was not indispensable. If something should come up that his subordinate couldn't handle, then Captain Felix, the precinct commander, would probably take charge. Nevertheless, Norah was anxious for him. "It's probably for me," she said as she answered, and, listening, nodded reassuringly.

Turning to complete his packing, Capretto didn't hear his wife's small, involuntary gasp and naturally couldn't see her sudden pallor and the pinched look of her wide mouth. He did realize that she was silent for a considerable time but assumed she was listening to a report.

"Thanks for letting me know," Norah said, and hung up.

The tone of her voice alerted him. "What's up?"

"That was Dolly. Pilar Nieves has been shot." She took a deep breath, held it, then slowly let the air out of her lungs, a trick to ease tension she'd learned from him. "I don't know if you remember Pilar. She was on the squad."

The squad Norah referred to was the unit she'd organized and headed, one of the first formed with the express purpose of protecting senior citizens from attack and also exhaustively investigating crimes committed against them. It had achieved marked success in both areas, but budget cutbacks had forced it to disband.

"How did it happen?" Joe asked, knowing that the blow was especially hard because the woman had at one time worked for Norah.

"She was acting as decoy when the suspect approached her. Instead of snatching her shopping bag he sidled up to her and started talking. It confused the backup team and the next thing they knew, Pilar was tumbling down the stairs and he was on the run."

"I take it he got away."

"Yes. Several busloads of children from Long Island unloaded at just that moment. They were between the men and the perpetrator. The men were afraid to use their guns."

"God!"

"Ferdi Arenas was one of them." Arenas had also been on the Senior Citizens' squad and before that he had worked in plainclothes on homicide for Joe. "Ferdi and Pilar were going together. I think it was serious."

He went to Norah and raised her to her feet, put his arms around her, and pulled her close till he could feel the throb of her body against his. There was no time for more than a kiss. "You'd better go."

"Now?"

"You want to, don't you?"

"I also want to come to the airport to see you off."

"It'll be a mob scene. We wouldn't have a chance for a real good-bye, not with the whole family there. It's better like this."

It would be their first real separation in five years of marriage.

Norah had joked about how she was going to let the house get dirty and the dishes pile up in the sink while she went out to see all the shows and movies that Joe hadn't been interested in. And how she was going to shop, shop, shop. She'd teased him about the money she was going to spend. Now that the moment of parting had come, she couldn't even manage a smile.

"I was going to drive you to the airport."

"I'll take a taxi."

"What will your mother say when I'm not there?"

"She'll be so excited she won't even notice."

Norah doubted that. "Are you sure you don't mind?"

"I mind like hell, so will you please get moving?"

By the time she arrived, Officers Gabig and Prentiss were gone. Ferdi Arenas sat in a corner of the squad room, elbows on the desk, staring at the unfinished report in his typewriter. Seeing him, Norah felt a most unofficial surge of sympathy. Arenas was twenty-five, dark-haired, sallow-skinned, and thin: no matter how much he ate, nervous intensity burned up the calories. Six years ago Arenas had left his native San Juan to find a job with dignity, a future, and enough pay so that he could help the family back home. Ferdi had been proud to be a cop, but having been raised in the old-fashioned virtues of hard work and respect for authority, he now found himself uneasy. His fellow officers no longer accepted the quasi-military structure and discipline of the department. The more they rebelled—going out on job actions, demonstrating, protesting hours and wages as they were doing then—the more uncomfortable Arenas felt and the more he clung to the letter of the "Patrol Guide." To offer Ferdi anything more than a formal expression of sympathy, here in the squad room anyway, would embarrass him.

"I'm very sorry, Ferdi."

"Thank you, Sergeant." Then, because it was Norah, because he'd worked for her, and because she was a friend, he added, "We were going to be married."

Now she put a hand on his shoulder.

"I saw it, Sergeant!" Her touch made him blurt it out. "The whole thing happened right in front of my eyes and I couldn't stop it. I saw the lousy bastard, but I can't describe him worth a damn." He tapped his forefinger on that part of the report form in his typewriter that dealt with the physical characteristics of the suspect and Norah noted that they were blank. "I could never pick him out of a lineup. I couldn't say, 'Yes, that's him.' I couldn't do it, Sergeant."

"Okay, Ferdi, take it easy. Just how much of a description can you give?"

"I can tell you what he wore," the young cop replied bitterly. "He had on one of those down-filled jackets that make everybody look like a barrel. Baggy brown, paint-stained pants, dirty white sneakers, and a fisherman's type wool cap pulled down to his eyebrows. His face, in the quick glimpse I got, was dirty, filthy—like he'd rubbed dirt on it on purpose, which he probably had."

"That's all?"

"His height—there's no way he could disguise his height. I'd say he was just under six feet, for all the good that does us."

"How about the rest of the team?"

Arenas shook his head. "We all saw him, but we have no idea what he looks like."

"You want to talk about it?" Norah asked.

Arenas straightened in the chair and began to recite in the official tone he used for a report. "Officer Nieves was down in the zoo by the seal pond. Officers Gabig and Prentiss were down there mixed in the crowd on either flank. I was up on the street, near the parapet, where I could observe her. I saw her leave the pond, and as she did she slipped the handles of the shopping bag off her arm and down to her hand—that was to make it easier to grab the bag and also to signal us that she'd spotted a possible mugger. So I moved in toward the top of the stairs and Gabig and Prentiss closed in below. The suspect followed her. He didn't approach Officer Nieves till she was nearly at the top of the stairs. Then, instead of reaching for the shopping bag, he spoke to her. I realized she was in trouble when I saw her go for her gun, but at the same moment several busloads"—though he was under stress he remembered to be specific—"four busloads of schoolchildren unloaded. The children were everywhere, running all over the sidewalk between me and Officer Nieves. The next thing I knew, she was down and the perpetrator was fleeing. I chased him into the traffic, but I lost him."

Norah frowned. "You didn't hear the shot?"

"He must have had a silencer."

Norah bit her lip and squinted thoughtfully. "How about the shopping bag, Ferdi? What happened to the shopping bag?"

"He shot her in front of my eyes and there was nothing I could do. Nothing."

"Ferdi, when you went to Pilar, did she still have the shopping bag?"

Blinking a couple of times, the young cop forced himself to recall a detail that seemed to him irrelevant. "The bag dropped out of her hand when she fell. Its contents spilled all over the stairs. People retrieved the stuff—it was all junk bits of string, extra socks, rags, half a sandwich . . . you know." His eyes filled. "The people picked it all up and put it back in the bag for her."

Norah proceeded briskly "So the perpetrator didn't take the shopping bag after all?"

"No. No, he didn't."

"You're sure?"

"Sergeant, I just told you."

"Are you sure it was Pilar who dropped the bag and not the perpetrator as he fled?"

Arenas frowned over the distinction.

"Let's just get the sequence clear, Ferdi. The perpetrator came up to Pilar on the stairs and spoke to her."

"Yes, Sergeant."

"*Then* she went for her gun. Are you sure that's what she was doing?"

"She reached her hand under her coat sweater and toward her shoulder holster."

"All right, good, I buy that. What I want is for you to be absolutely certain that at that point the perpetrator had not tried to take the shopping bag."

"No, he hadn't. Instead of taking it he spoke to her. We all noted it; we were all surprised."

"So if the sequence is correct, he must have threatened Pilar. There would have been no other reason for her to go for her gun," Norah pointed out. "And if he threatened her, and she went for her gun, then at the same time she surely identified herself to him as a police officer."

"Of course." Arenas couldn't see why the sergeant, who was so shrewd, should belabor the obvious. "When she identified herself, he panicked and shot her. My God, Sergeant, the man was strung out. Had to be. There's no other way to account for it. He was strung out. I saw him. I should have known."

"Did anybody in the crowd get a look at him?"

But Fernando Arenas had retreated into his grief. "What am I going to tell her people? How am I going to explain to her *mamá* and *papá* that I stood and watched while Pilar was killed?"

Norah had an idea, a theory, but she wasn't sure whether telling it now would ease or intensify his pain. She left him and, crossing the squad room, knocked on the captain's door.

Captain James Felix sat in a swivel chair with his back to the door, staring out the window as dusk fell. It was a rare indulgence to sit and do nothing. With his long, lantern-jawed face, wide mouth, penetrating green eyes, Felix was an energetic, hardworking man who could have passed for less than his forty-eight years except for the fact that his curly, roan-colored hair was beginning finally to turn gray. Jim Felix had been, once upon a time, the youngest detective lieutenant in the department. That distinction was a thing of the past, of course, but he'd garnered others during the years of service. To the brass, Felix was known as a skillful administrator and, what was of even greater importance in these days, a commander who could be counted on to maintain discipline. Not all commanders could control their men. Many countenanced relatively minor infractions, hoping to gain popularity and thus control. It seldom worked. Yet the men at the Two-O, and the women, too, accepted Felix's strictness because he was fair. And he backed his people. One of his detectives had been under investigation by the Knapp Commission on charges of taking bribes and Felix had stood by him—and had seen him finally cleared. The men and women of his command trusted Jim Felix.

A twenty-eight-year veteran, he'd seen it all, or as much as he ever wanted to see. If he'd stopped to brood over every case that crossed his desk, Felix thought, he'd never get any work done, and God knew there was enough work. Of course, every case was unique, but he would have been less than human if he were not particularly affected by this death of an officer under his command. Pilar Nieves had been both competent and enthusiastic, a combination rare in either male or female officers. For all that he tried to treat men and women alike, the fact the victim was a woman couldn't help but make a difference.

He had taken personal charge, going directly to the scene and throwing sixty detectives on the street to question everybody: pedestrians, taxi drivers, bus drivers—particularly the drivers of those parked school buses who had been in a position to observe the fleeing perpetrator—tenants of nearby buildings, doormen. Close to two hundred and fifty witnesses had been interrogated so far and the net result was a big goose egg. Jim Felix swung restlessly in the swivel chair.

His last hope lay in the ME's report. It was possible that Officer Nieves, in falling, had grabbed at her killer and perhaps had torn his clothing. Even as he thought about it Felix admitted that it would be close to a miracle if she had. To trace and identify such threads of fabric and link them to the suspect would require a second and even greater miracle.

"Come in," he said in answer to the knock. "Oh, Norah. Turn on the light, will you?"

Felix had known Norah Mulcahaney since she was a rookie working out of the women's pool and he had known her husband even longer. He was well aware that Joe Capretto was flying to Italy that evening and there was no need for him to ask why Norah wasn't at the airport seeing her husband off.

Norah wasted no time in explaining, either. "I just spoke to Ferdi, Captain. He thinks the perpetrator was high on something, that when Nieves announced, he panicked and shot her."

"So?"

"It couldn't have been like that."

Felix's green eyes narrowed. "Why not?"

"Nieves signaled that she'd spotted a possible mugger. The whole backup team made him. They were all waiting for him to grab the shopping bag, but he never did. Instead of grabbing the bag and splitting, he spoke to her."

Felix waited.

"Why should he speak to her? He wasn't trying to get the mink coat off the back of some lady on Park Avenue or drag some chick into a doorway to rape her. This was just a poor old bag of bones with maybe a few bucks hidden down among the junk in her shopping bag. Why didn't he snatch the bag and run?"

"Because he was no ordinary purse snatcher," Felix answered obligingly.

Norah nodded eagerly. "And he knew that she wasn't just any little old lady."

"He could have threatened her with the gun to make sure she didn't make an outcry when he grabbed the shopping bag."

"Unusual, but suppose he did? Nieves would then have identified herself. In fact, she did go for her gun, so we have to assume that she actually did announce herself as a police officer. Knowing that, would an ordinary mugger have killed her?"

"We're back to Ferdi's theory: he panicked."

Norah now delivered the clincher. "He had a silencer. Nobody puts a silencer on his gun unless he's pretty sure he's going to use it."

THREE

"It was premeditated, cold and premeditated murder." Norah's blue eyes were steady and her jaw was set in anticipation of having to defend her conclusion.

However, Jim Felix appeared only mildly resistant. "You think the perpetrator knew the old lady was actually a police decoy before he accosted her?"

"Yes, sir."

Felix passed the open palm of his right hand across his mouth as he considered. "Hell of a spot to choose," he commented. "Central Park Zoo on a bright, sunny afternoon with a couple of hundred people milling around, any one of whom could identify him later."

"And none of whom did," Norah pointed out. "Not one of them remembered him approaching the victim. Not one of those who saw him flee the scene can offer a description worth a damn —and that goes for Nieves' backup team also."

"All right, so the getup was a disguise, but the time and the place . . ." Felix shook his head. "Too risky. If he was well enough informed to know where she'd be and what she'd be doing, then he must also have known that she'd have plenty of protection."

"He got away with it," Norah pointed out. "You can't argue with success."

"Hm."

"I think it was pretty shrewd. If Ferdi hadn't observed the se-

quence of events with such accuracy, we would have written it off
as a case of a mugger who panicked."

"Probably."

The tightness across the shoulders and the hard knot at the
back of Norah's neck eased. He had bought it. She sat back in her
chair. "It could be somebody she'd busted, who had a grudge
against her."

"Maybe, but her busts didn't amount to much: juveniles who
got off with a mild reprimand, recidivists who knew the ropes and
got out on suspended sentences."

"Some psycho."

Once again Felix made that gesture of wiping his mouth with
his hand. "Let's try the easy way first; let's check out the personal
angle."

Norah and Fernando Arenas met the next morning at the coffee
shop around the corner from the West Eighty-second Street station house. Interrogating the dead girl's fiancé in the squad room
had seemed too unfeeling. When she saw Ferdi threading his way
through the tables toward her and saw how haggard he looked,
Norah was glad she'd arranged it this way.

"You know what gets me, Sergeant?" Arenas had hardly been
able to contain himself till the waitress took the order and went
away. "The way Pilar fought to get the damn job back. She
wanted it so badly. She loved being a cop."

"I know." Norah remembered both Pilar Nieves' enthusiasm
and her honesty. Pilar had freely admitted that being a policewoman gave her status in the community she would not otherwise
have had and that she savored it. "With my background and edu-
cation, what kind of work would have got me this kind of respect?
Well, being a nurse, but there's not much thrill to emptying bed-
pans."

She hadn't pretended to be any kind of superwoman, either.

"Sure, I'm scared sometimes, but that's part of the thrill. It
charges me up, keeps me alert," she'd confided to Norah after a
particularly hairy incident on the street. *Dios mío!* When I think
what it would be like to have a regular nine-to-five job. I couldn't
stand it. It would drive me right up the wall."

"She went to court to get the damn job back." Arenas moaned.

"I know." Norah sighed. The summer before, the city's budget problems had forced the firing of a large number of police officers. Naturally, the last hired were the first fired, and three hundred and ninety-nine women were among the first to be "furloughed," as the euphemism stated. That cut their ranks by nearly fifty percent from approximately eight hundred to the present four hundred and thirteen. When it became possible a year later to hire back some of these officers, the first group of sixty included only one woman. The women argued that not only were they being discriminated against in the order of rehiring but that they should never have been fired in the first place. They brought a class-action suit against the department, basing it on the fact that in the past the police quota limited the number of women it could hire and therefore the women's test was offered only once in every four or five years, while the men's test was offered every year. Therefore, the women who were finally hired lost a seniority that would have served to exempt them from the present layoff.

"Don't think about it, Ferdi."

"If she hadn't got the job back, she wouldn't have been killed."

"That's not necessarily the case."

She had his full attention as she explained her theory. Arenas went over it in his mind. "The getup, the silencer . . . sure, sure. That's it. You've got it, Sergeant. It was premeditated. It's the only way it makes sense. Even the buses . . . it's been eating at me that if those buses hadn't pulled up at that exact moment . . ."

"Let's not give him too much credit," Norah said, cautioning him, concerned at Ferdi's feverish look. "Let's just say he saw them coming and made good use of the opportunity they afforded. The question I have to ask you, Ferdi, is—why? Why would anyone have wanted to kill Pilar Nieves?"

"Oh, God, Sergeant, I don't know. I can't imagine. Everybody loved Pilar. You knew her, Sergeant. How could anybody not love Pilar?"

"Manolo! Manolo Costa!"

Sofia Nieves, Pilar's fifteen-year-old sister, cried out the name, then covered her mouth with her hands, aghast at having spoken.

They were in the small back room of the Nieves *bodega*, a mom-and-pop grocery store in Spanish Harlem. Norah had been surprised not merely to find it open but to see Mr. and Mrs. Nieves behind the counter. They were certainly doing a big business, she thought, then noted that few who came in were buying.

They were neighbors and friends who had come to give sympathy and support, which the bereaved parents accepted with quiet dignity. In the absence of the body, not yet released, it was nevertheless a wake. Here, amid the open sacks of dried comestibles, the hanging cheeses and sausages, the pungent aroma of spices, the tribute was especially poignant.

At Norah and Ferdi's appearance, the neighbors tactfully withdrew, the front door of the store was closed, the shades drawn. The two officers were ushered into the back room and small cups of thick, black Puerto Rican coffee thrust into their hands. Norah disliked the bitterness of it, but she would never have thought of refusing it.

The parents listened in a daze to what she had to say and she wasn't really sure that they understood, not until the girl, Sofia, blurted out the name of Manolo Costa.

Mrs. Nieves gasped, but Pilar's father frowned thoughtfully. "It is possible."

"I never heard of this Costa," Arenas said.

"He was Pilar's fiancé at one time," Nieves replied. "It was finished before she met you, Fernando."

Both mother and daughter looked anxiously at Arenas, as though assuring him of Pilar's loyalty.

"I didn't know she'd been engaged before."

"She never really cared for Manolo," the mother assured him. "We pushed her to accept him. We wanted to see her settled, married, out of that . . . terrible job." Tears momentarily choked her. "She was already twenty-four years old."

Arenas was not mollified. "She never said a word about him. She never mentioned his name."

"Did you give Pilar a list of all the girls you went with before you met her?" Norah asked.

He managed a fleeting smile before turning to Sofia. "If it was all over before she even met me, why did you cry out his name?"

Part American teenager and wise beyond her years, part sheltered and dutiful Spanish daughter, Sofia hesitated and looked to her parents for guidance.

"You must tell what you know, *chica*," José Nieves decreed.

"*Si, Papá.*" Obediently, the girl addressed Arenas. "When Manolo heard that Pilar was engaged again, he was very upset. He came to see her. He threatened her."

"She never told me that, either!"

"She didn't want to worry you."

"Worry!"

"Manolo said that he still loved her and if he couldn't have her then nobody could."

Very melodramatic, but also typically Latin, Norah thought. The girl's next words, however, shook her.

"He beat her up. He came over here and—"

"What?" Ferdi had turned pale.

"He tried to beat her up. She had to pull her gun on him."

"Just a minute," Norah began, but was interrupted by the father.

"*Maldito!*" the old man cried out. "When was this? When did this happen?" he demanded.

"Two weeks ago, *Papá*. It was the Wednesday. Yes, two weeks ago on the Wednesday, *Papá*; I had basketball practice."

"And she did not tell us! How is it that Pilar confided in you but not in her *mamá* and *papá?*"

"I only found out by accident, *Papá*. I came home late from basketball practice on the Wednesday and I saw Manolo leave the house. When I came inside, Pilar was crying. She had her gun in her hand and she was crying."

"*Madre de Dios!* You should have come to me and told me. It was your duty."

"She made me promise not to tell you, *Papá*. She didn't want you to know. She was afraid of what you might do."

"I would have given that *maldito* the beating he deserved. I would have given him a beating he would remember for the rest of his life."

"And you would have gone to prison for it, *Papá*. That is what Pilar feared.

"It would have been better, better for me to be in prison than for . . . ." He didn't finish.

"Oh, *Papá*," Sofia wailed. "I am so sorry, *Papá*."

The mother rose and drew her into her arms. "Don't blame the child, José. Don't blame the child."

"No, no. Sofia, *chica*, forgive me. You did what you thought was right. Forgive me." He put his arms around mother and daughter and the three clung together, as close physically as they were in spirit.

"I'm the one she should have told," Ferdi insisted. "I'm the one."

"She kept it from you for the same reason she kept it from her father," Norah reasoned. Because Ferdi's a police officer, any action taken by him would have been a serious breach of conduct. Had he inflicted any grievous injury on Pilar's ex-boyfriend, it could have finished Ferdi in the department. Norah had never considered the diffident Puerto Rican capable of violence, but with such provocation . . . Pilar surely had known him better than she.

"Where can I find this Costa?" Norah asked.

"At the hospital," Nieves replied "He works at the New York Hospital."

"Señor Nieves." Ferdi spoke with respect to the man who was to have been his father-in-law. "You must not yourself go near Costa. Be assured that we will take care of everything. He will pay for what he has done."

"When we know what he's done," Norah amended. She waited till they were outside for the rest. "I brought you along with me because I thought you had a right to help find Pilar's killer. I see it was a mistake."

"I'm sorry, Sergeant."

"I want you to check Pilar's arrest records. I want you to interrogate every person she ever brought into the station house."

"Sergeant—"

"Do it, Officer Arenas. And stay away from Manuel Costa. I mean it. If I find out you've so much as stood outside New York Hospital, I'll not only make sure you're off the case, I'll get you suspended. That's a promise."

Manuel Costa entered the second-floor visitors' lounge and looked around. He approached the only person there.

"Sergeant Mulcahaney?"

Norah rose from the seat beside the window. "Dr. Costa?" He was a slim young man, elegant, almost aristocratic-looking in his hospital whites; he didn't look like a killer, but then how many killers did? Norah asked herself. From the way José Nieves had spoken, Norah had been expecting an orderly, some kind of paraprofessional, not a doctor. Well, how many doctors turned killers? Too many.

Dr. Costa came over and held out a hand. "You're Sergeant Mulcahaney? This is a rare pleasure."

His smile was charming, consciously charming; what was wrong with that? Dr. Manuel Costa was quite aware of his own good looks. Why shouldn't he be? Norah smiled back, warned herself not to be prejudiced, and thought that as far as height was concerned, Costa could be the killer.

"What can I do for you, Sergeant?"

"Is there somewhere we can talk privately?"

"There's an empty room just down the hall.

She followed the resident and at his indication entered a single-occupancy room in which the bed was freshly made up and a woman's robe was lying on a chair.

"The patient is in OR," Costa explained. "Now, what's all this about?"

"You must know that Pilar Nieves was fatally shot yesterday afternoon."

"Yes. Of course. A tragedy. Incredible. I mean, because you never think such a thing can happen to someone that you know."

Trite, but true, Nora thought.

"I have been uncertain how to express my sympathy to the family," he confided. "My first impulse was to go over immediately, then I considered . . . perhaps not. Perhaps a letter would be more . . . tactful. Since obviously they mentioned me to you . . . It is the family who sent you?" Norah nodded. "Then perhaps I should pay a personal visit."

"I don't understand your hestitation."

"I feared my visit might cause them added sorrow. I assume they told you that Pilar and I were once engaged."

"Yes."

"Well . . ." He spread out his hands in a manner indicating that surely it should be clear. "If Pilar had married me she wouldn't have been working and she'd be alive."

For some reason that Norah couldn't explain to herself, she found that in very poor taste. "Just exactly why did you and Pilar break up, Doctor? Do you mind my asking?"

"Should I mind?" That charming smile was up front again, acting as buffer. "Of course I don't mind; it's no secret. We broke up because of her job. She wanted a career; I wanted a wife. I am not so old-fashioned that I would keep my wife in purdah, Sergeant. I was perfectly willing for her to have a job, but it could not be one that would take precedence over husband and home."

"Something like a hobby?" she suggested.

"No, Sergeant, but something she could keep in proper perspective."

"You knew she was a policewoman before you asked her to marry you, didn't you?"

"I didn't know that it was the main thing in her life, not till she sued for reinstatement. That told it all. When she got together with those other women to bring a class action—"

"Is that when you broke up? Or did you wait till the case came to court hoping she would lose?"

"She went against my wishes."

"That means you waited," Norah concluded. "You didn't expect her to win."

"To tell you the truth, no, I didn't. I never expected the judge to hand down such a decision. The suit was brought on the basis that the women's seniority had been affected by their not being permitted to take entrance exams with the same frequency as the men."

"I know the background, Doctor."

"All right, sure. The point I'm trying to make is that the decision is now a precedent which every other minority group can use to attack workers with more seniority and experience."

"What do you have against policewomen, Doctor?"

"Per se, nothing. Specifically, with regard to the woman I intended to marry . . . With all due respect, Sergeant—are you married?"

"Yes. My husband is a police lieutenant."

"Ah, well, there's no conflict. But a doctor, who has an unpredictable schedule himself, to be married to a woman who works the crazy hours you people take for granted . . . it's just not feasible. I want a wife I can count on, who'll be home when I get home. I want her there and waiting."

"And willing?"

"Certainly."

"And Pilar didn't see it like that."

"As a career woman yourself, Sergeant, perhaps you feel that I might have been the one to give up my profession? Let's say that neither one of us, Pilar nor I, cared enough about the other to make the sacrifice."

"In other words, you reached an amicable decision."

"Sad but amicable, yes."

"When was the last time you saw Pilar?"

"That was . . . let me see . . . early this summer."

"On that final occasion of your parting?"

"That's right."

"And you haven't seen her since?"

"Not in the sense you mean. We're members of the same community, go to the same church, attend certain functions. We have many friends in common."

"So you knew that Pilar was engaged again."

"Of course. I wished her well."

"That was generous."

He shrugged.

"Did you call her? Write her a note? Exactly how did you express your good wishes?"

Reaching into the pocket of the tunic, Costa brought out a pack of cigarettes and shook a couple loose. Having offered one to Norah and been refused, he lit up. She took the ritual as a sign of nervousness and a ploy to gain time to think.

"It seems you know that I went to see Pilar a couple of weeks ago. I suppose Sofia told you. Why don't you ask me straight out what you want to know?"

"Why didn't you tell me straight out that you'd gone to see her?"

"Because it's none of your business!" the resident snapped. He got up, paced around the bed, and went to stand and stare out the window. "I don't really know why you're here, Sergeant Mulcahaney. Pilar was killed by a mugger in the park. Considering the kind of work she was doing—that she insisted on doing—she just about asked for it. I realize that sounds callous; I can't help it. The point is that our past relationship doesn't enter into it."

"There's some doubt that it was an ordinary mugger who killed her," Norah explained, watching Costa closely. "We think the killer knew he was approaching a police decoy and knew who the decoy was."

"Incredible!"

Norah waited; sometimes silence was the best probe.

"You think I did it," he stated flatly.

"At this point, I don't think anything, Doctor. I am curious about what happened between you and Pilar at her house on the Wednesday afternoon two weeks ago."

"I have nothing to say."

"All right, then Sofia's version must stand." Norah got up, indicating she was about to leave. "Aren't you interested in what she said?"

He shrugged.

"She says she saw you leaving the building just as she was approaching it. When she got to her apartment she found Pilar sitting on the sofa, service revolver in hand. Pilar was crying. She told Sofia that you were enraged over her engagement, that you swore if you couldn't have her, nobody could. You attempted to assault her physically and she pulled the gun to defend herself."

Costa's mouth remained obstinately shut.

"Where were you yesterday afternoon at three P.M., Doctor?"

"Right here."

"On duty? Doing rounds? Working with a particular patient? Can you give me the name of a doctor or nurse who can corroborate precisely where you were?"

He glared. "I ducked into my call room for a nap. On this job you sleep every damn chance you get."

"Were you alone?"

"Yes, Sergeant. On hospital premises I sleep alone."

"How long did you sleep?"

"A couple of hours. Say from two to four."

"Plenty of time to get over to the zoo and back."

"I did not go to the Central Park Zoo and I did not kill Pilar," he yelled, his face livid, quivering. "Get off my back." Abruptly, he whirled once again to stare out the window as he struggled to regain some measure of control. "I told you that it was all over between Pilar and me. We parted friends. There were no hard feelings. Pilar got herself somebody new. That was no surprise; I haven't been exactly celibate myself. You can ask around, Sergeant. I've been dating some of the nurses. In fact, there's a special girl, the one I'm going with right now."

"Do you mind if I talk to her?"

"I don't give a damn what you do, Sergeant." Brushing past her in the narrow space between wall and bed, Manuel Costa strode out into the hall.

So, Norah thought, whether or not Sofia Nieves had told the truth about what happened between her sister and Costa, she had certainly been right about one thing: the doctor had a violent and explosive temper. And he had used that temper to his advantage in that melodramatic exit, which had served a double purpose: it had terminated a difficult interview and at the same time made it possible for him to avoid giving Norah the name of his new girlfriend.

FOUR

"You're not on till four; why do you have to leave so early?" Lorna Janssen demanded.

Her husband sighed. He pushed aside the plate of half-eaten franks and beans. "I told you. There's a meeting."

"Sure."

Lorna Janssen was a trim young woman with short light brown hair, a pert, upturned nose, and hazel eyes that were ordinary but much enhanced by thickly fringed lashes. She'd been exceedingly pretty once, with the good looks of youth, health, and high expectations. She still had the youth and the health—she was only twenty-four—but the expectations had long since evaporated. Her husband's long hours, low pay, combined with the responsibility of two children, a boy and a girl, kept her tied to the house. Discontent had already made her face sag; now suspicion put an ugly twist on her mouth.

"And you didn't get in till three-thirty this morning because you were out demonstrating in front of the mayor's house." She was heavily sarcastic.

"My God, Lorna. You heard it on the radio. You saw it in the paper." Janssen picked up a copy of the *Post;* a picture of the off-duty police demonstration that had taken place at Gracie Mansion the night before filled almost the entire front page. He slapped it on the kitchen table for emphasis.

His wife immediately snatched it up. "Where are you? I don't see you in the picture. I don't see where it says anywhere in this account that Officer Thomas Janssen took part, that Officer Jans-

sen was one of those fine, upstanding rowdies out there banging
garbage lids, yelling, and throwing beer cans in front of the
mayor's house."

"Oh, God." Janssen lowered his head between hunched shoulders.

That only increased the intensity of her harangue. "I do see that
the *riot* broke up around two A.M.. Two, not three-thirty."

"A bunch of us stopped for a couple of beers."

"According to this, you'd already had too much."

He winced. "Yeah, well, that's probably right. I guess we did
overdo it. We got pretty charged up."

"Okay, so now I'm charged up. It's my turn. I've got a right to
blow off steam once in a while." Instead, she now shifted from
ranting to whining. "I never see you anymore, Tom. You're never
home. This place is falling apart, and you don't do a thing. I had
to climb up to the garage roof to fix that leak yesterday. I couldn't
let it go any longer, not with the heavy rain we're supposed to get.
I was ashamed for the neighbors to see me."

"I'm sorry about that, honey, I forgot. Honest. If you'd just
make a list of the things that—"

"Sure. I'll write you a letter."

"Ah, Honey . . ."

Thomas Janssen was a big, heavy-boned man with fair hair and
light gray eyes. Like his wife, he had once had the typical American good looks based on a vitamin-rich diet, participation in
sports, an untroubled mind, and the economic circumstances that
made the preceding possible. Four years of riding patrol had made
him fat and sluggish. His wife's attitude made him nervous. At
first her jealousy had been flattering. Then he'd tried to laugh it
off. Now he simply endured it.

"The kids never see you anymore," Lorna Janssen continued.
"When's Daddy coming home? Is Daddy going to be home for
supper tonight? What can I tell them?"

"Okay, Lorna, that's enough, Knock it off. I'm on the contract-
negotiating committee and I've gone to a few meetings, that's all.
Maybe I have stayed out a little afterward for a few beers with the
guys, but that's no big deal, for God's sake. And it hasn't been
that often, either. You know the new contract is important. You
know we've got to make a stand. It matters to both of us, you as
much as me—in the pocketbook, in the hours, everything. But if it
makes you so miserable, I'll drop it; I'll get off the committee."

"Then what will you use for an excuse?"

"An excuse for what?"

"To be with the woman," she said shrilly. "Don't think you're fooling me, Tom Janssen. I know where you were till three-thirty this morning. You were with her."

"All right. All right." Janssen's pleasant, usually placid countenance was flushed. "If it makes you happy to think so, then go ahead. Okay. I wasn't at the demonstration last night; I was with her. I see her eight hours a day, but it's not enough." He grabbed his blouse from the back of the kitchen chair and his cap from the seat, and, without pausing to put them on, rushed out the back door.

"I'll show you!" she yelled after him. "You'll be sorry. You'll see." Lorna pounded her fists on the kitchen table in frustration and the tears coursed down along the already established runnels. By the time her husband's car was rolling down the driveway, Lorna Janssen's face was bloated and red.

The call seemed relatively innocuous. A neighbor was calling to report a family quarrel in apartment 2A, the sounds of a woman screaming and furniture being smashed. The complaint was logged at 1:22 A.M. Eight minutes later, Officers Janssen and Ochs pulled up in front of a somewhat seedy converted town house on West Sixteenth Street. The neighborhood was quiet and so apparently was the building. Most of the lights were out. Everything appeared normal except that when the two officers entered the vestibule the inner door was ajar. Ochs pushed the bell for Dimask in 5A, the complainant, but got no answering buzz. She raised questioning eyebrows at Janssen, who shrugged but took the precaution of drawing his gun before inching the inner door a little wider so he could see inside. The lobby was small, well lit, and empty. Motioning for his partner to follow, Janssen started up the sagging stairs.

Apartment 2A was at the front. All was silent within. In fact, the entire building was quiet, the inhabitants apparently tucked in for the night. Too quiet? Janssen wondered. Assuming the battle in 2A was over, everything had quieted down awful fast. A quick, sideways glance at Audrey Ochs reassured him. She no longer seemed concerned. Audry was okay, he thought, slow, maybe, but a good partner—she didn't argue, she did what she was told, and you could count on her. In the short time they'd been working together Janssen had got over his dismay at being saddled with a woman and had come to trust and even rely on Ochs. Must be his nerves, he thought, trying to throw off his uneasiness, the loss of sleep, the fight with Lorna. What he should have done, right at the beginning, was take Audrey out to see the house and introduce her to his wife, let her see that his partner was no glamour girl. Everything would have been different then. Lorna and Audrey might even have got to like each other, become friends. Wouldn't that have been something?

The two officers took up positions against the wall and on either side of the door of 2A, and Janssen rang the bell. Having waited a reasonable length of time without getting a response, Janssen rang again, holding his finger on the button. When that, too, failed he knocked hard and called, "Police. Open up!"

"All right, all right, I'm coming. Keep your shirt on," a woman answered.

She was a robust blonde in her mid-forties. Hair dishevelled, lipstick smeared, and mascara smudged under her eyes, she nevertheless did not look as though anybody had been beating her. She didn't look as though she'd been asleep, either.

"What's going on?" she demanded.

Janssen was embarrassed. "Sorry, ma'am. We had a report of a disturbance."

"Here?"

"Yes, ma'am. Apartment 2A. Family quarrel. One of your neighbors called and said a woman was screaming and furniture was being smashed."

"You've got to be kidding."

"No, ma'am."

"There must be some mistake." She was more mystified than indignant.

"Mind if we come in?" Audrey Ochs asked.

The blonde hesitated, then threw out her hands in a gesture of resignation. "I suppose you might as well."

The room was filled with ornate, cheap furniture and cluttered with souvenir-type bric-a-brac. Not that Janssen or Ochs was interested in either the taste or the quality. A glance between them was enough to note that with so much breakable stuff around, there was no way the place could have been cleaned up and put together again in the time since the complaint.

At that moment a man, bantam and balding, knobby knees and

hairy legs showing under a kimono-style bathrobe, appeared in the bedroom door, blinking nearsightedly. "What's going on?"

"One of your neighbors reported a disturbance, Mr. . . . ?"

"Weissman."

"Somebody called the police and said you were beating me up, Sam." The blonde chuckled.

"Yeah?" He grinned. "Maybe we were a little noisy, but we've never had any complaints before. No, Officers, I can assure you I was not beating my wife."

"Mind if we take a look around?" Audrey Ochs asked. "We have to be able to say we looked," she apologized.

Weissman made an expansive gesture toward the bedroom. "Be my guest."

One look inside convinced both officers that the only struggle in there had taken place on the bed.

"Did you hear any unusual sounds in the building during the last half hour or so?" Janssen asked.

"No," Weissman replied. "This is a quiet building. The walls are thick. We weren't listening."

"Who made the complaint?" Mrs. Weissman wanted to know.

"Sorry, ma'am, I can't tell you that. Sorry to have bothered you." Both officers edged toward the door.

"Maybe you got the wrong apartment," Weissman suggested as he accompanied them. "Maybe you got the wrong address," he called just before shutting the door.

Possibly but not likely, Tom Janssen thought. Probably the call was from a crank who had it in for the Weissmans. Still, it would have to be checked out. They'd have to go up to 5A and find out why the complainant hadn't answered his bell earlier and what he had to say for himself. With a jerk of his head toward Ochs, Janssen strode to the end of the hall and jabbed the elevator button. Once. Twice. No result. No sound to indicate the thing was working. "Damn," he muttered. "I guess we've got to walk. Come on." Without a backward look, he started up the stairs, Audrey Ochs faithfully trailing behind.

She was extra slow tonight, Janssen thought irritably as they climbed. God, she was so slow! She had complained at the start of the tour that she wasn't feeling well, so why hadn't she called in sick? He had to stop a couple of times to let her catch up and each time his irritation grew. She shouldn't have come to work. Actually, Janssen's impatience was aggravated by his anxiety. The situation had become increasingly suspicious. The out-of-order elevator made it look like more than just a crank at work. It smelled of a setup. He was nervous. He wanted to get up there to the fifth floor, talk to the complainant, and get the hell out. Fast.

By the time they reached the fourth-floor landing Tom Janssen could no longer contain himself. "I'm going ahead," he said over his shoulder, and bounced up the last flight, leaving his partner at her own pace.

Apartment 5A didn't answer. Though Janssen rang and knocked and finally called, there was no response. Automatically he tried the door and was surprised, then alarmed, to have it open at his touch. Hand on gun, he cautiously peered inside. It was dark. Not wanting to turn himself into more of a target, he didn't use his flashlight but waited till his eyes adjusted and then stepped into the narrow hall and followed it to the main room, where he got a second shock. The place was empty. Vacant. There was no furniture. Nobody lived there.

"Let's get out of here," he whispered to Ochs, backing out the way he had come. In the hall, carefully pulling the door closed, he turned abruptly to find himself alone.

"Audrey?" For some reason he himself didn't understand, he continued to whisper. Suddenly he became aware of it and called loudly, "Ochs! Where the hell are you?"

Now what? Janssen wondered. What was going on? "Ochs!" he called more urgently. He went over to the stairwell and looked down, expecting to see her sitting on the landing, resting. "Audrey, where are you? What are you doing?" He was all set to bawl her out, but she wasn't there. Panic seized Thomas Janssen. "Audrey!" he yelled.

A moan. Was that a moan? He froze. Just for a second. Two seconds? More? He had no clear idea how long he stood there while a montage of what might have happened to Audrey washed over him, while he visualized the possibilities. . . . He came out of it to find himself running down the stairs to the fourth floor.

"Audrey . . ." His voice was hoarse with desperation.

She was nowhere to be seen. The fourth-floor hall was empty; the apartment doors closed and secretive. A hard knot twisted his gut and reached up to squeeze his heart. What had happened to her? He hadn't turned his back on her that long. How could she have disappeared so fast? Already he was formulating excuses.

Where was she? Where could she have disappeared to? A hum from the elevator shaft was his answer.

The damn thing was running.

It hadn't occurred to Janssen earlier to check where the elevator was, since it had seemed to be out of order. The sound indicated it was on that very floor. Without hesitation this time, Janssen rushed to the end of the hall in time to see the elevator disappear on its way down. Instinctively he charged for the stairs again and plunged downward, determined to reach the ground floor first, to be there when the door opened. He didn't make it, and the door didn't open. As soon as the elevator hit bottom, it started up again.

From then on, every action was pure reflex.

Back to the stairs. This time he had no hope of winning the race. Never fast, not in his best days, Janssen was badly out of shape, but he tried. By the third floor he couldn't run, he climbed laboriously. By the fourth he was gasping. He heard the elevator reach the fifth floor and stop. He stopped, too—to listen. He heard the elevator door open and shut. He heard footsteps, light and quick but not a woman's, going up an extra flight. He heard another door, heavy, open and thud shut. The door to the roof.

Tom Janssen panted the rest of the way to the top and then down the hall to the automatic elevator. He put his hand on the doorknob, took a deep breath, and pulled the door open.

She was there—Audrey Ochs, his sensible, slow but reliable partner—on the floor, crouched on her knees because the elevator was too small for her to lie full length. Her head was bent forward and her fair hair had tumbled loose from her spinsterish bun and was hiding her face, so that for a moment he almost thought she was kneeling in prayer. He hoped that she'd had a few seconds to pray. Then he, too, got down on his knees and gently placed a hand under her chin to tilt up her head. She was bug-eyed, her mouth a round O gaping for breath, her complexion cyanotic. Then he saw the blood, a wide bright band around her neck. Cutting into the flesh of her throat was a length of rough twine. Janssen eased her head down again and, as he did so, the hair at the back of the neck parted to show the piece of wood that had been used to tighten the ligature. She had been garroted.

Tom Janssen backed off, out of the elevator, over to the stairs. He sat down and cried.

After a while he walked down the five flights and out into the street to find a phone booth.

Two cases do not constitute a series. The department took the position that the murders of the two policewomen within a week of each other were in no way related. The earlier death of Officer Katherine Chave was not even mentioned. A press conference was called, at which the two commanders under whose jurisdiction the cases fell—Kreps of the First Division and Felix of the Fourth—were ordered to appear and stress the differences between the two homicides. Much was made of the fact that the killings had occurred at different times and in different sections of the city: Officer Nieves had been killed in Central Park in broad daylight, whereas Officer Ochs had died in the dim hallway of a building on West Sixteenth Street after midnight. The principal discrepancy, the one that weighed most heavily with the press, was the difference in MOs. Nieves had been shot, and Ochs grabbed from behind and garroted. The fact that the murders had occurred while the women were on duty was used to stress the high element of danger that was a normal part of the police officer's job. By the time the session broke up at eleven in the morning, Louis Deland, chief of detectives, had already consumed his daily ration of cigars and was, with complete disregard for his doctor's admonitions, starting on the next day's. He ordered both commanders to give top priority to the solution of the two homicides and to cooperate with each other in all possible ways.

Returning to his office, Captain Felix called the people he most relied on for a briefing: Detectives Brennan and Schmidt, Sergeants Link and Mulcahaney.

"It was an obvious ambush," he announced. "The call was a fake. There was no family quarrel in 2A. If anything, the Weissmans were known throughout the building for making love, not war. The caller gave his name as Sylvester Dimask. There's no such person in the building. He was supposed to be living in 5A, but 5A was vacant and had been for six months. Furthermore, the name Dimask was inserted into the appropriate slot in the vestibule."

There was a collective sigh.

"Why didn't Janssen check with the complainant first?" Brennan, the veteran of the squad, asked.

"He says they did buzz Dimask but got no answer."

"So that should have made him suspicious and they should have gone up there first." Brennan shook his head morosely, indicating the tragedy was a result of a breach of procedure.

"He should have," Dave Link agreed. "But if it was an ambush, it wouldn't have made any difference. Somebody was out to kill a cop. It's getting to be quite a hobby."

"Just any cop?" Norah asked. "In that case, he could have got himself a gun and shot the pair of them anytime while they were prowling through the building. He could have bagged two for one."

"A woman cop, then," David Link amended. These two had worked together, knew each other's methods, respected each other's strengths, and allowed for each other's weaknesses. At the beginning, as the youngest members of the squad, they had been staunch allies; now they were friendly antagonists. David thought that Norah had become too cautious, a habit inflicted by her promotion and her conservative husband. Norah thought David too impulsive. The truth was they were much alike and just about everybody else recognized it, particularly Jim Felix, who was now content to let them kick the subject around for a while.

Link's eyes met Norah's. "You're saying that he was out specifically to kill a woman cop. Okay. How did he know that a woman would be part of the team answering the complaint?" He now answered his own query. "He could have known that a woman would be on duty that particular tour. Hell, on a busy day —and what day isn't?—anybody can walk into any precinct and get a look at the duty chart. Better yet, all anybody has to do is call up and ask for a particular officer and be told when that officer is due to report."

"You just said it—a particular officer."

"Sure. He knows she's on duty and he may even know which car she's riding, but how the hell does he know that car is going to answer his complaint?"

"If he knows that much, he knows what sector the car is working," Brennan put in.

"It would be easier still if he were personally acquainted with the victim," Norah observed quietly.

"In other words, the killer was not out to get a cop, male or female, but Miss Audrey Ochs," Link stated.

Norah swallowed. "It's possible."

"Ah . . ." David sighed and this time when his eyes met

Norah's they offered sympathy. "I hope that's it. We all hope so, but two policewomen, both killed on duty but for separate, personal motives . . ." He shook his head.

"The second murder could be an imitation of the first," Brennan threw in, but obviously didn't put much credence in his own suggestion.

Time to get back to hard facts, Felix thought. "Where do we stand on the Nieves case?" He looked from one to the other of his team, settling on August Schmidt. A stolid, unimaginative, but thorough and dogged researcher, Schmidt had been given the assignment of going through the murdered policewoman's arrest and conviction records and then, with Arenas' help, tracing those who had been arrested and convicted and those who had managed to beat the charges—in other words, everybody. "Gus?"

"Nothing, Captain. Nobody she busted got any kind of a heavy sentence. Nobody seemed uptight about having been collared by a woman or anything along those lines."

"Norah? Any more on Dr. Costa?"

"No, sir. He refuses to say anything about the last meeting with the victim. He claims it was all over between them, but the consensus around the hospital is that he still cared, and cared a hell of a lot. He also claims he's got a new girlfriend and that he's serious about her, but when I finally tracked the girl down she was surprised to hear it. But delighted, I might add. She's pretty crazy about Dr. Costa, but with his reputation for playing around, she didn't let herself even hope. It seems that after he broke up with Pilar Nieves it was all one-night stands for the doc."

"He still hasn't come up with an alibi?"

"No, sir."

"He's supposed to have a violent temper, isn't he?" Link interjected. "Wouldn't he have been more likely to do something like walk up to Pilar in the middle of the street and shoot her right there in front of everybody? Just pump lead into her and into Ferdi, too? The way it was actually done seems out of character for Costa."

"There could be a kind of Latin justice in killing her while she was engaged in the work that had come between them and in doing it while her new lover stood helplessly by," Norah said.

"Sure, but I don't think he'd either disguise himself or make a run for it."

"Neither one of you is a psychiatrist; I suggest you stick to what you know." Felix, who had been rocking thoughtfully, brought his swivel chair to rest in the upright position and leaned across the desk. "Let's just make sure there's no personal connection between the two victims and, through them, to Costa. David, that's yours. Find out if the women met socially, if they double-dated or anything like that. Brennan, get in touch with whoever's carrying the Ochs case over at the First and find out how he's getting along." He paused. Chief Deland had ordered cooperation between commands, but protocol demanded respect for jurisdiction. "Mulcahaney, call Captain Kreps at the First and request permission to take a look at the scene at West Sixteenth."

That Norah should get that particular assignment was neither unexpected nor resented; she'd had a great deal of success in solving crimes against women. The men credited it to her woman's intuition; Norah, to her skill in deduction. Both, if pressed, would have agreed that it was a combination. The meeting over, everybody filed out of the captain's office, with Norah hanging back.

"Captain?"

"What?"

"I just wondered if there was anything in the report, in Och's partner's report, that might be useful. Would it be okay for me to talk to him? Get the story from him before I look at the scene?"

Felix scowled. "I don't think you'll get much out of him." He swung sideways to the desk, crossed his long, lean legs, and tilted back. "I realize it was a shock for him to lose his partner like that, right from under his nose, but his behavior since just doesn't make sense. They hadn't been working together that long—say, three months. If it had been three years, then I could understand his being so broken up."

"Maybe he feels that way because she was a woman. Maybe he feels an extra sense of responsibility," Norah offered, wondering why Felix was so disturbed.

He passed a hand over his mouth. "He's sullen and resentful. Whatever you ask, he gets defensive."

"That's probably it, then; he feels guilty because he wasn't able to save her."

"I hope that's it."

What else could it be? Norah asked herself.

"Janssen's account is garbled, to put the kindest interpretation on it." Felix went on. "According to him, one minute Ochs was behind him, following him up the stairs, and the next she was gone. Disappeared without a sound. He starts to look for her and hears the elevator going down. He chases it. It stops at the lobby, but nobody gets out, and it starts up again. Again he chases it. This time, at the top, somebody does get out, climbs to the roof. He hears all that; he hears the roof door open and shut, but he makes no attempt to pursue the perpetrator. None."

"He was more concerned about the victim, hoped she was still alive, and figured the perpetrator would get away anyhow, down a fire escape or into another building."

"Yes, all right. So now let him pull himself together and make some kind of sense."

It really was out of character for Jim Felix to be so wrought up and to show it. Suddenly Norah realized the reason for his concern and it made her gasp.

"It is the simplest solution and the most logical, isn't it?" Felix knew she'd got it and replied to what she was thinking. "And the simplest answer is usually the right one—unfortunately, in this case. Assume that Janssen himself phoned in the complaint and everything falls neatly into place. There's no problem as to which car or which team is going to answer. The police operator would hardly recognize his voice whether or not he bothered to disguise it. It would explain why he didn't check out the complaint with the caller as he should have done. He was just going through the motions, waking up the Weissmans to verify the complaint, part of the con. He could knock her off anytime he felt like it."

Norah felt cold. Cold and sad.

"Not much of a choice, is it?" Felix asked bitterly. "One cop killing another or a madman hunting down policewomen. I don't know which side to root for."

FIVE

It looked like a nice place to live. The house was located just beyond the prestigious Gardens section of Forest Hills. Strangers wouldn't have known it was outside the incorporated perimeter because the streets were as luxuriantly wooded with fine old shade trees, the gutters as clean. The houses were perhaps a trifle older and not quite so ostentatious, but the difference was not blatant. Number 37 was considerably more modest than its neighbors, the poor relation on the block, and, though of the same vintage, had not undergone any face-liftings to bring it up to date as the others had. Yet it was not without its own honest charm, Norah thought as she mounted the four steps to an enclosed front porch and rang the bell of the Janssen home. The moment the door was opened, however, the tension and unhappiness spurted out like matter from an infected sore.

"Mrs. Janssen? I'm Sergeant Mulcahaney. Is your husband home?"

Lorna Janssen gave her a sharp, hard look of appraisal, then, without a word, turned and led the way across the porch and into a dark living room. On the brightest of days it would have been a gloomy place, for the light had to filter through overgrown shrubbery that blocked latticed windows, but today was not only overcast, the shades were pulled down so that it was actually hard to see. It was as though the Janssens were hiding from their neighbors.

"I'll tell Tom you're here." Mrs. Janssen left Norah standing in the half dark and went upstairs.

It wasn't a room you'd particularly want to show off, Norah thought as she examined the motley collection of castoffs with which it was furnished. Parents and grandparents must have searched their attics and donated what they found to the young couple to start them off, and the Janssens had never got around to replacing any of it. Probably didn't have the money: the children had come too soon, Norah thought, having examined Janssen's personnel file.

"Sergeant Mulcahaney?"

He stood with his wife in the doorway. Norah went to him, holding out her hand. "I'm very sorry about your partner."

Tom Janssen's handshake was limp. His entire posture was limp. Dressed in a pair of rumpled chinos and a plaid flannel sports shirt open at the neck to show a white T-shirt underneath, he looked not only dazed but physically sick. In shock, Captain Felix had remarked on his reaction to the murder, but Norah had expected to find him on the way to recovery by now.

Lorna Janssen made the first move. She walked into the room and sat, ensconced herself, in a shabby chair beside a fireplace with electric logs in it. Almost defiantly she reached down for the sewing basket on the floor beside the chair and prepared to do her mending.

Janssen stared; he swallowed a couple of times before speaking. "Honey, I think you better leave us alone."

"No."

The answer surprised both of them, Janssen and Norah.

"This is police business," he said, and his voice was a bit more firm.

"Then go somewhere else to conduct it. This is my home and my living room. I can sit in it if I want."

"Mrs. Janssen is quite right," Norah interposed quickly. "There's nothing formal about this, Tom. May I call you Tom?"

He nodded.

"Well, why don't we sit down?" Saying so, Norah took the nearest chair and, obediently, Janssen followed suit. "I just want to ask you a few questions about what happened last night. I'm sure you want to help in every way you can."

"Yes, ma'am."

"Could we have some light?"

Lorna Janssen got up, but instead of raising the shades, she turned on a couple of lamps. That done, she returned to her place and doggedly picked up her mending again.

"I made my report," Tom Janssen said.

"Yes, I've seen it," Norah answered. "You were under considerable strain, and so we thought that maybe, after some rest, you might remember additional details. You know how important some minor, apparently inconsequential thing can turn out to be."

"I didn't leave anything out. Anything at all. I put it all down."

Norah gave him a friendly smile. "Why don't we just go back over what happened, okay? According to your report, you were in the lead when you and Officer Ochs went through the building and you continued in the lead when the two of you climbed the last flight of stairs from the fourth to fifth floor."

"Yes, ma'am."

"You're sure that Officer Ochs was still with you when you started up that last flight from the fourth to the fifth floor?"

"Yes, ma'am."

"I wish you wouldn't answer quite so quickly, Tom. You're repeating what you put in the report. I'd like you to stop and think back to the actual situation."

"Ochs was with me when we started up to the fifth floor.'"

"All right. When did you first realize she was gone?"

"When I came out of the vacant apartment I turned, and suddenly she wasn't there."

"How do you mean, you turned?"

"I backed out and I assumed she was behind me."

"But she wasn't?"

"That's what I said."

"What do you think happened to her?"

"Somebody grabbed her from behind and dragged her away."

"Shouldn't you have heard something? Assuming the perpetrator covered her mouth to stifle any outcry, you still should have heard sounds of a struggle, scuffling sounds as he dragged her along the hall or down the stairs."

"I don't think she ever came up the stairs."

"You just said she was in the apartment with you. Right behind you, in fact."

Janssen's jaw hung slack; spittle appeared at a corner of his mouth and trickled down his chin. He appeared worse than confused, he seemed to feel cornered. Norah could understand Jim Felix's exasperation with this man. Was Janssen still so deeply in shock that he didn't realize his unresponsiveness would cause grave suspicion? "That's what I thought then. I realize now it couldn't have happened that way."

"I suppose you know that the complaint was a fake?" Norah asked. "That it was, in fact, an ambush?"

Lorna Janssen gasped. She had long since given up the pretense of sewing and was listening avidly.

"There was the name beside the downstairs bell," the police officer explained. "But when I discovered the apartment the complainant was supposed to be residing in was empty, I figured the whole thing was fake. I guess I'm lucky I'm as big as I am or he might have gone for me."

"Then you don't think the perpetrator was after Audrey Ochs specifically?"

"How could that be?" Janssen showed his first real concern. "How could he have known she'd be answering the call?"

He was quick with that one, Norah thought as she noted the furtive look Janssen cast at his wife. "You'd been riding with the victim for about three months. You must have got to know her pretty well."

He stared down at the worn carpet. "We didn't talk much."

"Come on, Tom, how could you avoid it?"

"Well, sure, we talked. We talked about the job, about the calls we answered, about the contract negotiations. Just shoptalk. Nothing personal."

"We know Audrey wasn't married and that she lived alone. Did she have a boyfriend?"

"She didn't mention one. I don't think she went out much. She was kind of a plain girl . . . and shy. She was real gung ho about the job. Proud to be a cop. It was all she had." He darted another quick look at his wife. "I felt kind of sorry for her."

Lorna Janssen muttered something under her breath and turned her head away.

"Mrs. Janssen? Did you want to say something? Did you know Audrey Ochs? Had you met?"

"No." It was a whisper.

"How did you feel about your husband riding with a woman?"

For a moment Norah thought that Janssen would object to the question, but he seemed to think better of it, though he waited anxiously for his wife's reply.

"Tom said she was a good officer."

"Some of the wives were very upset when the department started to assign women to patrol with male partners. In fact, a group of wives mounted a protest not so long ago. Did you take part in that, Mrs. Janssen?"

Tom Janssen was on his feet and striding to stand beside his wife. "I don't see that this is relevant, Sergeant."

Lorna Janssen ignored him. "Yes, I did, I did participate."

"You don't have to say another word, hon," he advised. Then he faced Norah. "She did it because she was afraid for my safety. It had nothing to do with being jealous or anything like that. She was afraid that a woman wouldn't be physically reliable in a crisis." The effort apparently had drained what strength he had because abruptly he sat down again. "Anyhow, the wives aren't the only ones who feel like that; plenty of the brass do, and I guess we know now there's some basis for it." He seemed suddenly to remember to whom he was talking. "Sorry, Sergeant, but that's the way it is."

"Where were you last night around one A.M., Mrs. Janssen?"

"I went to the movies . . ."

"She was at home . . ."

They both answered at the same time, stopped, looked at each other in consternation. Tom recovered first.

"That's it. We're not answering any more questions, either one of us."

"Well, you know your rights." Norah got up. "If you did call home last night, either before or after reporting . . ." she said to Janssen, then to his wife. "If you were somewhere that you shouldn't have been, then I suggest to you both, and I mean this in the friendliest way possible, that you let it all hang out."

If anyone had told Norah that anything, anything at all, could take precedence over the investigation of a cop killing, she wouldn't believe it. Certainly she would not have believed that she would be pulled off the case, albeit temporarily, because of a revolt of the rank and file. But that was what was happening. The bitterness over the new contract had festered too long. Small boils had erupted in the form of rowdy demonstrations by off-duty cops in front of Gracie Mansion and the march through Times Square, but they had done little to relieve the infection, seemed rather to cause it to spread so that each new protest was larger and more violent than the last. On Friday, September 28, the night of the

Ali-Norton fight at Yankee Stadium, two thousand off-duty cops turned out. They managed to circumvent police perimeters, forcing the on-duty cops to pull down barriers erected to control the crowds and thus letting in hundreds of rampaging youths. The gangs roamed at will, menacing, robbing, and assaulting civilians while the police, who should have protected them, looked on.

It was a night of shame.

There was little sign of morning-after penitence. Whether the men felt that, having gone so far, they had nothing more to lose by continuing or whether they were swept by sheer momentum, the demonstrations continued. A major protest outside Madison Square Garden on October 6, the opening of the hockey season, resulted in two suspensions. The next day one hundred policeman marched on City Hall to protest the suspensions. Worse was to come. On-duty cops in eighteen precincts of Manhattan, Brooklyn, and the Bronx participated in a job action by leaving the transmitting buttons open on their walkie-talkies, thus jamming police frequencies. Technicians were instructed to disconnect the portable radios carried by foot-patrol cops in those precincts, thus making it impossible for cops on the beat to radio for assistance. To eliminate any possible jamming of patrol-car radios the order went down that all radio cars would be staffed with one supervisory officer and one patrol officer.

Norah was one of those riding shotgun on a brother cop.

She was embarrassed. Also, she'd never been on car patrol before. Basically reserved, she got along well with people, particularly with her fellow officers, because she worked at it. The instances in which Norah Mulcahaney failed to establish a comfortable working relationship were rare. On meeting her new partner, Officer Charles Rhoman, Sergeant Mulcahaney extended her hand forthrightly, admitted she was new to the game, and offered to follow his lead. It got her nowhere. Rhoman's taciturnity told her plainly they were on opposing teams. Although Norah's feelings regarding the aims of the PBA were mixed, she was absolutely opposed to the methods being used to achieve the aims, so there was nothing further to be said. Under other circumstances, she would have welcomed a new experience. As it was, the hours dragged and she grew edgy in the unaccustomed confinement of the patrol car.

She was working the eight-to-four but usually went back to the office to keep abreast of her regular work. With Joe away, there wasn't much to go home for.

Her father didn't see it that way. "You can't go on trying to do two jobs at once," Patrick Mulcahaney scolded, claiming he'd called her eight different times before he finally reached her. "You're not getting enough sleep."

Norah was patient; she was used to this. "Eight hours every twenty-four."

"Then you're not eating right."

"Well . . ."

"Aha!" Mulcahaney jumped on the instant's hesitation. She was his only daughter, motherless since the age of thirteen, and Mulcahaney never would, never could, get over an extra feeling of protectiveness and responsibility for her. "I know what that means: you've been grabbing those lousy sawdust hamburgers and gulping them down on the run."

That was his new kick: pure food.

"Now, I want you to come on over and have dinner tomorrow night," her father ordered. "At least I'll know you've got one good meal inside you this week."

"Sorry, Dad, I can't."

"You have to eat. I guarantee to feed you and get you out as fast as your local greasy spoon. Well, almost."

He wasn't allowing for travel time between the precinct house and his place on Riverside Drive. Never mind, Norah thought, it was easier to say yes than to argue.

"Ah . . . Norah," he interposed before she hung up. "What do you hear from Joe?"

"Nothing yet. Mail service is supposed to be bad in Italy. Worse than ours."

No sooner had she put the phone down than it rang again. It was Lena, Joe's eldest sister, married to the accountant, Jake Sexton, who had offered to accompany Signora Emilia to Italy in place of Joe. "Well, you're home finally," she exclaimed. "You don't know how many times I've tried to get you."

"Sorry, Lena."

"You sound tired."

"I am."

"Okay, I won't keep you. I wanted two things: first, have you heard from Joe?"

Norah gave the same excuse she'd given her father about the Italian mails.

"I thought he might have cabled."

"What for? Mamma cabled to say they'd arrived safely."

"He could have called."

"From Italy?" Norah laughed and Lena had to join in because they both knew that Joe could be lavishly generous and pinch-penny in consecutive minutes. Still, Norah had half expected that he would have called and she was disappointed. "What's the other thing, Lena?"

"We want you for dinner tomorrow night."

"Sorry, I just told Dad I'd have dinner with him."

"How about Tuesday?"

"That's the night of the play-offs between the Yanks and the Royals."

"You going to that? I didn't think you cared about baseball."

"I don't. The PBA is planning a big demonstration at the stadium and I expect to be pulling extra duty."

"So when, Norah? When do you want to have dinner?"

Lena was not known for subtlety. Though they enjoyed each other's company, she was letting her sister-in-law know that she was under orders to issue this invitation, that she had been instructed to keep an eye on Joe's wife—by Signora Emilia, no doubt. Who else?

Knowing Lena would persevere, Norah thought she might as well accept gracefully. "How about Thursday? That is, if the Yanks clinch the pennant in four straight."

"Okay. Otherwise Friday." Mission accomplished, Lena hung up.

As it turned out, Norah didn't dine out on any of those nights and it had nothing to do with the Yankees' performance on the field. The night before the opening of the series of home games at Yankee Stadium, while she was putting in overtime on patrol, the PBA announced that they would have anywhere from two thousand to five thousand off-duty officers at the stadium to demonstrate. The next morning, the brass went into extended emergency session, drawing up plans to circumvent the kind of disaster that had marked the Ali-Norton fight two weeks earlier. They designated a virtual "war zone" around the stadium and in turn announced that a thousand higher-ups, principally sergeants and lieutenants, would be present to keep order. As she'd anticipated, Norah was assigned to cover at the precinct.

Eve Bednarski was one of the thousands who converged on Yankee Stadium for the first of the home games. But Eve was not interested in baseball. She couldn't have cared less. She was a big girl, big and luscious—six feet two, a hundred and thirty-five pounds of woman, with a natural blond hair that she'd tinted to strawberry. She squeezed herself into red tights, knee-high red boots, and a bulky red cable-stitched sweater. Big Red. She'd established an identity. Up to now she'd made only a few small buys, but the dealers remembered her; how could they help it? Big Red. At the Four-two she was Officer Eve Bednarski working out of Narco.

Surveying herself critically in the mirror, Officer Bednarski decided her working uniform wasn't classy enough for the occasion. True, tonight's audience wasn't going to be in the same league as the one for the big fight—that had really been something. The dudes in their minks and diamonds, peacocks next to whom the women looked like modest peahens. Still, the people passing through the gates would be wearing fancy threads, and Bernarski intended to pass through those gates with them. So from her closet she got out what she called her "hot-hots," red velvet knickers, white boots, and a white, curly lamb chubby, a variation of her trademark, though tonight her trademark was not all that important. Officer Bednarski felt a cold prickle on her skin. She was not so bold as she looked. In fact, the image had been created in part to bolster her own courage. How did the song go? "You may be as brave as you make believe you are."

Tonight, of all nights, there was no reason to be scared, Eve assured herself as she slipped the service revolver into the special pocket she had sewn into the satin lining of her fur jacket. She wasn't scared, a little charged up was all. Actually, she was looking forward to the meet. The precautions seemed unnecessary, but at the same time they appealed to her sense of drama. Everybody was always saying how routine police work was, how dull. They should be in her shoes—boots—now.

This time the image in the mirror of Eve Bednarski's studio apartment on West End Avenue was satisfactory. Leaving the discarded clothing on the floor where she'd dropped it, Big Red grabbed her imitation red leather purse, locked her front door, and headed uptown, where the action was.

As the crowds gathered at Yankee Stadium the city tensed for the confrontation between off-duty and on-duty cops. The game was secondary. Every precinct would monitor the events up at the Four-two. But whether the extraordinary precautions were inhibiting, or whether cooler heads prevailed, there was no repetition of the Ali-Norton debacle. The off-duty officers were there in the expected numbers and so were their superiors, but the anticipated clash did not occur. On that Tuesday, October 12, order was maintained. There were no untoward incidents. The home team won: Yanks 5, Royals 3. Everybody went home happy.

It wasn't till the cleanup crews moved in that the body of a woman dressed in red velvet knickers and a white fur jacket was discovered in a field-level women's lavatory.

SIX

The department took exception to everything. They could hardly deny that a policewoman had been stabbed and that it had happened at Yankee Stadium, but every other point was contested. A great deal of time and vehemence were expended in rebuttal of the description of the night as chaotic. The police demonstration had been orderly, the crowd under control, the department averred. *Three* policewomen had been killed while on duty during the past weeks, not four. The PR spokesman took care to underscore that the death of Officer Katherine Chave had been deemed an accident. There was no known connection between the *three* victims. The MO was completely different in each case. Therefore—portentous pause—there was no basis whatsoever for the allegation that a woman-cop killer was loose. The spokesman's scowl further punctuated the department's displeasure with the media's conclusions.

The fact that Public Relations, which issued the press release, was headed by the highest-ranking woman officer, an inspector, gave it added weight but did not squelch speculation. The story was too sensational. Every aspect of the Pilar Nieves and Audrey Ochs homicides was reexamined and compared with the details of the murder of Officer Bednarski. Policewomen all over the city were interviewed. As one, they adhered to the department line: there was no indication the deaths were connected; they were not afraid.

But not all believed what they said. And all were, if not afraid, at least nervous.

Now the press cooperated in toning down the description of the scene at Yankee Stadium. Whereas the newspapers had depicted the night of the big fight as a Walpurgisnacht of orgiastic violence in the ring and out, they were careful to assert that the disorder and confusion at the stadium were normal for any major sporting event that attracted large crowds. Unfortunately, it had been aggravated by the demonstration of the off-duty officers. The implication remained: the cops had permitted the climate of rowdyism and permissiveness in which the killer had struck. The cops themselves were responsible for the death of their sister officer.

The lid was clamped on further interviews or statements. Too late. The evil genie was out of the bottle. The brass themselves didn't know what to believe and therefore were uncertain what action to take. Should they take the women off the streets and off all undercover assignments? Keep them in the station houses? To do that would be to give credence to the theory that there was a Jack the Ripper loose, preying on policewomen rather than prostitutes. Not to do it would be to leave the women vulnerable to further attack and themselves to charges of negligence.

As always, there was also the danger of suggestion; some psycho, his own hang-up hitherto dormant, might be stimulated into the decision that killing policewomen was one hell of a good way to ease his tension. Then the assumption of a Jack the Ripper would become reality.

Norah Mulcahaney had learned the hard way to curb her impulses, observe routine, respect jurisdiction—in other words, get permission for practically everything. When she tried to contact Felix he was in conference. For how long no one could tell. It didn't take her long to rationalize her right to do what she'd intended to do from the moment she heard the report of Bednarksi's death—visit the scene. The first wave of investigators and technicians would have gone; she could read their reports later. What Norah wanted, needed, was to get a feel of the scene. Having staunchly held to the theory of personal motivation for each of the two earlier cases. Norah acknowledged to herself that for this third one also to be personally motivated was stretching coincidence. If the three murders had been committed by one perpetrator, then Norah, working officially on the Nieves case, had every right to go up to Yankee Stadium.

The guard posted at the door of the women's lavatory certainly didn't question it. Norah went in.

There wasn't much to see: the chalk outline marking the place the body had lain, bloodstains that suggested that Officer Bednarski had been at one of the sinks when stabbed in the back, then dragged across the floor and into one of the toilet stalls. Though why the killer bothered to hide her when there was an out-of-order sign on the rest-room door . . .

Nobody in Maintenance could tell her a thing about the sign. Nobody knew when or by whom it had been put up. Or even why. There had been no report of anything wrong with the plumbing in that particular lavatory.

"Would you mind coming up there with me and checking it out?" Norah asked.

The supervisor himself complied. He tested every faucet and flushed every john.

"There you are, Sergeant. Everything's perfect. Whoever put up that sign, he doesn't work in Maintenance." His satisfaction didn't last long. "Oh," he said, "just a second." He went back to the outer door. "This isn't even one of our signs."

"What the hell was Bednarski doing at Yankee Stadium?" Sebastian Honn demanded. Captain Honn was appalled at the murder of one of his people. Sorrow and frustration took the form of anger at Gerald Innis, who had been the dead woman's partner.

Innis squirmed. "I suppose she went to participate in the demonstration."

"Oh, for God's sake," Honn muttered. "I never figured Bednarski was into that. I thought her head was somewhere else."

"She was right into the whole contract thing, Captain." Innis was obviously nervous. "She took part in the demonstration outside the mayor's residence and she was at the Garden on the sixth."

"Amazing." Honn, commander of the Narcotics Squad, shook his head over it. "So what was she doing inside the stadium? The demonstration was supposed to be outside."

"I don't know, sir."

Honn kept shaking his head. "I can't believe this."

"I saw her, Captain. I saw Bednarski on the other side of the barricades."

That rocked the commander. "You? You were there?"

Too late Innis realized he'd made a serious error. He was twenty-nine but tall and lanky as a teenager with small, neat features and a clear complexion a girl might have envied. He was wearing a pearl-gray Italian-style suit with vest, jacket nipped at the waist, flame-colored Qiana shirt and flowing white cravat, black patent ankle-high boots: his working clothes. Under the captain's penetrating look, Gerry Innis lost the confidence that went with his outfit, the confidence he had on the street. His face was shiny with sweat and matched the rose glow of his shirt.

"It was my first time, Captain. I didn't take part in any of the other demonstrations."

Whatever remark Sebastian Honn was about to make was cut off by a knock at the door. "Yes?"

Norah stood at the threshold. "Captain Honn? The desk sergeant said it was okay to come up. I'm Sergeant Mulcahaney."

He looked her over. "You used to work in the Fifth Homicide. You married Joe Capretto. Right?"

"Yes, sir."

Norah remembered him, too. She remembered Sebastian Honn as big, strong, vibrantly attractive, a man with a surprisingly impish sense of humor. He had changed. When the Knapp Commission had investigated the Narcotics Squad, Honn, then a lieutenant, was one of the few given a clean bill of health. Then came the bitter irony of his only son's death. The boy, a brilliant student who had won a Rhodes scholarship, became addicted and OD'd on heroin. That, along with his reputation for integrity, classified Honn as above temptation in the eyes of his superiors. He was promoted to captain and put in charge of the newly structured unit. It was four years since Norah had seen him but he appeared to have aged fourteen. His dark, curly hair was almost completely gray, his color the parchment ivory of old age, the lines of his lean face etched with the acid of personal suffering. Yet he couldn't be more than forty-five.

"You're as pretty as ever, Norah. Am I allowed to say that now that you're a sergeant?"

Somehow that rolled the years back for both of them. Her blue eyes alight with pleasure, Norah returned his smile. "You certainly are, Captain, and thank you."

"So, Norah, sit down and tell us what we can do for you."

"Yes, sir. I've just come from Yankee Stadium. I looked over the scene."

"Did you?"

Was that condescension or a reprimand? Because he had made her feel so easy, Norah now overreacted. "I'm working on the Nieves case and also the Ochs case, Captain. I don't think it's too farfetched to wonder whether or not the Bednarski murder might be connected."

"Not at all farfetched."

He'd ignored her sarcasm. "I wanted to ask a couple of questions about Officer Bednarski," she said, chastened.

"You've come at an opportune moment. This is Officer Innis, Bednarski's partner. In fact, he was at the stadium last night himself."

Norah could tell when a man was under his boss's displeasure and she wondered what Innis had done.

"Were you and Bednarski on duty?"

Honn answered. "No, they were not. They were demonstrating. Both of them."

"Sir, I never went inside," Innis reiterated. "I kept within the designated area, and I left early, right after the game got under way."

Norah looked to Honn as though she expected him to put the obvious question, but he nodded, deferring to her.

"Had Bednarski already gone into the stadium at that time?"

"I don't know, Sergeant. I wasn't with Bednarski. I saw her, but I wasn't with her. I caught a glimpse of her, that's all."

According to the newspaper descriptions, her outfit surely made her easy to spot. "Just where did you see her?"

"On East 161st Street. Just across from the stadium."

"Security was pretty tight. How do you suppose she got in?"

Innis shrugged.

"She must have had a ticket," Norah suggested.

"I suppose so."

"If she had a ticket then she wasn't going up there to demonstrate," Honn barked.

"Sir, I don't know that she had a ticket. The sergeant suggested it and I . . ."

A wave from Honn silenced him.

"Could she have had a date to meet somebody inside?" Norah asked. "A snitch, maybe?"

"Why would she meet him inside? Tickets weren't exactly cheap or easy to get. Besides, Bednarski hadn't been around long enough to recruit informants."

"Could she have been meeting someone to make a buy?"

"Alone? Without a backup?" Honn implied she should have known better than to ask.

"How about her personal life?" Norah asked Innis. "I know she wasn't married, but did she have a steady boyfriend?"

"She had a lot more than one, Sergeant. Eve wasn't what I'd call beautiful; what she had was sex appeal. She was stacked. Wonder Woman. The guys were all on the make. You want to check her boyfriends, you'll have to go through the phone book."

"I don't see a lover or ex-lover killing her in a ladies' room of Yankee Stadium," Honn observed. "More likely to do it while she was in bed—with another man."

Norah shrugged. "The only thing that's sure is that she was set up."

"Could she have happened to walk into that rest room at the wrong moment?" Innis asked. "In the middle of a mugging or something?"

"You're forgetting the sign on the door. That sign is the linchpin. It tells us the murder was premeditated. It was not one of the standard signs used by the stadium crew and had to be put up before the crowd entered for the game. Officer Bednarski went into that particular rest room, ignoring the sign because she had a date to meet somebody there. That somebody was her killer. Was she working on anything particularly sensitive?"

"I told you she was new," Honn replied.

"Could she have got hold of information that might have made her dangerous to the mob?" Norah persisted.

"She was still learning the ropes."

Something inside Norah's subconscious sent a signal. "When did she join the squad?"

"As close as I can remember, August, early August. Now let me ask you something, Sergeant. It was your suggestion that these homicides of policewomen could be connected."

"Yes, sir."

"Then shouldn't you be looking for a motive that would apply to all the crimes, not just this last one?"

"I've got to start somewhere."

"It seems to me you have a logical and obvious place to start."

"With the fact that they were all policewomen." Norah shook her head. "Killing a policewoman is not a random thing. You don't find a policewoman on every corner."

"You don't even find a policeman on every corner," Sebastian Honn observed dryly. "That's part of the problem."

"You know what I mean, Captain. The killer would have to know when and where a policewoman would be likely to turn up and in what capacity."

"So each crime had to be carefully planned in advance. I don't see that as an obstacle to a psycho theory. These people are capable of great cunning and willing to take great pains."

"How about the different MOs?"

"Makes it a lot harder for us to get a line on him, doesn't it?"

"True," she agreed. "If there is a fanatic out there who has a grudge against policewomen, hates them enough to ambush and kill them, why isn't he announcing himself and his gripe to the world? Why isn't he calling us or the newspapers, writing letters, bragging, threatening?"

"Maybe he will. Maybe he's waiting."

"For what?"

"For us to find out on our own. And if we don't, to show us up for fools and incompetents."

A cold shudder passed through Norah. She took a deep breath and held it an extra-long time before exhaling. "Let's assume that the killer has some sort of grudge against policewomen in general, he still has to make a selection of a victim. As we agreed, he can't just put in a call for a squad car and expect a woman officer to show up. So on what does he base his choice?"

Honn looked at her a long time. He wet his lips. "What I'm going to tell you, Sergeant, is confidential. For the time being, at least. You remember Katherine Chave, killed in the bomb blast?"

"I remember."

At Honn's glance Gerald Innis picked up the account. "Chave and Bednarski were classmates at the Police Academy. Actually, they went back a long way before that; they grew up in the same neighborhood, went to the same high school, double-dated, like that. Naturally, Bednarski was all cut up about her buddy's death. She felt kind of responsible."

Norah thought of the dead woman's husband, Loy Chave; he'd felt responsible, too. "Why was that?"

"Well, Bednarski felt she was the reason that Chave was on the force in the first place. Seems Chave had kind of a schoolgirl crush on Bednarski and tried to do everything she did. So when Bednarski went over to the local high school to take the entrance exam, Chave tagged along and took it, too."

"Get on with it," Honn ordered.

"Yes, sir. So they both got hired at the same time and they both got fired at the same time."

It took a couple of seconds for her to grasp the significance of what he was telling her. Then, jaw set hard, Norah waited for the rest.

"When LEAA funds became available to rehire some of the cops that had been laid off, only one woman was on the list."

"She knows all that," Honn said.

Norah was very still.

"Well, ma'am, Bednarski was one of the women who went to court to get her job back. And she urged her friend, Katherine Chave, to do the same. Chave wasn't all that anxious; in fact, she didn't want to do it. She didn't really care about getting the job back. Bednarski insisted, told her she had an obligation to the other women, that they had to present a united front, that Chave would spoil it for all of them if she didn't bring suit."

That had to be the root of Loy Chave's sense of guilt, Norah thought with a sudden flash of insight. Not just that he had urged her not to stay home the morning of the bombing, but that he had urged her to sue for reinstatement to a job that it was now apparent she'd hated.

One woman had started it all by bringing a class-action suit against the department, charging discrimination on the basis of sex. She won, but the court decreed that the decision was not a blanket one and that each case would have to be judged on its individual merits. At the moment, as far as Norah was aware, there were approximately a hundred cases pending—the number wasn't important. What was of concern was that on August 13 thirty-eight policewomen had been rehired. Chave and Bednarski among them. And Nieves, Pilar Nieves, too. Three out of the four that had been killed. How about Ochs? Norah didn't know about Ochs; it hadn't come up.

"May I use your phone?" she asked Honn.

"We've already checked," he replied. "Each one of the victims had applied to the court for reinstatement."

His voice sounded far away; the scene itself—the bare, functional office and the two detectives—receded. Though outwardly calm, Norah was in turmoil. Of the women who had challenged the rehiring policy of the NYPD, brought suit, and won, thirty-eight thus far had been offered their jobs back. Six had declined, having found other employment or for personal reasons. Thirty-two went back to work.

Four of them were dead.

Thirty-two men had been dropped to make way for the women.

Four of them had been, or soon would be, rehired.

Monstrous as it was, she believed it, and her reasoning rendered her numb. Conditioned reflexes took over, sorting through the possible avenues of investigation.

"Norah? Are you all right?" Honn shot out of his chair and came around to her. "Here, you'd better sit." Gently, he eased her back into her chair. He glared at Innis. "Don't just stand there; get some water." He groaned with exasperation as Innis brought it, managing to slop half the contents on the floor.

They say anticipation is worse than the actual happening. Not always, Norah thought, not this time. The reality was beyond anything she had anticipated. A psycho with a hate on for all policewomen indiscriminately was a lot more dangerous and a lot harder to run down than one with a grievance against a specific group. Knowing the motive suggested where to look. It should have made it easier, but in this instance it magnified the horror. Norah gulped the water and handed the cup back to Innis with a hand that was steadier than his.

"May I use your phone?" she asked Captain Honn a second time,

He started to say yes automatically, but something warned him. "What for?"

"I have to call the women. I have to warn them." She was reaching for the instrument.

"Just a minute, Norah. Hold on. What I told you was in confidence."

Intuitive, always quick to grasp even an elusive concept, Norah was nevertheless totally confused by this. "I don't follow."

"Chief Deland is the one to decide how this should be handled."

Norah gaped at him. "The women have to be informed."

"Of course. There's no question. They will be."

"They have to be warned."

"Naturally."

"Now." She'd emerged from the miasma of doubt about the case. She herself in hand and she was sure of what she had to do. "They have to be warned that they're potential victims. Every one of the twenty-eight has to be told." She reached for the telephone.

Honn put his hand over hers. "You promised."

"No, Captain, I did not. You told me the information was confidential and then you went ahead and divulged it."

"I naturally assumed you'd respect . . ."

Norah looked him straight in the eye. "That was your mistake, sir."

"All right, all right, but be reasonable, Norah . . . Sergeant. There's no argument about the women having to be warned. My God, you can't seriously think that the chief would keep them ignorant of developments? If that were so, I wouldn't have passed the news on to you, would I?" A slight dip of her head indicated he'd made his point. "There are a lot of aspects to consider. The reputations of the men who were passed over in favor of the women, for example."

"They're going to come under suspicion no matter what. It's too bad, but—"

"The whole department is going to come under suspicion, every man in it."

Norah sighed. It was true.

"So give the chief a chance to work it out, to formulate some kind of policy. Then he'll inform the women. It is his prerogative."

"How long? How long before he tells them?"

"I don't know. I'm only a captain." Sebastian Honn tried a smile but met the wall of Norah's anxiety. "I'm sure that by the end of the day he'll be ready to—"

"Are you sure that by the end of the day another policewoman won't be dead?"

They stared at each other, neither willing to give way.

"I'm sorry, Captain, but I can't take that chance. I'm phoning our women's adviser to urge an emergency meeting for this afternoon." She glanced at her watch. "I think we can get hold of the women directly affected before the end of the current tour. The word will spread and probably we'll have most of the membership in attendance by five P.M. As long as we can contact the twenty-eight, though, that's the main thing." This time she actually picked up the receiver, then paused before dialing. "I won't say where or how I got the information."

"Do you think I give a damn about that!" Honn exploded. "I'm ordering you to put the phone down, but not because I'm concerned about being embarrassed."

"I don't work for you, Captain Honn. Even if I did, I'd have to go ahead." Norah still held the receiver in her hand. "If you won't let me use your phone, I'll walk straight out of here and use the first pay phone I can find. You can't stop me. Of course, meantime, you can use your phone to call my boss, Captain James Felix, Twentieth Precinct. Call Chief Deland, call the commissioner, but you can't stop me."

Norah was now calm, Honn was not. "Do you realize the position you're putting yourself in?" he demanded. Then he noticed Detective Gerald Innis, standing there gaping at this flouting of his captain's authority, and he bellowed. "Out, out! You've got work to do, haven't you? Go ahead and do it." As Innis scurried from the presence Honn added, "I'm sure as hell glad you don't work for me, Sergeant Mulcahaney."

Norah wasn't sure whether he was saving face for himself or for her or for both of them, but she waited till Detective Innis had eased himself out and pulled the door, very quietly, as unobtrusively as possible, shut behind him.

"So am I, Captain Honn."

He grimaced. "Sergeant, I have an idea. Why don't you let me call the chief and tell him you want to notify the women's association and call a meeting? He might want to appear and address you all. At least, let him know what he's going to have to deal with."

"In other words, ask his permission."

"No, no . . ."

"That's what it amounts to, Captain."

"All right, so what's so bad about that?"

Norah's blue eyes gleamed coldly. Her jaw was set. She trembled with anger. She had never been an active women's libber. Norah believed in individual initiative; she thought that those women who had ability and diligence would achieve whatever they were after. Banding together was good, but it was not a substitute for each woman's putting out her best. She had joined the force at the time of transition, while the women still worked out of a "pool" and were called upon to perform the routine, innocuous chores of matrons and clerks rather than police officers. Some of them were still in that rut. Nevertheless, she had thought that the women in the police department had definitely come a long way. Was she wrong? Honn's attitude clearly indicated that the rights the women thought they'd won on merit and hard work, standing beside the men, working the same hours, taking the same risks, were rights not earned but conferred. Conferred by the grace and favor of the men. She had never been so angry in her whole life.

"I don't need permission, Captain."

Norah was seething. "I've been a cop for seven years. Maybe you don't think that's long, but it's long enough for me to have observed the red tape, the duplication of effort, the waste of manpower, of time, money, the unfairness, the dissipation of enthusiasm among the ranks . . ." It was all spilling out. Now that she'd started, it was hard to stop. "I realize that some of it is inevitable in an organization this size. I realize you can't have people going off in all directions and conducting law enforcement according to their own criteria, that there has to be supervision and direction, that there has to be a chain of command. There have to be rules. Fine. I accept all that. But this has nothing to do with department regulations. The women have the right to know what they're up against. Not at the end of the day, not at the end of one hour— now. They have the right to take their own decision about what steps to take to protect themselves."

Honn sighed.

"And you have the right to call Chief Deland or Captain Felix or anybody else you damn well please and tell them what I'm up to. If I get kicked off the force, well, then, that's the way it's got to be."

"Okay." Sebastian Honn took a step back and with a grandiose gesture indicated she should go ahead and make her call.

"You're going to let me use this phone?"

"You might as well use this one as the one down the hall."

"But don't you want to use it?"

Sure, I intend to, but . . ." He made her a slight bow. "Ladies first. Oops, sorry about that, Norah. I hope you don't mind, but at heart I'm still kind of old-fashioned."

SEVEN

"Maybe I'm wrong. I can't this moment offer you proof that the women were murdered because they brought suit to get their jobs back, but it is a reasonable inference. Can we afford to ignore it? Do we dare call it a coincidence?" Sergeant Norah Mulcahaney appealed to her audience.

At the beginning merely a sorority group, the Policewomen's Endowment Association had recently been reorganized with a view to representing the rights of its members, although the PBA remained the official negotiating body for the women as for the men. As they paid two sets of dues, the funds available to the women's group were limited and so there were no permanent offices. The meetings, six times a year, as called for by the bylaws, were held in the halls of churches, schools, or benevolent associations that were willing to lend the premises without charge. The department also granted use of its facilities from time to time, in fact was very generous in this regard. Usually the women used the department's second-floor press-conference room, but tonight, expecting a full turnout of the membership, they had requested the use of the larger auditorium on the first floor of police headquarters and the request had been granted. Considering the circumstances, a change of policy at this moment would have been unthinkable in terms of public relations. It was on the dais in this room that Norah now stood facing almost the entire membership.

"We can't ignore the possibility that the murders may continue and that those of you who brought suit and were reinstated may be in danger." The group that had sued sat directly in front of her, huddled together not through preplanning but out of instinct.

Having scrupulously reviewed the four cases, making sure that everyone understood what was fact and what conjecture, she now summed up.

"I could be wrong. I could be jumping to conclusions. It's up to you to decide. It's up to you to decide what action, if any, you want to take." She paused and looked out at the completely female gathering. None of the brass had showed up. None had even asked to attend, much less address the gathering. Had Sebastian Honn warned them off? Norah wondered. Had the Narco commander advised that the women were in a highly volatile state and that interference, no matter how benign, was likely to be resented? The assembly and its purpose were by now common knowledge not only with in the department but throughout the city.

"Any questions?" Norah asked, and when no one responded resumed her seat at the side of the platform.

The chairwoman, Adele Schloss, who would not have been at a loss presiding in the boardroom of General Motors, now took over. "The meeting is open for general discussion," she announced.

The twenty-eight seemed to draw even closer together. After an interval intended to give one of them the first opportunity to speak, a strident voice was raised at the back of the hall.

"How do we know this creep is going to limit himself to the women who were fired and then rehired?"

There was a sharp intake of breath as each woman silently answered the question.

The speaker now got up so she could be seen and could also gauge the effect of what she'd said. "We have to protect ourselves. If we don't, nobody else will."

She was afraid, Norah thought, watching her, but would not admit it. She was agitating the others in order to appear to be merely sharing in their weakness.

"How can we do that? How can we protect ourselves? By getting off the streets, *that's* how. That's for starters."

"Right. Right!" Approval rang from every part of the auditorium.

"No more patrol."

"No decoy or undercover."

"Not while a maniac's on the prowl."

Norah sought and got recognition from the chair. "I just want to remind you all that while three women were killed on duty, the latest, Eve Bednarski, was not."

One of the group at the front timidly raised her hand. Officer Elizabeth Taggert was a self-effacing young woman of twenty-five with an odd kind of face, the two halves of which seemed microscopically out of line, as in a Picasso painting. Meeting Betty, one had the tendency to underrate her, to wonder what anybody saw in her, why she had so many friends. Norah knew the answer: Betty Taggart liked everybody; they couldn't help liking her back.

"You mean he might not be limiting himself to women on duty anymore?" Taggert suggested in her high, little girl's voice.

"I don't know." Norah was honest. "I just want you to be aware of all the possibilities." She underscored the "all," glancing toward the back.

"Wasn't Eve Bednarski out demonstrating?" Officer Mary Sussman, gray-haired, heavy-set, an eighteen year veteran who went back to the days when such a meeting would have been inconceivable, found the new assertiveness exciting and somewhat intimidating.

"She was supposed to be, yes." Norah replied.

Sussman, who in those eighteen years had never volunteered an opinion to a superior, now cleared her throat. "Is it possible that from the perpetrator's point of view it amounts to the same thing as being on duty? It was a police action."

"It could be," Norah agreed. "The point is a good one."

Mary Sussman flushed and sat down, proud of having taken part.

Again Betty Taggert asked to be recognized and this time stood up, as the others had done. "I've wanted to be a policewoman for as long as I can remember. I took the exam in '69 and had to wait nearly four years for appointment. Meantime, I worked for the telephone company. It was a good job with good money, plenty of security, regular increases, all kinds of benefits, but when I got the appointment, I quit without a minute's regret. Then in '75 I got fired. I was lucky because the telephone company took me back, but I wasn't happy. I guess police work is in my blood. I wanted my badge back. I fought to get it back. Out of the seven years since I applied I've only worked three as a police officer, but I refused to give up. Now I'm scared. I admit it, but I'd go on fighting . . . if I could. I've got an invalid mother. She has no one to look after her but me . . . If anything happens to me . . . ." Taggert swallowed, looked around at the strained, anxious faces. "I'm sorry." Her lopsided face twisted as she struggled to hold back the tears. "I'm sorry . . . I'm going to have to resign."

There was a moment's silence, then a long, collective sigh.

Another of the group of twenty-eight spoke. "Me, too. I'm going to resign, too."

And another, in a louder voice, defiantly. "Like Betty said, I wanted this job. I fought for it. But I'm not going to die for it."

"Right on!"

"You said it."

"Who needs it?"

The uproar grew, then divided into separate arguments. The chair pounded for order. In the center of the room, Officer Dollinger got up and waved both arms over her head and was recognized. She shouted.

"Sick leave. Why not take sick leave?"

Some heard and were willing to listen.

Dolly Dollinger was able to lower her voice. She addressed the women in the front, but she wanted to be heard by all. "You could take sick leave and stay out till the perpetrator is caught."

There were murmurs of assent and relief. It was a reasonable compromise put forth in a sensible, matter-of-fact manner. Dolly Dollinger, chubby and short, with straight hair cut in china-doll bangs, had once been a member of Sergeant Mulcahaney's Senior Citizen's Squad and was known to be sensible and level-headed. Her suggestion seemed to stem the tide of hysteria.

Officer Joanna Feliciano was not impressed. She had been silent up to now, listening. She was a woman slow in making up her mind, but once having done so, she was hard to change. "He wants us off the force and he'll come after us whether we're on active duty or not. I think the way he got Bednarski is an indication of that. *He wants our jobs.* I say, let him have them. He can have mine." With that, Feliciano began to edge her way out of the row. Reaching the aisle, she stopped and surveyed the assembly. "If you're smart, you'll follow me."

In that moment of uncertainty, many eyes looked to Norah. "I can't advise you; nobody can. I don't question your right to resign, but I have to say that in my opinion every resignation increases the risk to those who stay on."

"Tough." Feliciano, standing in the middle of the center aisle, spit out the word. "Then let's all resign."

"Maybe some of us don't want to."

A fresh, young voice challenged. It belonged to a small girl with delicate features, gold-flecked hazel eyes, and a soft cloud of red hair framing her piquant face.

"Easy for you to be brave Mairead Quinn. You work in the property clerk's office. Not much danger there. Besides which, you've got four big strapping brothers in the department to protect you."

Quinn, Norah thought, Quinn? Of course, Sergeant Frank Quinn, who she'd met at the site of the department-store bombing. This had to be his sister.

Meanwhile Mairead Quinn's face got as red as her hair. "I've got twenty-seven thousand brothers in the department and so do you," she retorted stoutly. "And every one of them is ready to protect us."

That brought murmurs of approval, few laughs, and a light round of applause.

Eagerly, Dolly Dollinger seized on the shift in mood. "Don't forget that we're a lot nearer to a solution of the case than we were, say, eight hours ago. The detectives now know why the crimes were committed and so they know where to look. Before, it could have been anyone in the city. Now we know that it's probably . . ." She stopped, aghast at having put into words what was lurking in every woman's mind but that so far none had dared express.

Joanna Feliciano had no such qualms.

"It has to be one of the thirty-two men whose jobs were appropriated."

That pronouncement was met by a dreadful hush. In despair, Dolly looked to Norah for help in repairing the damage she'd inadvertently caused. Norah tried.

"It could be anybody, anybody at all who is angry at so-called reverse discrimination, anybody who feels that the class-action suit is a threat to his own seniority . . . Even someone outside the department."

But this time they wouldn't listen. She was drowned out.

"It could be any *man* in the department."

It didn't matter who said it. The woman didn't stand up; she didn't speak loudly, but everybody heard. All other comments were stilled and what she'd said was repeated in hushed murmurs and passed along: *any man in the department.*

"Somebody who knew the victims."

"Somebody who worked with them."

"In the precinct."

"On active duty."

"Not laid off. Not one of the guys who lost his job, somebody on active duty."

"Right, right. Somebody who knew when and where the women would be and what they'd be doing."

"Somebody who hates us."

"Somebody who wants us off the force, not just those of us who were rehired but all of us."

"Somebody who knew the victims personally."

"No. Listen. Hold it. *Listen.*" Norah, Dolly and Mairead Quinn shouted; the chairwoman pounded the gavel; nothing served to counter the uproar. Norah went over to the podium and stood beside Adele Schloss.

"Who knew the victims better than their partners?" Norah shouted. "Who knew better than each woman's partner just exactly where she would be and what she'd be doing at any specific moment? When she'd be the most vulnerable. Isn't that right? Don't that make sense? The partners." She was making herself heard; she was reaching them. "Four victims, four partners, four possibilities. Four: Guy Felcher, Fernando Arenas, Thomas Janssen, Gerald Innis. Not the whole department, not *any man* in the department, but these four!"

She found herself shouting into a shamed silence.

"Okay, which one? Or are they in it together? Does one commit the actual murder while the others set it up? Or do they take turns? Why don't we get them down here and sweat it out of them? Let's not leave it to the detectives—they're men and they'll protect the suspects, won't they?"

Joanna Feliciano's face was sullen because she knew she'd lost. "Okay, but as far as I'm concerned, that puts us back to square one. So I'm resigning." She turned and strode down the aisle and out of the hall.

Her exit was followed by an uneasy stirring. A couple of the women started to put on their coats.

"Sergeant Mulcahaney," Mairead Quinn said, appealing to Norah. "You've been on the case from the start. What would you do if you were in our shoes?"

Norah had come to the meeting with the firm intention of not offering advice, of taking no sides. She shook her head.

"Just tell us what you think, Sergeant," the redhead urged. "We don't need to go along with it."

Norah took a breath. "All right. I think the safest place that any of us can be right now, and I mean all of us, is in our own station houses. I do think that we should get off the streets, but stay on active duty. I'm sure all commanders will go along with that. And when you go home, don't be alone. So far there's been no attack in the home, but we should all take reasonable precautions. Nobody stay home alone even for a short time. Don't go to and from work alone. Ever. Don't run down to the corner for cigarettes or a newspaper, or whatever, alone. Use the buddy system. Settle in for a long siege."

The mood changed.

"Hang tough."

"Bring him out into the open."

"We're cops. We're supposed to take care of other people, we ought to be able to take care of ourselves."

Euphoria bloomed.

"We'll get him."

"Say, Sergeant . . . suppose a woman's living alone?"

"Get a roommate," Norah replied.

"Male or female?"

"That's up to you."

Laughter. The tension was broken.

"Does that go for all of us? About not being alone?"

"Sure. Never hurts to be careful. We're dealing with a psycho and there's no telling how he'll react. If we make it too hard for him to attack the original group, he could turn his attention elsewhere."

The chair went through the motions of parliamentary procedure in adjourning, but it was perfunctory; the crisis had passed. Collecting their belongings, the women broke up into chatty small groups. Dolly Dollinger joined Norah.

"So which is it going to be—your place or mine?"

"What?"

"Do you want to move in with me till Joe gets back, or should I come over to you?"

"Come on, Dolly . . ."

"I could always go to my folks, or course." Dolly made a face. "And you've got your dad or any one of Joe's sisters . . ."

Norah grinned. "I don't think our man is interested in a couple of old war-horses like us."

As they walked out into the first-floor corridor Norah was handed a telephone message: Captain Felix wanted to see her right away. Honn must have gone ahead and snitched, she thought, and felt a sharp stab of disappointment.

James Felix looked up as Norah entered his office. "How was the meeting?"

She had come girded for battle. Back straight and stiff, shoulders square, jaw thrust characteristically forward to maintain her outward composure, Norah nevertheless felt her stomach doing flip-flops. "All right," she answered. "Pretty well, actually. There was talk of mass resignation, but in the end only one woman walked out. I'm hoping she'll change her mind."

"Good. Very good. I'm glad to hear that."

No mention of her part in calling the meeting, nor of divulging privileged information, nor of disobeying a direct order.

"The women will stay on the job but request desks duty."

"Much better for them to request it than for the commissioner to impose it."

There was a twinkle in Felix's green eyes and a twitch at the corner of his mouth. Either Honn had not made any complaint against her or Felix had chosen to ignore it. Either way, she could relax, Norah thought. "Yes, sir, much better."

With one thing settled, Felix prepared to tackle the next. "I had a talk with Chief Deland, and here's how it stands. Each homicide will be handled within its own jurisdiction. Tactical will be responsible for running a check on the alibis of the thirty-two men who were dropped when the women won their court cases. Tactical will also organize the test-firing of all weapons of all police officers—including superior officers."

The autopsy on Pilar Nieves had revealed that she was shot by a .38 S and W police special. "Would a cop have used his own weapon?" she asked.

"Frankly, I don't think so, but it has to be checked out, for everybody's sake."

Norah sighed.

"Tactical will also run a computer check on all arrests made by all policewomen, going right back to the time the women moved from the central pool into the precincts."

Going right down to the bone, Norah thought. Then she wondered why Captain Felix was taking the trouble to fill her in. Her earlier qualms returned in a rush.

"We'll be the nerve center," Felix went on. "Since the first homicide occurred in our division and we're already tied to the others, all information will feed in to us."

That was good, even gratifying, but not what Norah was waiting to hear. "What will we be *doing,* Captain?"

"What we usually do—dig."

She couldn't hold back any longer. "What will *I* be doing?"

"Ah . . ." Felix sighed, leaned back, and, making a temple of his long, tapering fingers, thoughtfully regarded Norah over the tips. "That's what I wanted to talk to you about, Sergeant." He paused.

She held her breath.

"Do you intend to request desk duty?" Felix asked.

"What? Me?"

"Because if you do, there's plenty of work available. Somebody has to monitor the information that comes in, evaluate it, make sense out of it. You needn't think you'd be left out."

"Thank you, Captain, but I had no intention of requesting any change in assignment." Her jaw hardened. "No change, sir."

"Just asking, Sergeant." Felix grinned and tipped his chair forward. "I might add that the chief was very impressed with your work in uncovering the link between these cases. He authorized me to tell you so."

"With *my* work?"

"He also told me to tell you that he understands your motives in calling the women together but that he would have preferred you to file your report first—according to procedure."

"But . . . sir . . . I didn't . . . What gave the chief the idea . . ."

"That you were the one who figured out the connection? Captain Honn told him."

"Captain Honn did?"

"That's right. He said you're both intuitive and shrewd. He said your observaions at the scene at Yankee Stadium were perceptive and that you followed up with all the right questions."

"That was very nice of him."

"He's a very fair man. Plenty of officers owe their promotions to Sebastian Honn's generous commendation. What he's been through the past couple of years would have soured plenty, made them bitter and hard to get along with. Honn has kept his troubles to himself and hasn't allowed them to affect his work."

Norah was torn. Sebastian Honn's gesture was certainly magnanimous, and it had also got them both off the hook. If she now admitted the truth, that in fact she'd had little if anything to do with the discovery of the link between the victims, that it had been made by Honn himself, and that he had revealed it to her, it would not only be ungrateful but might make trouble for him. She didn't want to do that.

"In fact," Felix continued, "Captain Honn was staunch in your defense. He suggested that since you had in fact informed him of your discovery, you had in essence reported it." Felix paused. "It satisfied the chief."

But it did not satisfy James Felix, obviously. She owed him an explanation and he was waiting for it. Norah bit her lip. "I got carried away, Captain. I should have reported to you, sir."

"Don't let it happen again."

"No, sir."

He nodded, dismissing the matter, and Norah knew that he would not mention it again or hold it against her.

"So." He rubbed his hands together. "Before anything else we've got to clear up the Janssen situation. What we want is a straight story from him finally. We have to know, once and for all, just what the hell went on in that building on West Sixteenth. Captain Kreps agrees with me that you're the one to find out."

She flushed with pleasure. "Thank you, sir."

"And Norah . . ." Felix picked up the telex report of the women's meeting, which he'd been reading when she entered. His voice moderate. "You gave your colleagues good advice; be sure you follow it yourself. Don't take unnecessary chances."

"No, sir."

"Also we're setting up an emergency number for all policewomen to use in case they get any information or notice anything at all. On the job or at home, anywhere. At any hour of the day or night."

He didn't say in case of attack. He didn't need to.

EIGHT

Getting murdered is one way of attracting your neighbor's attention, even in New York.

People who barely acknowledge the existence of their next-door neighbor, who refuse to nod in the elevator for fear of surrendering their privacy, seize on the slimmest of contacts when that neighbor becomes a victim of violence. Unfortunately, as Norah well knew, they then magnify and color what little information they possess according to their own imagination. Therefore, she did not expect to get much of value from a canvass of the building in which Officer Audrey Ochs had lived. It was merely a place to start, for Audrey had no family in the city and no close friends at the precinct. As far as members of the Tenth were concerned, Ochs had kept to herself. What she did and whom she saw in her off-hours was completely unknown. What Norah had not counted on, and what came as a pleasant surprise, was that being a police-woman had conferred distinction on Ochs among the tenants of the five-story building. They had pointed her out to one another, had made a point of making themselves known to her. She had been both a curiosity and, in a building with no doorman or eleva-tor man, lacking even minimal security, a reassuring presence that made it easier to sleep at night.

Paul Heddringer lived on the same floor as Officer Ochs had and had been most aware of her comings and goings. He also had plenty of time for a friendly gossip. Lucky, Norah thought, and weren't they due for a bit of luck in all this mess?

"She came and went at all kinds of hours," Heddringer

confided, having ensconced Norah in a blue velvet chair beside a small table covered with a lace cloth. "Of course, that was because of her job."

Heddringer was about six four, a hundred and ninety pounds, and despite the dyed auburn hair and walrus mustache that didn't quite match and the suntan makeup, he was probably over sixty, and looked it.

"I must say that Officer Ochs was quiet and very considerate about her comings and goings; she never banged doors or talked in a loud voice in the halls. After some of the people we've had in this building . . ." He threw up age-spotted hands whose finger-nails flashed a pearly polish. "Twenty-five years I've lived here. I was born right across the street." He pointed through white lace curtains at a massive edifice with every possible stonework orna-mentation. "When my mother died, naturally I didn't require an eight-room apartment, so I moved over. I don't know if you noticed the small art shop half a block down. That's mine. Now I don't even have to cross the street to go to work."

"How nice."

"Those needlepoint pictures in Officer Ochs's apartment . . . over her sofa? She had them framed in my shop. Perhaps you no-ticed?"

"I haven't been in there yet. I'm waiting for the super to come with the key."

"Good luck!" Heddringer snorted derisively. "Syd's what's called a 'floating superintendent,' which means he's never around when you need him. Would you believe he has an answering serv-ice? Which makes sure he never gets a message." The aggrieved tenant sighed. "This building was sold about a year ago and it's been down hill all the way since then. You should have seen it before—a jewel. Clean, beautifully maintained. Now—the pits."

Though she sympathized, Norah didn't want him side-tracked into complaints against his landlord. "About Officer Ochs—did she have many visitors? Living on the same floor, perhaps you no-ticed?"

"She didn't give any parties, I couldn't have missed that. As to just the odd visitor, well, I'm in my shop most of the day, but somehow I don't think she did. I don't think she made friends easily. She was rather shy."

Janssen had said the same thing.

"She was kind of plain, I guess." Norah had the official photo, but one couldn't tell much from that.

Tilting his head to one side, Heddringer considered. "Of course, that's a matter of opinion, but I thought she was rather . . . engaging." He was patronizing. "Her problem was that she had no style. I don't mean her clothes; she was usually in uniform when I saw her, but even in uniform she could have carried herself with more . . ." He thrust out his right shoulder and flung his chin high. "Panache! Know what I mean?"

"Oh, yes."

"She was sweet. Not at all what one would imagine a policewoman to be. Now you, Sergeant Mulcahaney, the moment you identified yourself, I accepted you as an officer of the law."

"Thank you."

"Frankly, I don't know why she was so determined to get back on the force. What she should have been was a nice housewife, married to some nice, middle-income man, living in the suburbs and having babies."

"I guess she hadn't found the right man."

"Oh, but she had."

"Really?"

"It seemed so to me." He shrugged. "She'd started going with him only recently, but from the amount of time they spent together . . ." He leered.

What do you mean by 'recently'? A month, two months?"

"Hm . . . about three months."

"Did you ever meet the boyfriend?"

"I ran into the two of them a few times going in and out of the building. We spoke, but she didn't introduce us—no reason why she should."

"Can you describe him?"

Heddringer put forefinger to pursed lips. "About my height, a little heavier . . . I try to stay in shape." He sucked in his stomach self-consciously. "It's not easy; I do enjoy good food and I'm a good cook."

Norah nodded her admiration of such self-discipline. "His coloring . . . do you recall?"

"His hair was kind of a darkish blond."

"Anything else you can remember about him? Distinguishing marks of any kind?"

Forefinger to lips once again, Heddringer slowly shook his

head. "I'm sorry. Half the light bulbs in the lobby are out and the halls are so damned dark."

"You've done very well, Mr. Heddringer, very well." Norah made it a point to compliment witnesses. "I have some pictures here that I'd just like you to look through. Perhaps you could pick out Officer Ochs's friend?"

Heddringer squinted. He grimaced. He shuffled through the pack, stopped at one. "Just a moment," he murmured, and, getting to his feet, strode to a small ormolu-decorated desk, where he extracted a stylish pair of horn-rimmed spectacles from a drawer. Putting them on, he returned to his seat and reexamined the photograph.

"Yes, that's the man I saw with Officer Ochs. That's her friend."

"You're sure?"

"Absolutely."

"Forgive me, Mr. Heddringer, but were you wearing your glasses on any of the occasions on which you met Officer Ochs and her friend? As you said yourself, the halls are quite dark."

He sniffed. "I only use the glasses for close work, Sergeant. I'm not dependent on them. I know what you look like without them, but if I had to pick out your photograph from an assortment, then I would use them to avoid error."

"Of course." The identification would not stand up; she hid her disappointment. Could she nail it another way? "You seem to have excellent recall, Mr. Heddringer, really unusual. I wonder if you could fix the dates on which you saw this man with Officer Ochs. I know it's not easy, but I'd really appreciate it if you'd try."

Of course he was flattered, but uncertain.

"Let's work backward," Norah suggested. "Did you see them together this past week?"

"No. And not the week before, either. At least . . . no, I'm sure not. I'm sure that I didn't see either one of them, because I wanted to speak to Officer Ochs about getting the landlord to put a grille behind the glass panels of the downstairs door and I was particularly looking for her."

Good, Norah thought, he'd got the idea. "Perhaps we can connect it with a particular occasion—a night when you'd been entertaining perhaps or had been out."

"Yes, yes!" He was excited, the previous pique over his nearsightedness forgotten. "I'd been out to dinner and came home late on this particular night. When I stepped out of the elevator I jumped at finding people in the hall—in this building one always expects the worst. Then I realized that it was only Officer Ochs and her friend. They seemed startled to see me. I assumed that they were saying good night, and I just nodded and came straight inside. Naturally."

"Do you recall the date?"

"I can look it up in my engagement book."

"Wonderful, I'd appreciate—"

"But I don't really have to. There's more, Sergeant, if you're interested?" He came close to smacking his lips. "I was hurrying home that particular night because there was something on the *Late Show* that I wanted to see. It was *Casablanca*. I never miss it. I was glued to the set for the whole thing and when it was over I was just getting myself a snack when I heard sounds outside in the hall. Normally I would have assumed it was Officer Ochs coming home, but as I knew that she was already home . . ."

"You thought it might be a prowler," Norah suggested.

"Exactly. So I looked through the peephole and it was the boyfriend." He watched Norah to see if she appreciated the significance.

"So that when you saw them at the door earlier, he was not leaving Officer Ochs but going in with her."

"Right, that's right." Heddringer paused. "As it happens, Sergeant Mulcahaney, I wear my glasses when I watch television." He tossed his head. "I still had them on when I looked through the peephole."

They smiled at each other: he, because he'd been vindicated; she, because his testimony would now stand up.

"I could have come to your house, but I thought this would be more convenient for both of us," Norah explained to Officer Thomas Janssen as they entered one of the interrogation rooms. With a deprecating gesture, she added, "I hope you don't mind; I couldn't think of anywhere else that we could be private."

Janssen's puffy face showed no reaction.

In fact, Norah had chosen the interrogation room specifically because she was no longer interested in making things easy for Janssen. To the contrary. She pulled out a chair and sat down at the plain deal table and indicated he should sit also. She waited.

He waited. Evidently he was prepared to wait her out. Okay, Norah thought. She had a good hand; she didn't mind making the opening lead.

"I want to be straight with you, Tom, so that you'll be straight with me. Your original report on the Ochs homicide left a lot of holes. Now, everybody from Captain Kreps and Captain Felix down understands that you were under considerable stress after your partner was killed. But now that you've had a chance to pull yourself together we expect a coherent account of exactly what happened."

"I'm sorry if the report isn't satisfactory, Sergeant. I did the best I could with it. There's nothing I can add."

"Are you willing to try?"

He mumbled something like "It won't do any good." Norah ignored it. "First, let me ask you this: how did it feel to have a woman for a partner?"

She had asked it so casually that he had to look at her, make actual eye contact for the first time in order to gauge her intent.

"Okay. She pulled her weight." Quickly he looked away again.

"Good. I'm glad to hear it. You felt that in a crisis you could rely on her?"

"Sure."

"And, of course, she could rely on you." It was a low blow, as Norah had intended. "Did you go out together? I mean, for a couple of beers after work, as you would with a guy?

"Oh, yeah, like that, sure."

"No more than that?"

"We worked together. We were partners. Period."

Norah took a deep breath, exhaled. "I don't know whether you realize it or not, Tom, but you're in trouble, really bad trouble. That report of yours—"

"I'm goddamned sick and tired of being hassled over that report."

"I'm trying to help you, Tom, I mean it. If there was something between you and Audrey Ochs . . ."

"No! How many times do I have to say it? No!"

"Your wife thinks there was."

"Leave Lorna out of this! Leave her out of it."

That had got a rise out of him, anyway, Norah thought. "I'd like to leave her out; that's one of the reasons we're meeting here instead of at your home, but you've got to stop sitting there like a

lump and start cooperating. Your report stinks and you know it."
She paused. "We've got a witness who saw you going in and out
of Audrey's apartment—frequently. He's already made a positive
ID of your photo and, believe me, it will stand up. So. You give
me the straight story or I'm going to Lorna and start matching up
dates and times with her."

Janssen groaned. "I used to take Audrey home sometimes, after
the late tour. She was a woman. I felt responsible."

"You mean when you worked the four-to-midnight? No other
times?"

"We went to the PBA meetings a couple of times. I took her
home from those."

"Her neighbor says you went in with her."

"Once or twice for a nightcap."

"How about October first? Was there a PBA meeting that
night? It was a Friday."

They both knew there had not been a meeting and Janssen and
Ochs had worked the eight-to-four.

"Some of us got together informally."

"I see." Norah paused. "Do you like old movies, Tom? Do you
watch old movies on TV? I do. I get really caught up in some of
those oldies. Like *Casablanca*. That's a real favorite of mine."

Befuddled, he shook his head. He was a cop, too, after all, and
knew he was being set up . . . but how?

"So you weren't watching *Casablanca* when they ran it a couple
of weeks ago? Mr. Heddringer was; he's a real buff. That's
Audrey's neighbor who lives on her floor, the one who made the
ID on you. Seems he'd been out to dinner and ran into you and
Audrey in the hall when he came home. He had the date marked
in his engagement book. He got home just in time to catch the
start of the movie. It was no sweat to check the date and time with
TV Guide to make sure he had it right. When the show was over
he heard a noise in the hall and looked out just in time to see you
leaving. The movie went for over two hours: that's quite a while
for one nightcap."

"Okay. So what? It's nobody's business."

"That might have been true once, but no more. My God, man.
Your partner was snatched from behind your back, dragged away,
and garroted. Don't you give a damn? Didn't you have any kind
of feeling for her at all?"

He began to sweat. Rivulets ran down his face. A dark rim appeared around his collar. He gave off a rank odor of fear. Norah would not give him respite; there were no excuses for Thomas Janssen.

"According to the autopsy report, Audrey Ochs was pregnant."

He put a hand over his eyes.

"You must have known it would show up in the autopsy."

He groaned.

"She was a plain girl and she had no friends. Just you."

Saliva trickled from the corner of his mouth and down his chin.

"She expected you to get a divorce and marry her, didn't she?"

"Nobody gets pregnant by accident, not nowadays," he complained. "It was a lousy thing to do."

Norah wanted to slap him. Looking into his darkened, surly face, she was revolted. Anger churned inside her to the point where she felt that she must get some kind of physical release. She fought it, gritting her teeth, clenching her hands, waiting till the inner trembling passed. "Maybe she loved you."

The silence in the interrogation room was absolute. The second hand of the electric wall clock swept a full circle.

"Was she threatening to tell Lorna?" Norah asked.

"Yeah." He refused to look at her.

"You couldn't let that happen."

He was too immersed in his own thoughts to grasp the implication. "I offered to pay for the abortion."

"Fair enough." The anger coursed through her blood, throbbing at her temples, pulsing like the most relentless of headaches. "But she didn't want an abortion."

"No."

"So you killed her."

"What?"

Finally, finally he realized his situation, Norah saw. And it shocked him. And so now maybe he'd talk.

"No. *No.* Is that what you think? I wouldn't do that. Never. I swear. Is that what this interrogation is all about?"

"Where were you on the afternoon of Saturday, September fifteenth, at three in the afternoon?"

"Saturday, September fifteenth, at three in the afternoon? I can't remember. I don't know. Off the top of my head, I just . . ."

"How about this past Tuesday, October twelfth? Two days ago? Off the top of your head, can you remember what you were doing then?"

"Two days ago? I suppose I was home. I've been home ever since . . . That was the night of the demonstration at Yankee Stadium. I didn't go. I . . ." He stopped, mouth open, eyes bulging. She wasn't out just to pin Audrey's murder on him, she was out to nail him for the whole damn series of murders. God, God! He knew her; he knew Norah Mulcahaney. She had a big reputation for solving these multiple-murder cases. Well, she wasn't going to add his scalp to her string. She wasn't using him as a rung up the ladder to make lieutenant. No way. The sweat was so heavy on him that he shivered. His teeth chattered. He couldn't speak.

Norah read his anger and his confusion. If he'd killed Pilar Nieves and Eve Bednarski he'd surely have had some sort of alibi ready. She didn't even think he'd killed Audrey Ochs; she never had thought so. He'd behaved badly to Ochs and he knew it. Inwardly he acknowledged it and it made him defensive. He was relieved that Audrey Ochs was no longer a problem and he was ashamed of being relieved. In fact, he was glad that she was dead. In one intuitive flash Norah had it. She understood what was behind Tom Janssen's taciturnity, why he had written that vague report and why he doggedly refused to discuss it. It made her sad. Very sad.

"Tom?" She spoke quietly.

Instinctively he pulled back, eyes narrowed. He didn't trust her. He never should have trusted her, not even for a second.

"You must have realized pretty early on that the complaint you and Audrey were answering that night was a fake."

"I'm not going to say any more. I'm entitled to my rights like anybody else. You should have read me my rights," he said accusingly.

"You must have realized it as soon as the complainant failed to answer his doorbell. Weren't you the least bit suspicious when the elevator didn't come? Didn't that make you extra cautious climbing the stairs? Knowing that the call very probably was a fake, you surely must have been sensitive to every sound, every footfall, every crack in the stairs as you went up. How can you persist in saying that you didn't hear a thing when Audrey was grabbed from behind you?"

Janssen's lips were clamped in a tight, hard line.

"Obviously the perpetrator covered her mouth when he grabbed her so she couldn't cry out, but there had to be sounds of a scuffle, some kind of noise when he dragged her along the hall, down the stairs, and into the elevator. You did say that the elevator was on the fourth floor while the two of you were on the fifth?"

"I left her behind on the fourth floor. I told you that," he shouted, provoked at last. "I was inside the apartment when she was snatched. I couldn't hear anything."

"Oh, yes, you heard, Officer Janssen, you heard, all right, but you ignored what you heard. Maybe you were inside the apartment when it happened, but by your own account the building was very quiet. You heard. Maybe you didn't know what it was, but you heard and you didn't investigate till it was too late. Hadn't you secretly been wishing that something might happen to Audrey? That somehow she just . . . wouldn't be around to bother you anymore? Hadn't you fantasized about something happening to her, an accident of some kind? And here it was, the wish being realized. You let Audrey Ochs die."

"I didn't mean to. I swear. Audrey was slow, lagging behind. I got impatient and went on. I thought she'd caught up with me and was behind me when I entered the apartment. Like I told you, I didn't know she wasn't there till I backed out into the hall again. I swear. I did hear a moan . . . a couple of times . . . down below. I froze for a couple of seconds. No more than that. Okay, I admit it did go through my mind—what you say—that if anything did happen to Audrey, if she had an accident or lost the baby, then I'd be off the hook. But when I realized that she might be in real danger, then I ran down those stairs as fast as I could. I got to the fourth floor just as the elevator disappeared. It wasn't more than a minute. It couldn't have been."

Nora sighed. "That's why you didn't follow the perpetrator out on the roof. That's why you didn't give chase. You didn't want to apprehend him."

"I wanted to help Audrey. That was more important. I thought she was still alive."

"You knew she was dead. One look was all you needed to know she was dead. You didn't want to catch the perpetrator. You were afraid that if you did catch him he'd talk and he'd tell us just how long you waited before going to your partner's assistance." She paused. "And it was a hell of a lot longer than one minute."

He bowed his head. "All right. Yes. I admit it. She's dead now. What difference does it make?"

"I'll tell you what difference it makes, Officer Janssen." Norah's eyes burned, her jaw trembled. "If you'd done your sworn duty,

Officer Ochs might still be alive and the baby she was carrying, too. Your baby. Having failed that, you might have collared her killer. If you had, Officer Bednarski would be alive."

"I didn't realize . . . I didn't think . . . I'm sorry."

"Shut up," Norah snapped "Don't you dare say you're sorry."

"I am."

"Then pray to God that no more women die."

NINE

Thomas Janssen made a full statement, which was taken down by a police stenographer. Temporarily suspended while his conduct was under investigation, he surrendered shield and guns. It was not likely that he would ever get them back.

Norah was supposed to be making out a report, but she sat at her desk, chin in hand, brooding. The Janssen business depressed her because it was an indication of the degeneration of the department. When she first joined the force, only seven years before, spirit had been high. In Norah's eyes every man had been a hero, defender and avenger of the poor and helpless, and most policemen had at least tried to live up to that image. Bad cops had been one in a thousand. That ratio had shifted considerably in recent years, she thought bitterly. She was less naive now; she realized that cops were only human, but that didn't give them the license to lie, cheat, even steal; to sleep, drink, and fornicate on the job. It was this moral rot that was responsible for Thomas Janssen's fatal hesitation in going to the aid of his partner. Who was to blame? Norah wondered. Had the cancer been there dormant, waiting for the right climate to grow and spread? Or was the public to blame, in part, anyway? Having permitted scorn, abuse, and vilification to be heaped on their police, could they expect every man to stand staunch and incorruptible?

Yet the whole department wasn't rotten; not every officer was self-seeking. There were plenty of good, dedicated men and women. Names and faces of cops she'd known and worked with passed across Norah's mental screen. There was Joe, of course.

Sebastian Honn belonged in that group. Thinking of Honn reminded Norah that she owed him a call.

"Well, Sergeant Mulcahaney." Honn's voice was warm and friendly. "This is an unexpected pleasure. What can I do for you?"

"I want to thank you for what you did."

"You mean for what I didn't do," he said teasingly.

"Considering how strongly you felt, it was very generous. I appreciate it."

"We both made too much of the problem. What matters is that the women are staying on the job but taking all prudent precautions. That's what we were both after, isn't it?"

"Yes," Norah agreed. "I just don't feel that I should take credit that isn't due. I feel bad about depriving Detective Innis."

"Detective Innis made a chance remark about the friendship between Officers Bednarski and Chave. One thing led to another and we put it together. It was neither brilliant deduction nor a blinding revelation."

"Still . . ."

"Don't worry about it. Innis is getting full marks where it'll do him the most good—in my book."

"If you say so."

"Look, Sergeant, I haven't the time right now, but if you insist on discussing your qualms then it'll have to be over dinner.

"Dinner?"

"That's right. I'm asking you out to dinner with me, Norah. I understand that Joe's in Italy, that you're alone."

"Yes. Joe's in Italy."

"That's what I heard. So?"

She didn't know what to say to him.

He pressed. "Well, he wouldn't mind, would he? Surely Lieutenant Capretto wouldn't mind if you and I had dinner together?"

She decided to put it on the line "Joe wouldn't, but how about your wife? How would she feel about it?"

There was a moment's silence at the other end of the line. "My wife is dead. Margo died nearly a year ago—last November."

"Oh. I'm sorry, Captain. I didn't know."

"No reason why you should." He took a breath. "I'll pick you up at your place at seven."

"Fine."

"Oh. Where do you live?"

She gave him the address.

No sooner had she hung up than she remembered she was supposed to go to her father's for the dinner she'd canceled because of the extra duty. So she'd just have to call Honn back and explain. Maybe they could make it for tomorrow night? No, tomorrow she had Lena. Then, the day after that, Anna . . . She could hardly ask Sebastian Honn to wait half a week. The invitation had been proffered spontaneously: to postpone it for that many days would be to turn it into an obligation for both of them, even an embarrassment. She'd just have to cancel. She reached for the phone.

She didn't want to cancel: she wanted to see Sebastian Honn. Despite their difference, Norah liked him. In fact, she found it stimulating to argue with him, exciting. So instead of calling Honn, Norah called her father. Patrick Mulcahaney, catching the pleasure in his girl's voice, made no fuss about yet another change in plans.

Now Norah attacked her paperwork with gusto. As she pecked at the typewriter her mind wandered. It was odd that the friendship between Eve Bednarski and Katherine Chave should have been the clue that led to establishing the link between the homicides and the killer's motive: odd, because Katie Chave's death was an accident and therefore couldn't be part of the series.

She'd stopped typing and was staring out over the desks and the men in the squad room, completely oblivious of the routine confusion and even of the man who now stood in front of her, waiting to catch her attention.

He spoke finally. "Sergeant Mulcahaney. I don't know if you remember me. Frank Quinn?"

She looked up into the tawny, nearly yellow eyes. Most particularly she remembered his eyes, which seemed not to belong in his pudgy, freckled face. "Considering how we met, I could hardly forget you. In fact, I was just thinking about Katherine Chave."

"Oh?"

"It all began with her."

"How's that?"

"I wish I knew. I just have the feeling . . ." She shrugged it off and fixed her attention on her visitor. He looked very pale, she thought, almost as strained now as he had been on the occasion of the discovery of the mutilated body. A cold chill passed through her, and Norah shivered. She changed the subject. "I had the pleasure of meeting your sister the other day. Uh . . . Mairead. A lovely girl."

"Thank you. It's Mairead I came to see you about, Sergeant. I have a favor to ask."

Norah eased back in her chair. "I'll do it if I can. Glad to. I was very impressed with Mairead. The women were just about ready to walk out in a body. She stopped it."

He was not pleased to hear that. "I want her to resign."

Norah folded her arms and waited.

"She's in danger and she won't admit it."

"I don't agree. I think your sister is an idealistic young woman but also a sensible one. It struck me at the meeting that she was very much aware of the danger but that she had a lot of courage and was determined to meet it."

"She's got too much courage and too much determination. That's the problem. Always has been. You see, Sergeant, Mairead is the only girl in a family of four boys. Naturally she was always the pet. She could have had all kinds of privileges, but she didn't want them: she didn't want to sit around in pretty dresses, go to dancing school, or learn embroidery. She wanted to play with us boys, do what we did. Everything. Well, you know how kids are: the older boys think it's sissy to play with the younger ones, and to play with a girl—that would be a complete loss of status. Mairead, being both the youngest and a girl, didn't have a chance. But she kept trying and she got plenty of bumps and bruises and skinned knees and a broken leg and a fractured wrist to show for her efforts. But she never gave up.

"We've been a police family going back three generations, so it was natural for the four of us men to join the department. It was the one thing we never expected Mairead to try to imitate. But we were wrong. On the first try she was excluded by the height requirement, but once that was dropped, Mairead rushed to take the exam. She passed in the top one percent."

Though she knew what was coming, Norah didn't interrupt.

"We didn't oppose her, not at the time: there wasn't any particular danger in being a policewoman in those days. Actually, we were kind of proud of her—our little sister, a cop. And there was Dad to see to it that she got a good and safe assignment."

"She still has a good and safe job in the property clerk's office."

"The atmosphere has changed. The attitude as far as women in the department is concerned has changed."

"True," Norah agreed, but forbore to point out that the women had fought hard to bring about those changes he deplored and that, from what she'd observed, his sister had probably fought as hard as any.

"The women are out and exposed to danger as they never were before," Quinn continued. "I'm not referring to this specific series of attacks but to the fact that policewomen face physical violence as a matter of course and they don't have either the physical strength or skill to cope with it. Forgive me, Sergeant Mulcahaney, but in this job brains aren't enough. That's the way I feel."

"You're entitled to your opinion."

"In any case, Mairead is too sensitive, too compassionate. Some of the things she sees, the people she comes into contact with . . . It's too much for her."

Once upon a time, when Norah had first joined the force, her father had used those same arguments, she recalled. "Does she say so?"

"She doesn't have to. I know. I'm her twin. They say twins have a strong empathy and, believe me, it's true. I know how Mairead feels, sick or well, happy or sad. It's kind of eerie sometimes. I know that some of the things she has to deal with actually make her sick, that she has to go outside and throw up. I don't have to be there. I know. I feel. I get sick, too."

Norah supposed he was talking about her job before she was assigned to the property department and made no comment. Certainly Mairead and Frank Quinn were physically similar, though the red hair and amber eyes became the girl far more than they did the man. Temperamentally the girl was all buoyant optimism and courage, whereas the man was introverted and pessimistic.

"Have you discussed this with Mairead?" Norah asked.

"She won't talk to me about it."

"Is the work still making her physically sick?"

"Yes."

Again, because Norah herself had gone through the same thing, though to a lesser degree, she had to sympathize with the girl. "If she hasn't overcome it by now, then I should think your parents—"

"No. They don't understand. See, when we were kids I knew what trying to play in our league was costing Mairead and I tried to make them see it then, and couldn't. It's a lot worse for her now, but they don't see that it isn't cute for her to be strutting around trying to keep up with her brothers. They say it's her decision; she has to make up her own mind; she's got to do what she thinks is right."

"I'm afraid I agree."

"But she's *not* doing what she wants," Quinn exclaimed, his face flaming with the frustration of not being understood. "She's doing what she couldn't do when she was a kid."

"You don't know that. You're not a psychiatrist."

"I've explained to you—"

"That you're her twin and that therefore you have a special empathy, yes."

"Well, then, Sergeant Mulcahaney, would you talk to Mairead? She respects and admires you. She values your judgement."

"I appreciate that, but I can't tell her what you want me to, Frank. May I call you Frank?"

He nodded. "Why can't you?"

"What you want is for me to advise her to resign, right?"

"Yes."

"If I did that I'd be advising her to go against every principle and belief she stood up for at that meeting."

"So? She's entitled to change her mind."

"And in which I tacitly supported her," Norah pointed out. "Besides, if she resigns now it'll look as though she's afraid."

"She *is* afraid. That's what I'm telling you."

"You're afraid for her, that's what you're telling me," Norah said, correcting him. "Your sister's a brave woman; don't turn her into a coward."

"Quinn got up. "Thanks for your time."

"I'm sorry, Frank. I honestly am."

"Sure. You stick to your principles and your high ideals, Sergeant Mulcahaney. Never mind what it costs. You just stick to them."

"All right, all right, I'll at least talk to Mairead. I'll try to find out how she really feels."

Frank Quinn turned and was on his way out.

Norah sighed. The encounter had disturbed her. She couldn't get it out of her mind. It engrossed her so completely that she forgot to stop at the market on the way home for the milk, eggs, and bread she'd need for tomorrow's breakfast. Never mind, she'd get them later or go out for breakfast. Why not? With Joe away, Norah's housekeeping was becoming sketchier everyday and the more she neglected her usual tasks, the freer she felt. She was like a kid playing hooky—for the first time since she was thirteen and her mother died, Norah was without household responsibilities. It did occur to her as she dumped pine oil into her bath water that she'd be offering Sebastian Honn a drink when he called for her and that she had nothing in the way of snacks to go with it. So? All that fancy cocktail junk was just that—junk. You put it out when you were entertaining another couple, mainly to impress the woman. Without another thought to the snacks, to Mairead and Frank Quinn, to the case, Norah put a foot into the tub to test the water. Perfect.

Norah Mulcahaney had a terrible singing voice; she could hardly carry a tune and knew it, but she was humming happily as she slid into the hot, lavishly scented bath.

"Pardon me, I'm looking for Sergeant Mulcahaney. I must have the wrong apartment."

Sebastian Honn looked so blank as he stood in her doorway that Nora fell for it. "I'm Sergeant Mulcahaney," she began, and ended laughing. She had taken pains with her dressing and was wearing the new Qiana. It was a shimmering beige and she knew she looked well in it, but her pleasure at his compliment was spoiled by the awareness of having betrayed how unaccustomed she was to flattery.

"How did I ever snare such a beautiful creature into having dinner with me?" Honn wondered aloud as he handed her a small bunch of miniature roses.

She accepted them, feeling the glow in her cheeks, and, being Norah, gave up trying to play the game. "You're embarrassing me, Captain."

"I certainly don't want to do that. However, I do think that we have to establish a couple of ground rules here. One, my name is Sebastian. Two, don't be embarrassed; I meant what I said. Did you know that I was once one of the judges at the beauty contest in Atlantic City, no less? So kindly respect my opinion."

She laughed.

"Three . . . well, I'm not sure about three. That's open to be filled as needed, okay?"

"Okay. Sebastian. What will you have to drink?"

"Whatever you've got. I'm not fussy."

An old-fashioned phrase. She liked it. "Scotch, rye, a martini?"

"Scotch and water's fine. Why don't you let me fix the drinks while you put out whatever you're going to serve with them?"

"Ah . . ." She was embarrassed again.

"You should blush more often, Norah; it's very becoming. What did I say to upset you this time?"

"I don't have anything to go with the drinks."

"I don't believe it."

"I'm sorry. I didn't think you'd care. I could run out and—"

"I don't believe I'm not going to have to force myself to swallow those slimy little messes on soggy crackers and pretend I like them. Those things spoil good booze—assuming you're serving good booze?" He opened the liquor cabinet she'd indicated. "And I see that you are. Those damned little things also spoil the appetite—assuming there's a good meal coming. And there is. So what can I fix for you, Norah?"

"Scotch and water will do fine," she replied happily.

* * *

He took her to a small restaurant that offered good food, well served, that permitted the diner to set his own pace in consuming it without being either rushed or kept waiting. It was after ten when they left and Sebastian didn't suggest going anywhere else. They'd come in a cab, but by mutual consent they set out to walk back to Norah's place. They strolled; they looked into shop windows; the conversation lagged. For the first time during an evening that had flowed without effort on either side, the rapport faltered. Norah's building was one of the many small, remodeled town houses abounding in the East Sixties. There was no doorman. The front door was locked after six. Sebastian unlocked it for her. He was taller than she and as he held the key out to her he looked down into her eyes.

"Want me to come up with you?"

He was leaving the interpretation to her. Deliberately, she chose the old-fashioned one. "No, thanks, I'll be okay. I had a wonderful time, Sebastian."

"Me, too." He inclined his head slightly, accepting her decision. "It was the most pleasant evening I've had in a long time." He hesitated. "Are you sure, Norah? Are you sure you don't want me to come up?"

Her blue eyes darkened; she dropped her gaze. "I'm sure," she said, and slipped through the partially opened front door and into the inner lobby. Honn made no attempt to follow. The door clicked shut between them.

So, that was it, Norah thought when she got upstairs and inside the apartment. He hadn't mentioned seeing her again. Why should he? She'd indicated clearly enough that she wasn't interested. And she wasn't. Was she? Of course not. Norah didn't believe in having affairs. She wasn't the type, anyway. She wouldn't know how to behave. With Joe away she'd been lonely, so she'd gone out and enjoyed herself. Period.

But it had been a lovely evening, she thought, sweeping through from living room to bedroom turning on lights she didn't need. Lovely . . . *loverly*. She put on the record player, swaying to the music. It had been fun to be flattered and catered to, to be out with a good-looking man, to be treated like a woman—a very special woman. Taking her clothes off, she let them fall to the floor and for the first time in years stood completely naked before the mirror and surveyed herself. Not bad. She would have liked to have a narrower waist and perhaps slimmer thighs, but on the whole . . . She had a good body. Even beautiful. No man would be disappointed.

The phone rang

Reaching for her robe, Norah put it on before answering "Hello?"

"Sergeant Mulcahaney?"

It wasn't Sebastian. It was a woman and she was whispering.

"I am Mrs. Rogoff. Natalie Rogoff from downstairs? You know me, Sergeant?"

Norah belted and tied the robe. "Yes, Mrs. Rogoff, of course." Automatically she glanced at the bedside clock; 10:46. "What can I do for you?"

"I am sorry to disturb you but . . . I hear a noise . . . outside my door."

She was a little Russian lady, retired for many years, living alone, and literally bent over with arthritis. She spoke English haltingly at best and now she was having more trouble than usual. "What's wrong, Mrs. Rogoff?"

"Somebody is trying to get into my apartment." Her voice quavered. "Somebody is trying to open my door. I can hear him. I can hear him . . . doing something to the lock. I think he has a key . . . Oh, help me."

Her voice sank lower and lower in her fear so that by the end Norah could hardly hear her. "Is the door bolted on the inside, Mrs. Rogoff? Now, Mrs. Rogoff, you go and make sure that the door is bolted, and that you've got your chain on. You do that. I'll hold the phone." In moments the woman was back. "They're both in place? Good. Good. Now, I'm coming right down, Mrs. Rogoff, so don't be frightened. But I may need some help, so you call 911 right away. Right away, Mrs. Rogoff, as soon as I hang up. And talk loud so that he'll know you're in there and that you're calling the police." Norah was more concerned with saving her neighbor further fright or shock than in apprehending the would-be burglar. "You call 911 and *talk loud*. I'll be right down."

As she grabbed a pair of pants and a sweater and stuffed her feet into loafers it occured to Norah that it was odd for a burglar to be attempting a break-in without first having ascertained whether or not there was anybody home. It was a lot less trouble to do a job when the apartment was empty and most burglars were really not interested in hurting anybody; what they wanted was to get in and out fast, with as much loot as possible. This one could be an amateur or too high on drugs to bother taking precautions, or maybe for some reason he thought the place was empty. Once he found out he was wrong he'd beat it. Grabbing her gun from her purse, Norah raced for the door. She'd opened it and was just about to shut it quietly behind her when she remembered her keys. Damn. By now the suspect was probably gone anyway and it wouldn't help anybody if she got herself locked out. She was just about to go back inside . . .

An arm was thrown around her neck and a cloth saturated with a pungent, sweet-tasting liquid held over her mouth and nose. She struggled, trying to remember just exactly what she was supposed to do to break this kind of hold. Visions of the judo instructor flashed before her, but her body refused to respond. Her limbs were so heavy. She tried to pull the hands away and the harder she tried, the more deeply she breathed and the more of whatever that rag was impregnated with she sucked into her lungs. She felt as though she were falling, falling. Faces looked down and watched her fall. It was as though she were tumbling down a well and they were looking for her from the rim—Joe . . . Sebastian . . . Mrs. Rogoff . . . grinning, all grinning—and their faces were diminishing as she fell farther and farther down There was a loud thud. A lid placed over the well mouth? Then darkness. Absolute.

TEN

"Drink this, Sergeant."

Norah blinked a couple of times before bringing the scene into focus. She was in her own living room, sitting on her own couch, and wrapped in a blanket. A young black man wearing a white jacket with a hospital insignia on the sleeve sat beside her holding a cup of . . . something to her lips. She sipped. Coffee. Standing and looking down at both of them was a patrolman. She couldn't make out his nameplate. She could hear talking outside the apartment, sounds of movement. The other tenants milling in the hall, probably. Then she remembered.

"Mrs. Rogoff? Is she all right?"

"The old lady who put in the call?" the patrolman asked. "Sure. But whoever was trying to get in was gone."

"Naturally." Norah winced at the sound of her own voice setting up a violent throbbing inside her skull. Also, the coffee had a vile taste, though she suspected that was actually the aftertaste of the drug that had been used to knock her out. Her nose and throat were raw from its fumes.

"Okay, Sergeant, let's just drink the rest of this so we can get out of here." The emergency technician coaxed her as he would a child.

How did he know who she was? Well, the tenants had told the patrolman and he had told . . . or maybe the patrolman had gone through her purse and found her ID . . . and what the hell did it matter anyway? Suddenly the import of what the technician had said got to her. She threw up her head, then grimaced at the waves of pain that caused. She kept her voice low to lessen the echoes inside her head. "What do you mean, so we can get out of here?"

Orderlies entering with a stretcher were the answer. They moved the coffee table out of the way and set the stretcher alongside the sofa.

"No way," Norah said. "I'm not going to any hospital."

"Look, Sergeant . . ."

"Save your breath, young man. I'm not going. You can't make me. You know that."

"For observation, that's all."

"No." She intended to stand up and walk away from him, but all she accomplished was to throw off the blanket, knocking the cup out of his hand and spilling coffee all over the rug, her rug. She was more interested in proving she could get to her feet than in the damage, but her legs refused to work.

Clifford Jones watched. "You were chloroformed, Sergeant. I don't know how much of that stuff was absorbed into your system or in what concentration, okay?" He was trying hard to curb his impatience: as a police officer, she should know better than to resist; as a woman, what could you expect? "Chloroform is a very unpredictable substance, Sergeant. You might feel fine in a couple of hours and then have a recurrence of dizziness, difficulty in breathing, and all the rest of it, tomorrow, the day after, or the day after that. Symptoms can recur in as many as four or five days. People die from the stuff, Sergeant. I don't think you got a heavy dose, but I damn well am going to take you in so the doctors can find out."

He'd impressed her. "Well . . ."

"Fine." He gestured to the orderlies.

"But I'm not going to be carried out of here."

"Oh, yes, you are." Jones was fed up. "You are going to behave like a mature, sensible police sergeant and not like a dumb civilian."

Norah gritted her teeth, thrust out her jaw, and, using every bit of her strength and will, managed somehow to get to her feet. The whole room swayed. She closed her eyes for just a moment, fighting incipient nausea, and felt Jones's hand on her elbow. She opened her eyes.

"If behaving like a dumb civilian means walking out of here under my own power, then, yes, that's exactly what I'm going to do." She looked down at his hand. "But I could use someone to lean on."

Norah had to spend the rest of the night in the hospital; of course, she'd expected that. They took the various samples they needed—blood, urine, and so on and so on. Then they had to wait for the lab reports, didn't they? Of course. Then there were chest X rays and cardiographs and kidney scans. Nevertheless, as soon as she awoke the next morning Norah started to agitate for release. She honestly did feel perfectly fit and she wanted to get out before her father and all of Joe's relatives found out where she was and came rushing over to fuss and cluck. Mainly, though, she wanted to get out and back to work for the same reason she'd insisted on walking instead of being carried into the hospital—to prove to herself that she was okay. For Norah was under no illusion about what had happened to her, and for one of the few times in her life her confidence in her own ability to control her destiny was shaken. Norah Mulcahaney was frightened.

She'd been in tight spots before, certainly. Plenty of times. Like every police officer. On each occasion she'd managed to work her way out. This time she hadn't been given the chance. The option had not been hers but the attacker's. She had been completely at his mercy. A little stronger concentration of chloroform, the rag held over her mouth and nose for a little longer, and she'd have been dead.

A cold chill passed over her.

She threw back the covers, swung her legs over the side of the bed, and reached for the floor. With or without formal release, she was leaving.

"Hi."

Dolly Dollinger stuck her head in the door, black bangs dangling over her eyes, and grinned. "Hey, you're up. That's great."

"How did you know I was in here?" Norah asked.

"It's all over the grapevine."

"How about the papers? Is it on the radio?"

"No. Not yet."

She sighed with relief; all the more reason to get moving. Norah walked over to the closet to get her things.

"What are you doing?"

It didn't take long to pull on the slacks and sweater she'd been wearing the night before. Taking the mirror out of her handbag, Norah gave herself a quick look. Awful. A flip of the pocket comb and a slash of lipstick didn't help.

Dolly watched with growing disapproval. "You can't just walk out of here."

"Want to bet?"

"Come on, Norah." Seeing that it would do no good to remonstrate, Dolly strode to the door. "I'm calling a nurse."

"Fine. Tell her I want to sign myself out."

"Ah, Norah . . ."

The phone interrupted Both women were relieved. Norah sat on the edge of the bed, glad to be able to rest for a moment, for she felt slightly dizzy. "Get it for me, will you, Dolly? If it's the family, I've gone home. Dolly, please?"

With mouth pursed, her friend picked up the phone. "Police Officer Dollinger. May I help you?"

"I'd like to speak to Norah, please. Tell her—Sebastian."

Covering the mouthpiece, Dolly simply said, "Sebastian."

Norah's eyebrows shot up. She held out her hand. "I'll take it. Hello . . "

"Norah. God, it's good to hear your voice," Sebastian Honn exclaimed. "How are you feeling?"

"A little shook up but not bad. Actually, it's the best night's rest I've had in years."

"I blame myself. I should have insisted on seeing you to your door."

"It wouldn't have mattered. I was safely inside, just about tucked into bed, and he lured me out. One of my neighbors, a Mrs. Rogoff, I think I mentioned her to you—a Russian lady crippled with arthritis? Well, she heard somebody at her door and she called me for help. Naturally, I went. He must have been waiting outside my door, because as soon as I stepped into the hall he grabbed me."

"God. When is this going to end?" Honn groaned. "I hope you're getting off the case."

"What?" Norah was stunned. "You're kidding, of course," she said in a carefully controlled voice.

"I am not."

"Would you say that to me if I were a man?"

"Let's not start that."

"I didn't start it."

"All right. If you were a man and a member of a group threatened by some psycho—yes, very probably I would."

"So now it's your opinion that every woman in the department, not just the ones who were rehired by court order, is in danger and should disappear into the woodwork?"

"Oh, hell." There was a long pause. "I don't want to argue women's rights with you, Norah. I just . . . I just want you to be safe."

She knew he meant it and that she was being touchy and ungracious and she couldn't help it. "Yes, well, I appreciate that. Thank you. Thank you for calling." She hung up.

Dolly, who had listened and observed, now spoke with brisk and cheerful determination "All righty . . . which is it going to be, your place or mine?"

Norah frowned. "Not you, too."

"Yup."

"Look, Dolly, the man didn't intend to kill me. He could have if he'd wanted to. He didn't want to."

"Good. Great. So how about next time? Maybe he'll change his mind. So do you want to move in with your dad or with one of Joe's sisters? Of course, Joe could be back . . . in hours, that is, if somebody were to get in touch with him and let him know that you need protection, which somebody is bound to do. If not one of the family, then surely one of your friends . . ."

"That's blackmail."

"Right. So which is it going to be?"

Norah sighed in exaggerated despair. "My place."

"Good. I was hoping you'd say that. I'm having the painters, so it was either you or my folks."

While Dolly moved her things Norah said she'd go on to the precinct. Of course first she had to go home and get decently dressed. But having done that and picked up her car, she decided to take a detour. To the Rockaways. It was a clear, brisk afternoon, and long before she reached the sea Norah could smell the salt tang right through the gasoline fumes. Once she reached the area of dunes and salt marshes and sea gulls swooping and cawing overhead, the sea dominated. Norah walked up to a squat brick house on Seagirt Avenue, overlooking the waters of the East Rockaway Inlet, and rang the bell.

Mairead Quinn's eyes lit up when she saw who it was. "Gee, Sergeant Mulcahaney, this is a surprise. I was just reading about . . ."

Norah shivered.

"Are you all right?" Mairead asked.

"That's a pretty sharp wind you've got here. May I come in?"

"Oh, sure, of course, I'm sorry. Yes, please come in." Mairead stepped aside to let Norah pass.

As soon as she walked into the middle-class living room with its busy wallpaper and lumpy, faded furniture, its overheated air tainted by cigar smoke, and the inevitable clutter left by the men who used it, Norah felt at home. Having herself grown up in such a male-dominated atmosphere, she had a warm empathy for this girl in a family of five men. She could also understand Frank Quinn's concern for his twin, for Mairead was indeed small and delicate. In fact, Norah wondered how she'd made it through the physical part of the training program—on sheer determination probably. Yet beneath the redhead's almost fragile prettiness, Norah sensed a tough-mindedness equal to her own. The way the younger woman had stood up at the meeting had impressed Norah, created a bond between them, made them allies in a common cause. It was why Norah had come.

"Are you home alone?" she asked.

"No. Ma's in the kitchen."

"You shouldn't have answered the door. You made a perfect target, standing in the doorway."

"I . . . I didn't think."

"I know. You have to, though." Norah smiled to ease the criticism. "Is your brother home?"

Mairead grinned. "Which one?"

"That's right, you have so many. Frank. I was told he's off duty."

Mairead nodded. "Francis is out fishing. He goes out whenever he can. He's just crazy about it. He and Dad. They're on the boat and they won't be putting in till four-thirty. Then they'll probably stop for a couple of beers; if they had a good day they'll stay swapping stories till suppertime. You could meet them there, at Henning's, if you want. It's only about half a mile down the road, on the other side of the bridge."

"Well . . ."

"Is there anything I can help with?"

"Frank . . . Francis came to see me yesterday. He was very concerned about you, about your safety."

"Oh, no!"

"He felt that you should resign from the force. He thinks that you would like to resign but that you're afraid to let the other women down."

"No. no. That's not so." Mairead shook her head violently. "I don't want to resign."

"He asked me to talk you around. To use my influence. I told him I couldn't do that."

The redhead blushed.

"I said exactly what I'd said at the meeting—that every woman has to make her own decision. I say it again to you now, Mairead. Every woman has to consider her own personal situation. There's no disgrace in quitting if that's what you want to do."

"But I don't want to, I don't. Oh . . ." The girl groaned with exasperation and embarrassment. "I wish Francis would stop interfering. He's always fussed, always. I'm really ashamed that he went to you, Sergeant Mulcahaney."

"No need."

"It's nice of you to say so, but I am. I wish he hadn't done it. He had no right to involve you in our family squabbles. Francis means well, but he always thinks he knows what's best for me." There was a touch of childish pique in her manner.

"He cares for you. It's nice to have someone care."

"I know that, but he's fussed at me ever since we were kids. Every time I got a scratch he . . ." Suddenly Mairead Quinn grinned. "Here I am doing exactly what Francis did—unloading on you." She sighed. "Your'e easy to talk to, Sergeant."

"Then why don't you call me Norah?"

"Thanks, Norah. And again I apologize for Francis."

"Forget it. What I'm worried about is that he might do something rash—like going after the killer himself."

Mairead gasped. "How could he do that?"

"If he had some idea of his own . . ." Norah watched the girl carefully. "After all, he was acquainted with at least one, maybe more, of the victims. Through you." She hurried on. "You knew them. You went to the Academy together; you were classmates. Did you ever have any of them to the house?"

"No."

"Could Francis have met any of them at a party, a police function? Maybe he occasionally stopped by to give you a ride home after class. Did he give any of them a lift?"

"Well . . . sure. Yeah, of course he did. Eve—he would have given her a lift because she and I were buddies. I suppose he gave all the girls a lift at one time or another, but I can't remember specific instances and I'm sure he can't. It was a long time ago. He didn't really *know* any of them."

Norah pursed her lips in thought. "Has he talked about the case?"

"Of course. We all have. I mean, we're a police family and under the circumstances we'd be bound to talk about it. If Francis had any specific knowledge about the case or any ideas, he'd report them. He would have told you yesterday when he went to see you."

"I hope so."

Mairead stiffened. "He would. Francis is a good cop."

"I'd like to believe that."

The girl drew herself up, eyes flashing golden shards of indignation. "Just what are you getting at, Sergeant?"

"I wonder where Francis was at ten-thirty or so last night."

"I didn't know this was an official interrogation."

"It isn't."

Mairead's control slipped. "You think Francis is the one who attacked you. You do. You *do*."

"I want to make sure that he didn't."

Tears filled the golden eyes. "Francis went to you for help."

"Which I had to refuse."

"And you think he attacked you in retaliation? Well, he didn't. You can forget it, Sergeant Mulcahaney, just forget it. Francis and I went to the movies last night. We went to the Central in Lawrence. We saw *Rocky*. We didn't get home till after midnight. I'll swear to that."

"All right, Mairead."

"And if that's not good enough, my mother will tell you what time we came in. And my father, too; he was home and he was still up. My father's retired, but he was on the force for thirty-two years. He's not a liar." No longer able to hold back the tears, Mairead Quinn ran from the room.

Norah waited a few moments, then let herself out.

"I thought you were coming straight over from the hospital," Felix remarked as Norah entered his office.

"Sorry, sir, I had an errand."

He glanced at the clock on the wall. "Took a hell of a long time."

"I stopped for a bite to eat," she lied.

"So how are you feeling?"

"Fine, thanks, Captain, just fine." Another lie, because actually Norah felt slightly queasy and certainly food would have helped. She thought Felix was more annoyed than the situation warranted. Could Sebastian have gone over her head and suggested she be taken off the case? She squared her shoulders. "I won't be scared off."

"I never thought you would," Felix replied mildly.

Relief was immediately followed by the wry acknowledgment that she was getting very uptight. "Aside from anything else, it would be just one more boost to the perpetrator's ego. I think everything we've done so far has been feeding his self-confidence and sense of importance, making him feel invincible. We're playing the game his way—huddling in the station houses and in our homes."

Felix had a pretty good idea where she was heading. "I don't see that we have any other choice."

"We've got to take the initiative away from him. We've been letting him call the shots, choose a time and place at his convenience. It's our turn to set the stage."

Indeed, Felix had already considered and rejected such a ploy, but Norah often came up with ingenious schemes and he was willing to listen. "How?"

"The reporters have been after me with all kinds of questions about last night: how I felt, do I think it's the same perpetrator that killed the other policewomen, and so on. Suppose I were to give an interview? Suppose in it I said he hadn't frightened me one bit and he hadn't really frightened any women in the department. I could call on all policewomen to keep their courage high, to stick in there."

"In other words, you want to provoke him into going after you a second time?"

"Yes, sir."

"Hmm . . ." Felix tilted his head to the side thoughtfully.

"He's not going to let me get away with that kind of talk. Up to now I've counseled caution and that was an acknowledgment of his power over us. This would be a direct challenge, and if I read him right, he couldn't let it pass. He'd have to punish me. That would give us the chance to set him up the way he set those women up."

"Well, psychologically I think you're right, but practically I don't see how we can do it."

"We've done it before, a dozen times, in all kinds of—"

"When we had some kind of pattern to go on. We've got no handle on this guy. How can we establish control when we don't know what kind of attack to anticipate? Each homicide has varied drastically from the others in time, place, and above all method. Under optimum conditions setting a trap is risky business, but in this instance . . ." Jim Felix shook his head.

"As long as we're expecting . . ."

"Have you considered that, smart as he is, this may be exactly the move he expects and wants us to make? That while we're guarding you he'll strike somewhere else? And be having a good laugh at the same time? We just don't know how many steps ahead of us he may be."

He was right, Norah thought. He was right.

"I interpret the attack on you last night not so much as a personal thing but as a warning to all women in the department that they can't hide from him, that he can get to whomever he wants, whenever he wants."

Norah waited.

"Suppose you were to publicly acknowlege that."

She gasped. "I thought we agreed that whimpering only fed his ego."

"And makes him complacent and perhaps quiets him—for a while. It could buy us some time." Felix knew that to even appear to knuckle under, to back down on her principles, deeply distressed Norah. "Nobody's even going to ask you to do it unless it's absolutely necessary. Then it will be your decision. But I want you to think about it."

What could he say? If the need arose . . . She could only pray that it would not. "So what do we do in the meantime?

"Check out the suspect, naturally."

"What suspect?"

"The man picked up leaving your building last night."

Norah's eyes widened even farther. "After I was assaulted? A suspect was apprehended? Why didn't anybody tell me?"

Felix grinned. "You didn't give anybody a chance." Then he added, "Of course, he may not be the killer."

"So then what was he doing in the building right at . . ." Something told her to slow down. "Who was it?"

"Manuel Costa."

"Costa?" He was the last person she'd expected to hear named.

"Naturally he claims he had nothing to do with the assault, that he didn't even know about it. But he was leaving the building just as the patrol car drove up in answer to your neighbor's 911 call. He was picked up for questioning. He admits going around to see you but insists that he rang your bell a couple of times and when you didn't answer he left. According to him, he never got past the vestibule."

Norah frowned and shook her head. "I just can't believe Dr. Costa was the one who attacked me."

"Chloroform was used. He's a doctor."

"You don't have to be a doctor to get hold of some choloroform."

"It makes it easier. There's also the matter of timing."

Norah's eyebrows went up questioningly.

"It's tricky, don't you think?" Felix asked. "The old lady makes her call for help, which is logged at 10:59 P.M. The squad car responds by 11:04. In that five minutes the perpetrator has to leave the old lady's door, go up one flight to your door, wait for you to come out, grab you and hold you till you're unconscious, then run downstairs and make his getaway. How come your friend Costa, hanging around by the entrance, didn't see him?"

"Does he say nobody passed him?"

"That's right."

"Well . . ." Suddenly her face cleared. "It's very simple: the perpetrator was gone by the time Dr. Costa arrived."

"That's cutting it real fine."

"No, sir." Norah was the one smiling now. "You say the call to 911 was logged at 10:59 P.M. and the squad car arrived five minutes later. But that doesn't mean Mrs. Rogoff placed the call at 10:59. We both know they don't exactly pick up on the first ring."

Unfortunately, that was true. Complaints about how long it took the emergency operators to respond were coming in all the time. Some citizens claimed it took them almost twenty minutes to get through. Felix scowled. "We have no way of knowing."

"Yes, sir, we do. I know for a fact that Mrs. Rogoff called me at 10:46. I made a special note of the time and I was out of my door in two minutes, or three at the very most. So that makes not a five-minute but a fifteen-minute lapse. Plenty of time for the prepetrator to knock me out and get away before either Dr. Costa or the squad car arrived." She waited for the Captain's reaction. "We could ask Mrs. Rogoff how long it took her to get through."

He shrugged. "I don't suppose she wasted any time in trying to place the call."

He accepted it, Norah thought. That being so, she moved on to the next point. "What did Costa want?"

"I was wondering when you'd get to that." Felix regarded her quizzically. "He wouldn't say. Claimed it was personal and had nothing to do with the homicides."

"Is he in detention?"

"His lawyer sprung him."

Norah got up. "I'll catch him at the hospital."

"Hold it, Sergeant, one minute." He motioned her back to the chair, waiting till she was seated and attentive. "I'm assigning Gus Schmidt to work with you on this." Though he knew she understood his purpose, Felix was nevertheless at pains to spell it out. "When I say I'm assigning Schmidt to work with you, Sergeant, I mean *with* you. I mean that you should be together at all times. You're not to divide up the work; you're not to send Detective Schmidt off on one job while you do another. You're to stick together."

"Yes, sir."

"Right. I've already explained to Gus that he's not to leave you for any reason or to lose you. If he does—no excuses; I'm holding him directly responsible. Remember that if you're tempted at any time to give him the slip."

Detective First Grade August Schmidt, a stocky, grizzled veteran in his fifties, was an excellent choice for this kind of watchdog assignment. He worked always to the letter of the rule. He had little imagination to lure him into deviating from an order. He revered rank. In case of a conflict between orders, he could be counted on to obey Felix over Norah.

Not that Norah had any intention of trying to shake Schmidt. On the contrary, she was very glad that he would be with her.

"One more thing, Sergeant." Felix's green eyes narrowed.

"However you may have analyzed Dr. Costa's character and whether or not he assaulted you, just remember one thing—he's still under suspicion of murder."

ELEVEN

Norah had never seriously considered Manuel Costa a suspect even in the murder of Pilar Nievas, the girl he'd loved and of whom he'd been insanely jealous. The old premeditation of the crime was too much at odds with the resident's passionate temperament. Now that Pilar's death was deemed to be one of a series, the suspicion against Costa was, in Norah's opinion, just about wiped out. So why had he gone to her apartment to see her? He'd had no alibi for the time of Pilar's death; could it be that he had one for one of the other occasions? Clearing himself of one homicide would clear him of all. Then why hadn't he simply told Captain Felix? Why had he insisted that he could talk only to Norah Mulcahaney?

Maybe the girl to whom he was supposed to be engaged would know?

The first time around, Ellen Hansen had been surprised to learn of the dashing doctor's interest in her. This round, it was Norah who marveled that the interest continued. Nurse Hansen was a plain young woman of about twenty-five and she made no effort to improve her looks or to glamorize herself. Face scrubbed clean and devoid of makeup, drab blond hair pulled back into a tight, little girl's ponytail, soft brown eyes betraying intense shyness, she was not the type to be carrying on a casual affair. Nor was she the kind to tell lies for a man—unless, of course, she were completely besotted by him. In which case, Ellen Hansen was precisely the kind of girl who would stop at nothing to protect her man.

There was no question that Nurse Hansen was in love with the handsome resident. At the mere mention of his name her face glowed, her entire being was suffused with joy. However, she made no attempt to provide an alibi for Manuel, not for the time of Pilar's death or for any of the other times. In fact, she readily admitted that it was only recently, after the tragedy, that she and Manolo had started to see each other on a steady, serious basis.

"I think, terrible as it was, that Pilar's death freed Manolo. After they broke up, he played the field. He had a reputation . . . well, either the girl put out or he dropped her. I think he was trying to show Pilar he didn't need her. He knew that what he was doing would surely get back to her and he wanted to hurt her."

According to orders, Detective August Schmidt was with Norah on this visit to Ellen Hansen in her tiny apartment in the nurses' residence. Ordinarily Schmidt had a stern authoritarian look, but he gave the witness such a kindly, paternal smile that his presence seemed to reassure Ellen Hansen rather than intimidate her. "You did date Dr. Costa before Officer Nieves was killed?" he asked.

"Oh, yes." She was eager to explain. "He kept after me. Oh . . . not because he was that crazy to go out with me but because he just couldn't bear to have anybody turn him down—not after Pilar. Finally, to stop him bugging me, I had to say yes. But I didn't enjoy myself, not on that first date. I was so nervous, so uncomfortable with him. I guess he sensed it and felt sorry for me, because he didn't make a pass."

"Before Pilar's death that was your only date with Manolo?"

"That's right, Sergeant. After that we'd run into each other in the hospital, in the halls, sit together in the cafeteria, and like that, but it was all much easier and more relaxed than before. After she was killed, he changed; the tension seemed to ooze out of him. I could sense it, anybody who knew Manolo could. When he asked me to go out with him again, I was glad to accept."

"Were you with Manolo the evening of October eighth?"

Of course Hansen knew why she was being asked. She made no coy evasions but went for her handbag and consulted what appeared to be a pocket diary or appointment book. "No, I was on duty that night and so was Manolo."

"And on the twelfth?"

It needed only another glance, then the blood drained out of Ellen Hansen's plain face, making her look old and ugly. "No," she admitted, then paused, reached a decision. "We were both off duty, but Manolo said he had business that night and couldn't see me. He called later, around eleven, to wish me good night. He was not in the state that a man who . . . who had done what you suggest . . . would be. Manolo has a violent temper; it's well known. Actually, it's a safety valve, you know? Basically, he's gentle, a good person. He's a very good person."

As far as Norah was concerned, there was nothing more to be said. After they'd left, with the door of the nurse's apartment shut behind them, it was Gus Schmidt who summed up the inconclusiveness of the interrogation.

"At least she didn't lie."

"No," Norah agreed. "Not to us, anyway."

As he had before, Manuel Costa received Sergeant Mulcahaney in the second-floor visitors' lounge. On this occasion she was accompanied not by Schmidt but by Ferdie Arenas. Norah hoped that confrontation with the man who had supplanted him in Pilar Nieves' affections might shake the young doctor. It was a calculated risk.

"You wanted to see me, Dr. Costa," she stated. "Here I am."

"I wanted to see you alone." The resident refused to look at Arenas; the muscles of his lean face were tight, the pulse at his right temple throbbing visibly.

"Detective Arenas was Pilar's backup," Norah explained. "He was present when she was shot. He saw it happen."

"I read that." He paused, then almost against his will his eyes turned to Ferdi and, once on him, couldn't let go until they'd dissected him square inch by square inch. Then his look softened. "It must have been terrible for you."

Norah let a soft breath of air escape: that was the first hurdle accomplished. It did not occur to the suspect that Ferdi Arenas could make an eyewitness identification of him as the killer. Or perhaps he realized that if he could make a positive ID, Arenas would have done so long since. Norah's impression about the young resident didn't match his fiancée's; she thought not that he was less tense but less self-centered than before.

"Why did you come to see me at my home the night before last?" Norah persisted. "You must realize that you're under suspicion for what happened to me?"

"I had nothing to do with that. I went to see you because my fiancée, Ellen Hansen, thought I should."

"Why didn't you call me up first?"

"I hadn't really made up my mind. I was kind of walking around in your neighborhood, getting up my nerve."

"To attack me?"

She could see the surge of anger; she could see him fight to control it. "I can understand why you might think that I killed Pilar." His voice shook, but only slightly, the only indication of the struggle he'd fought with himself. "I was very jealous of Pilar and I did actually threaten her. But why should I hurt you?"

"Then why don't you tell me what you wanted to see me about?"

Abruptly, Costa turned his back on both detectives and strode to the window.

"We spoke to Ellen," Norah told him. "She says you were both on duty on the night of the eighth. That was the night Officer Ochs was killed. On the twelfth, however, the night Officer Eve Bednarski was murdered in a ladies' room at Yankee Stadium, you were both off duty." Norah paused. "But not together. She says you told her you had business that night."

With a heavy sigh, he turned around. "No, that wasn't true. I didn't have any business. I wanted to be alone, to get my head together."

"So you have no alibi for that night, either?"

"What do you mean, that night, either? I didn't even know those women. *Dios mío*. What is going on here?"

"Read him his rights," Norah ordered.

Arenas took out the much worn plastic-covered card and began to intone, "You have the right to remain silent—"

"Does this mean you're arresting me?" Costa interrupted. "You can't do that. I'm innocent." His voice rose, his eyes flashed, but his fists, clenched at his sides, indicated he was still trying to control his temper. "For Gods sake, Sergeant, give me a break. I've already been picked up once for questioning. If you take me in on suspicion of murder . . . Do you know what that could do to my career? Even if I'm released immediately, the stigma . . ."

"What did you want to see me about?"

"So. That's a low trick, Sergeant. I wouldn't have thought it of you."

"It's no trick, Doctor. You don't seem to grasp the fact that you really are under suspicion for these crimes. Admittedly, you have no alibi for the eighteenth of September or for the twelfth of October. You were on duty on the eighth, the night Officer Ochs was killed, but unless you can account for the hours of one to two A.M. specifically . . ." She waited but he remained silent. "Under the circumstances, the fact that you were coming out of my building immediately following the attack made on me, well, you can see that the explanation becomes crucial—to you. Evidently you were willing to tell me privately. But it could never have remained private. I would have had to report what you told me."

Costa wavered. He looked to Arenas. Norah intercepted the look and thought she understood. "You wanted to tell me about the last time you and Pilar saw each other; is that it? You don't want Detective Arenas to know. But not only will he know in the end, he has the right to know, and of all people, he is the one who will best understand."

Costa swallowed. "The child—Sofía's story of what happened —it was what Pilar told her, I'm sure."

"You're saying it was not Sofía but Pilar who lied?" Arenas bristled, but at a warning glance from Norah subsided.

Costa directed his answer to Arenas, however, apparently as eager now to make his rival understand as earlier he had been anxious to ignore him. "When I heard that Pilar was engaged again, I was shocked. I believed that we were destined for each other and that somehow we'd get together again. Suddenly I realized that it wasn't to be, that I had really lost her, and I couldn't accept it. I wanted her back. I was wild with anguish. Wild. So I went to see her. I waited in the street till she came home from work and then I followed her inside. I made a terrible scene, but she stayed calm. Cool. Detached. In the old days, she would have yelled and screamed back at me; she would have cried, and we would have fallen into each other's arms. That was what finally got to me—that she stayed cool. That told me more than anything else could have, that she didn't care, that finally it was over, finished. And it drove me crazy." He ran trembling fingers through his dark hair. "*Crazy.*"

"What did you do?"

"I went for her gun. Her handbag was lying on the coffee table between us, and I knew her gun was in it."

Norah, who carried her own weapon in the handbag slung over her shoulder, instinctively clutched it closer to her side.

"I got the gun before she could stop me. I jumped back and held it to my head and threatened to kill myself."

Norah glanced at Ferdi; he was watching Costa.

Costa was breathing heavily. "I threatened to kill myself right in front of her unless she promised to break off the engagement and come back to me. I even took the safety catch off."

"And she disarmed you," Norah stated.

"She threw a heavy ashtray which knocked the gun right out of my hand. It fired as it hit the floor."

"What happened to the bullet?"

He shrugged.

"We'll look."

But Costa was waiting for Ferdi Arenas' reaction.

"We'll find it," Ferdi assured him.

"If it's still there," Norah murmured.

"There'll be traces," Ferdi said, and gave Manuel Costa an encouraging nod.

"I take it you buy his story," Norah remarked as she and Ferdi inched their way crosstown at the start of the rush hour.

"Yes, I do."

"How do you square it with the sister's version?"

"I think Costa's right, that Sofía did get her story from Pilar. The child came home right after Costa left; in fact, she saw him leave. Probably Pilar was pretty upset. After all, she had once cared for the guy. The place was also probably still a mess and she had to tell the kid something. It was easy to say she and Manolo had quarreled; it happened all the time. All that was left was to concoct some kind of explanation for the bullet mark."

"Why not tell the truth?"

"The truth would have shamed and humiliated Costa. Pilar cared enough to conserve for him his pride."

"His *machismo,*" Norah said, and couldn't help sounding patronizing.

Arenas shrugged, admitting the weakness but not apologizing for it.

Neither mentioned that the story, true or not, had little bearing on Costa's status as a suspect. It neither cleared him nor served to implicate him more deeply. However, thoughts of Manuel Costa were driven from their minds when they turned the corner of Eighty-second Street and saw the fire engines lined up along the curb in front of the station house. Whatever had happened was over, for the crowd was pretty much dispersed, the hoses were being rewound, the street hydrants, turned off, though water still flooded the gutters. All buildings appeared intact, including, most particularly, the precinct house, so probably . . .

"What in the world?" Norah began, then gasped. "Stop. Ferdi, stop the car. Let me out." She had her door open and was running as soon as Arenas hit the brake. She ran to where she'd parked her car when she came to work that morning.

"Oh, no," she moaned when she reached the place she'd left it, just down the block from the station house. "Oh, no." Her first and only lovely little dark green Pinto was a twisted, mangled, water-sodden, total wreck.

"Damn shame," David Link, standing there, commiserated. The cars in front and back were scarcely damaged.

"What happened ?" Norah wailed.

"I think somebody's trying to tell you something."

"What happened?" Norah repeated in a woeful plaint as she surveyed the wreckage of her car.

"A kid threw a primitive version of a Molotov cocktail into it," David Link told her. "Threw it under the car—under the gas tank, I guess, and ran like hell. There was a witness. A man on the other side of the street just getting into his own car saw him. He didn't realize at the time what was happening, but instinct made him dive for cover as the thing went off. After the explosion, when he raised his head and looked around, the kid was gone, naturally."

"Naturally." Norah sighed. "Any description?"

"Sure. Black, with an Afro, blue jeans, and a leather jacket, maybe ten or eleven years old."

She groaned.

"Lucky to get that much."

"Captain wants to see you."

"What? Oh, yes, sure. Thanks, David."

* * *

"I'm sorry about your car," Jim Felix said. "But better the car than you."

"What does he want?" Norah wailed.

"That should be obvious.'

She flinched, not only because it was the second time within minutes she'd been told that, not only because this time it came from the boss himself, but because she could no longer deny it. Also because she knew why Felix had sent for her and what was coming next.

"If he wanted to kill you, all he had to do was rig a device that would be triggered when you got in the car and turned on the ignition or stepped on the brake or a half dozen other simple booby traps. No, this was a warning. The second warning," Felix added.

"All right. I'll get off the case."

"That's not what he's after."

Norah bit her lip and remained silent—and miserable.

"The third warning may not involve you. He could be threatening to commit another murder."

"What am I supposed to do? Get up and urge the women to resign in a mass?"

"Not all of them. Just the twenty-eight."

Norah shook her head.

"We can't fire the women just because they're in danger," Felix reasoned. "We could suspend them, but that's not going to placate this fanatic. If you get up there and tell the women that you were wrong, that you think they should resign, it might work; it might placate him for a while anyway. I don't know. I think you have to try. You have to try to buy us some time." He waited. "I'm authorized to assure you that the resignations will not be processed until the case is solved. That anyone who wants to rescind her resignation at that time will be allowed to do so without question or prejudice."

"If the case is ever solved."

"That doesn't sound like you, Sergeant."

"They'll think I'm doing it to save my own hide."

"Some will. But not those who really know you. Not your friends."

"Everybody will. Everybody in the department."

"I know it's hard for you to make yourself look like a coward."

"How do we know that what I say will have any effect on the women? Why should we assume I have that kind of influence?"

"Because *he* does."

"Suppose it doesn't work. Suppose they don't listen to me. Suppose they don't resign."

Felix looked hard at her. "It's up to you to convince them."

TWELVE

WOMAN COP REVERSES HERSELF

Sergeant Norah Mulcahaney, heroine of many encounters, an acknowledged leader among women police officers, and in the forefront of the fight to "hang tough" as a fanatical killer stalks them, now tells her fellow officers their jobs are not worth their lives. Two nights ago Sergeant Mulcahaney was assaulted outside her apartment and rendered unconscious by the use of chloroform. This afternoon her car was firebombed where it was parked outside the Eighty-second Street station house. Asked whether the two incidents had anything to do with her change of mind, Sergeant Mulcahaney refused to comment.

Asked whether she would turn in her own resignation, the sergeant again refused to answer. . . .

The interview had been bad enough. Reading the account made Norah hot with shame, but the full impact of what she'd done really hit when she saw herself on television. She and Dolly watched together. As soon as the segment was over, the phone started to ring.

"Want me to get it?" Dolly asked.

Norah shook her head. She knew that she couldn't run from the comments and queries both friendly and snide; nevertheless, she had an overwhelming urge to lay the receiver on the table and leave it there. She put it to her ear. "Hello? Dad. Oh, Dad, it's you, How are you?"

"Proud of you, sweetheart, that's what I am. Proud that you had the courage to speak out."

Her heart sank. She should have told him first, explained the reason for what she was about to do.

"I know that you're not afraid for yourself. I know you did it for the other women. I want you to know that I understand."

"Oh, Dad."

"Just remember, darlin', that I'm with you, no matter what. Now, uh . . ." Patrick Mulcahaney cleared his throat. "Don't you think it would be a good idea if you let Joe know what's going on?"

"No. No, I don't I don't want you to do it, either. I don't want you to write or call him or anything. There's no need. I don't want you to. Promise me."

"Why not?"

She couldn't answer. She wanted Joe back, but she didn't want to send for him. She could hardly expect him, over there in Italy, to know what was going on back here. Sensational as the case was, it probably hadn't made the Italian newspapers. What she wanted was for Joe to return spontaneously because he missed her or because he had some kind of psychic intuition. Illogical. Ridiculous. Irrational. "Please, Dad."

"Whatever you say, sweetheart."

As soon as she put the phone down, it rang again.

"How's it going?"

Norah caught her breath. Sebastian. "We'll have to wait and see."

"That was a damn good interview you gave. It didn't fool me, but I'm sure it did everybody else. It was a smart move and it took a lot of guts."

"I don't know what you're talking about." The tears quivered in Norah's eyes.

"Can I see you tonight?"

To the gratitude for his understanding and support was now added pleasure that he wanted her company. She started to say yes spontaneously, then remembered. "I have a roommate now; she shouldn't be left alone. I'm sorry."

"Okay. I'll take you both to dinner. See you at seven."

Thanks to the efforts of Sebastian and Dolly, Norah was in a much more cheerful frame of mind when she went to bed that night. The next morning, she awoke with traces of that cheer to support her till she turned on the radio for the morning news.

. . . in the wake of Sergeant Norah Mulcahaney's advice to her sister officers the resignations have started to pour in. There have been six so far, and it is still early. High-ranking officials in the department have refused comment. Unofficially, the concensus is that the entire group of twenty-eight women directly threatened by the unknown killer will have resigned by the end of the day, and that perhaps some other—

She snapped it off.

A heavy pall fell on Norah. A few years back, in order to lure another killer, Norah had voluntarily agreed to have a story planted that she was on the take. It had not been easy to bear the ostracism of her colleagues then, but as she'd been suspended—ostensibly—she'd been able to stay home for most of the period. This time she couldn't hide. Having branded herself a coward, she was going to have to go to work, walk into the precinct and the squad room, and face her colleagues.

Dolly didn't say anything over breakfast. Sympathy at that point would only have aggravated the situation. Dolly didn't need to be told that her friend had not voluntarily given that interview and that the views she'd expressed were not what she really believed. Anybody who knew Norah should have been able to figure it out, but Dolly was very much afraid that most wouldn't take the trouble.

Unfortunately, the chubby, very practical policewoman was right. As she and Norah entered the station house every man and woman stared. No one spoke to either of them. Maybe they were embarrassed and didn't know what to say: a "Hi" or a "Good morning" would have been welcome. Dolly cringed on Norah's account, but there was nothing she could do. She had to withdraw the support of her presence to go into the locker room and change into uniform. Norah entered the squad room alone.

There were men in that room she knew were on her side. Just a glance would have brought David Link, Gus Schmidt, Roy, or Ferdi over to her to show his faith, but Norah, cheeks burning, looked obdurately ahead, as though warning them off, and made straight for her desk. Somebody was sitting beside it, waiting for her.

"Mairead."

She was not only surprised to see the girl, she was startled by the dark circles under her eyes and her generally drawn look. "What's wrong, Mairead?"

"I came to apologize for the way I acted the other day."

It took a couple of seconds for Norah to think back. When she did remember, the meeting seemed to have taken place a lot more than two days ago and was not particularly important. "Forget it."

"I can't. You came as a friend and I was nasty. I got so upset. Then, last night, when I saw you on television, I wondered if anything either Francis or I did had anything to do with your changing your mind and urging the women to resign."

"No."

"Because if it did, if I thought either one of us was in any way responsible, I couldn't forgive myself."

"You had nothing to do with it," Norah assured her. "Don't worry about it."

"I'm glad." The redhead's amber-flecked eyes remained fixed on Norah. "I'm glad because you see, I'd already decided to resign even before Francis came to see you."

"Oh?"

"Yes, I had. I know I didn't act like it, particularly at the meeting. I guess I got carried away. I've always admired you, Norah, and I wanted to support you."

"You don't have to explain to me," Norah said; nevertheless, she was disappointed. She liked the young woman, had seen a lot of herself in Mairead Quinn.

"When I got off the high of the meeting, I was just plain scared." The younger woman's voice quivered, "I guess my brother knows me better than I know myself. I guess I never did belong on the force."

"So now you're going to quit. Well . . ."

"I've done it. I've already gone ahead and done it."

Suddenly Norah had enough whining self-justification. "Maybe it's the best. Good-bye, Mairead. Good luck." She held out her hand.

"Thank you, but that's not what I came to see you about. At least it's not the main reason."

"What, then?" Norah asked with an edge of exasperation, indicating her cluttered desk. "I've got a lot of work."

"It's about the case. I want to help. I don't mean with the investigation; I know I can't do that now. I couldn't have even before while I still had my badge. What I mean is that I think I've come up with something."

"What?"

"You put me onto it. You asked me if Francis had known any of the victims and I said he hadn't, not really. Then it came to me that I had. I mean, we were classmates."

"So?"

"So I started thinking about them, about the women who were killed. I put everything down on paper about them that I could remember." She opened her handbag and pulled out a sheaf of papers covered with a big, undisciplined, schoolgirl's scrawl. "I thought you might want to look these over, but the main thing that I remembered is about Eve Bednarski."

"What about her?"

"I knew Eve better than the others. We double-dated a couple of times."

"Go on."

"She arranged the dates. The men were detectives. Narcotics division."

Norah waited some more.

"You have to understand Eve Bednarski. She looked like a real sexpot: the way she dressed, the way she moved. It was a real come-on. Every guy at the Academy was after her, even the instructors, and she loved it. The women resented her, naturally. They figured she was man-crazy, that she'd joined the force just to be around men."

"But?"

"Eve Bednarski could have attracted men from the inside of a convent. I'm not saying she didn't get a kick out of the effect she had on men, but she had brains, too, more than anybody gave her credit for, and she was very ambitious." The redhead paused. "You know how it is on a double date—the girl the guys are hot for drags along somebody plain who won't be any competition. It used to be Katie Chave—Henderson, she was then—but after she met Loy she wouldn't go out with anybody else, so Eve picked me."

Norah didn't think that Mairead fitted that category, but perhaps compared to the highly charged Bednarski, she had seemed quiet.

"I didn't mind," Mairead continued. "I knew I couldn't compete with Eve and I didn't try. Actually, I got a kick out of sitting back and watching her operate. That's when I realized she wasn't just out for a good time, that it wasn't just a casual date with her. She had picked those detectives for a purpose. She got them talking shop, which wasn't hard. But she teased and wheedled more information out of them than they realized."

Now Norah was alert. "What kind of information?"

"About cases they were on, busts they'd made, drugs they'd confiscated."

That was all of three years ago, Norah thought, and sat back again.

Mairead didn't seem to notice that her listener's interest was flagging. "Eve told me afterward that she thought the guys were on the take but that they were dumb and would probably get caught."

"What's the point of this, Mairead?"

"The point is that one of them did get caught, was hauled up in front of the Knapp Commission and was fired off the force. The other is . . ." She hesitated. "He's still a cop. His name is Gerry Innis."

Norah made sure not to show how startled she was. "Bednarski's partner?"

"Yes, ma'am."

"Well, that's interesting, Mairead. But why didn't you mention it before?"

"I didn't know. What I mean is, the date was a long time ago, and I didn't know who Eve's partner was. Somebody happened to mention Gerry Innis—I don't remember who—and it struck a chord. One thing led to another and I put it together. It's probably just a coincidence, but I thought I ought to tell you."

"I find it hard to believe that Eve Bednarski had larceny on her mind while she was still at the Academy." Jim Felix had listened to Norah's account with growing skepticism.

"I agree. I think she just enjoyed leading those two detectives on, making fools of them, showing off to her friend, maybe. At the same time, I don't think there's any doubt that Eve was attracted to the kind of work they were doing and that she made her mind to get on the Narco Squad herself one day. And she did. She made the squad three months before she was laid off," Norah pointed out. "With Gerry Innis for a partner," she added.

"According to Captain Honn, she still had plenty to learn. She'd made a couple of small buys, She didn't have the expertise or the time to get anything going."

"Maybe Innis already had, and she caught him at it," Norah suggested.

Felix raised an eyebrow. "And demanded a piece of the action,"

"And the payoff was supposed to take place in the ladies' room at Yankee Stadium. Maybe the 'out-of-order' sign was a signal that the deal was on."

"Maybe." Felix scowled. "She got paid off, that's for sure."

*　*　*

"Why didn't you mention that you'd dated Bednarski?" Honn, facial muscles tense, eyes fixed on a squirming Innis, demanded.

"It was a long time ago, Captain, and it didn't mean anything. It was nothing serious, a couple of casual dates, that's all. I didn't think it was important." Gerald Innis had started out with high color, which diminished as he offered up each sentence of defense, pausing, hoping it had satisfied his commander, and having to offer up one more segment of explanation.

Honn was not placated, far from it. "Oh, now it's more than one date. How many more?"

Both detectives had forgotten Norah Mulcahaney, who sat over to the side and wisely took no part in the exchange.

Innis winced. "Sir, whatever had been between us was finished before she ever joined the squad. She was a girl who got bored easily; no hard feelings, but she just moved on." Again Innis paused, hopeful that he'd given satisfaction, and again his chief's dour expression told him that he had not. Desperate, he could only counter attack. "I didn't think it was anybody's business."

"It wasn't," Honn agreed, "till she got killed. You were quick enough to mention the friendship between Bednarski and Officer Chave and to mention the coincidence of their both having sued to get their jobs back."

"Yes, sir, I thought that was important. I didn't think the fact that we'd gone together three years ago had any bearing." The color was returning and his girlishly rosy skin glowed once again. "You had to know Eve, Captain. She had to keep moving. No guy could hold her for long."

Honn's rigidity cracked; he slumped in his chair, face sagging into fissures that were not due to appear for years yet. "Okay, Innis, you can go."

Surprised, but not waiting to be told a second time, Innis fled.

Honn looked at Norah. "Now, you," he said. "The answer to you is—no. Absolutely not. No way. I've already told your boss that I do not want you on my squad."

"I thought you told Captain Felix you'd be glad to take me on anytime?" She made an attempt at lightness.

Honn refused to be diverted. "Not on this kind of assignment. And that's final, Sergeant. Personal feelings do not enter into it. Well . . ." He paused. "All right, they do, of course. Inevitably. But I'd say the same even if we didn't see each other on the outside. It's too dangerous. I wouldn't let any woman . . ."

Norah opened her mouth.

"All right, all right, I take that back; forget I said it. Just consider that every man in the division knows you're a homicide detective and working on this case. Suddenly you get transferred. You really think they're not going to know what you're up to?"

"Will the pusher and dealers out on the street know?"

"You bet your sweet life. You'd had your pretty face plastered all over TV and the newspapers. Every small-time hood is going to recognize you. Unless you intend to adopt a heavy disguise— say, a blonde wig and dark glasses?" He was heavy on the sarcasm.

"I don't think I'd look good as a blonde."

"So, then, I'm sorry, but you're out," he snapped, again ignoring the attempt at humor. "I told you that Bednarski wasn't around long enough to get connected for a payoff and I'm sticking to that. As far as her catching somebody else at it is concerned, I've been around a long time—I was a narcotics cop before you graduated from high school; I've had personal experience of how drugs corrupt, how they rot the moral fiber, how they turn decent men and women into criminals, and I tell you that Bednarski was clean and so is Innis and so is every other officer in my department."

It was the first time Sebastian Honn had alluded even obliquely to his son and his son's drug addiction, and it touched Norah deeply. "I'm not interested in posing as a nark. I just want to follow the routine Bednarski followed, daily, as myself, without pretense. If you believe in your people, where's the danger?"

"The danger is to *you.*" He threw up his hands. "I can't argue with you."

"Then don't."

He stabbed his forefinger at her. "Let me ask you something. If Eve Bednarski was killed because she was taking graft or knew somebody who was taking graft, how do you explain the two other murders? Why were the other policewomen killed?"

Norah had the answer ready. "As a cover-up for the real motive."

THIRTEEN

"A cover-up for the real motive?" Honn repeated, scowling. "All the murders? Including the Chave bombing?"

"No, not that," Norah admitted. "There's no way that could have been anything but an accident." It was so clear to her that she thought it should be equally clear to him. Maybe it was and he didn't want to admit it; he could be stubborn sometimes. "Chave's death was what gave the killer the idea. The publicity surrounding the bombing suggested a series of policewomen killings to mask the key murder, which was that of Eve Bednarski."

"Speculation." Honn shrugged, but his face was grim. "Pure speculation."

Norah wasn't offended. If her theory was true then the corruption was in Sebastian's own command; it must have grown and flourished without his having the slightest suspicion. That had to rankle. "It makes a lot more sense, to me anyway, than some fanatic cop running around killing women cops so he can maybe get his job back. I never really believed that."

"And you believe this?"

"If the other women hadn't been killed first, if only Eve Bednarski had been murdered, then the investigation would immediately have honed in on her drug connections and on this squad. But as it was, with her death apparently one in a chain, the drug suspect was not considered important." She waited a moment. "The killings have stopped," she pointed out.

"Because the purpose has been achieved?"

"Yes."

"Okay, so they've stopped. So now you come poking your nose in, and what does that make you? Honn demanded. "The next victim, that's what. This time the killer is not going to be satisfied with administering a whiff of chloroform or firing an empty car. He'll go all the way. Sorry, Sergeant, the answer is still no, you're not working on my squad. I will not countenance the risk." He glared. "You're a good detective, but there are others equally good—of course, I'd never suggest better. Don't worry, be at ease, we'll get the job done."

"Yes, sir. Captain Felix said it was to be your decision."

"Ah . . . well . . . I'm glad you understand."

"Yes, sir, I do. You don't want to be held responsible in case anything happens to me."

"Damn it. You know that's not it."

"It would have been easier working directly, but I can handle it out of Homicide as I would any other case."

"You're the most stubborn, exasperating . . . If you were working for me, I'd be a nervous wreck. I can't stop you?"

"No, sir."

"Then I suppose I'd better help you. Okay, then, you're on. I make only one proviso—stay away from Gerry Innis."

"How can I? He was Bednarski's partner."

Honn formed the word silently. *No.*

"I thought you were so sure he's innocent. There's nobody I could be safer with. Gerald Innis isn't going to let anything happen to me. If it does, he's bound to be the prime suspect and he knows it. Gerry Innis is going to be *soooo* solicitous of my safety."

"He's also going to take infinite precautions to keep you from meeting anybody who's liable to tell you anything, or from going anywhere you're likely to learn anything of significance—always assuming he's involved, of course."

"Always assuming—how's he going to do it?"

Before Honn could reply, Norah whipped out a small spiral notebook. "How's he going to do that when I have Officer Bednarski's casebook? I can trace every contact, every buy, every bust those two were involved in."

"How'd you get that?"

"From the property clerk, of course," Norah replied evenly. "I went down to the property clerk's office and asked to look at Bednarski's effects."

"I guess I know when I'm licked." At last a grin eased the harsh lines of Honn's face, but did not erase them.

As it turned out, there was nothing of particular significance in Eve Bednarski's notebook, at least not at a casual perusal. It was the typical police officer's aid to memory, intended to be used when preparing a report. Nevertheless, it was a guide to what Bednarski and Innis had done, where they had gone, and whom they had interrogated. Whatever ideas Gerald Innis might have had about his new partner and how to handle her were dispelled at the outset when Norah produced the book.

"I want to start with the last entry and work backward," she announced. "You introduce me as Officer Bednarski's replacement."

"Whatever you say, Sergeant." He was less than enthusiastic.

"Never mind whether they buy it or not. I don't care. And never mind the 'Sergeant.' Call me Norah. You're showing me the ropes just as you showed Eve. Okay?"

"Yes, ma'am. Yes, Norah."

The area hadn't changed much since Norah had worked as a rookie on the prestigious Homicide North, except in degree. Everything looked, smelled, and was—worse. The places to which Gerald Innis took his new partner were much like the places Joe Capretto had guided her through then—tenements, cheap bars, rat-infested alleys with mounds of garbage for the rats to sustain themselves except when the people got to it first. There was less hope. More crime. Now the crime was out in the open, in full view of the cop on the beat. The people to whom Innis introduced her —black, white, Hispanic—were mostly pushers, small-timers, some just one jump ahead of supporting their own habit; if busted, they couldn't have come up with the cash for a bribe. In presenting her, Innis was never at ease. His eyes constantly shifted back and forth between Norah and the subject and over the shoulder to see who might be observing them. Beside Innis, in what she privately dubbed his "pimp outfit," Norah knew she looked out of place, but she wasn't good at role-playing, so she just didn't attempt it. She played it straight. Let them laugh at her, let them think she was scared. Meanwhile, along with Innis, she continued to work her way through the cases in Eve Bednarski's notebook.

By the end of the week Norah began to wonder if she hadn't missed the clue she was looking for. Questions and answers, faces and places, were piling into a blurred, meaningless montage. The nerve ends of her intuition were rubbed raw as Jimmy Valentine's fingertips but relayed no signals. At night Norah pored over the entries in the little book, comparing them with her own notes, staring at them as if they were a Rosetta Stone that contained the secret of the crimes. She remained convinced that she was on the right track, that they were dealing with a series of cover-up murders of which the central object was the death of Officer Eve Bednarski. Two things reinforced her conviction: Gerald Innis' growing unease and the cessation of further crimes against police-women.

The second frightened her. If the killer thought they were getting close, if he followed their reasoning, might he not kill again just to prove it wrong? It was a constant, gnawing fear that Norah managed to shake only for brief periods during the day and that kept her awake into the night. She didn't mention it in her verbal reports to Felix or to Sebastian, not even when she and Honn met privately, which they now did on a regular basis. It was harder not to confide in Dolly Dollinger, for now that they lived together their friendship and rapport were growing and Norah knew that Dolly sensed her uneasiness.

Dolly did, indeed. Having been with Norah on other cases, she knew how deeply involved Norah could become. Usually, though, Norah liked to discuss a case; these days she was silent. Dolly put it down to Norah's involvement with Sebastian Honn and Joe's imminent return from Italy. Certainly Captain Honn had gone out of his way to be nice to Dolly, yet she couldn't warm up to him; she supposed she resented him on Joe's behalf.

Joe's return was also very much on Norah's mind. Once he was back—well, she could hardly go on seeing Sebastian. Sebastian was not the type to fit the "faithful friend of the family" mold. Nor was Joe the *ménage à trois* type. Not that the situation had reached the point where it would fit into the category. Sometimes Norah let herself imagine what might have happened if she'd given in and let Sebastian come up with her that first night. Then she reminded herself that it wouldn't have mattered, for Mrs. Rogoff's call would have interrupted, and then she smiled ruefully at the images that brought up. Of one thing she was sure: if Sebastian had come up with her, Norah would not have been chloroformed in the hallway—not that night. And the relationship with Honn would have been very different, for by now they would surely have finished what they'd begun. The blood surged and her heart pounded at the mere speculation of what it might have been like. She hadn't told him yet that Joe was coming home. She kept putting it off, afraid that it would catapult them into each other's arms or into saying good-bye.

The family was getting suspicious. Norah was never home when any of them called, and between Joe's sisters and Patrick Mulcahaney, someone was always calling. They got Dolly who, after going out a couple of times with Norah and Honn, had insisted that she was perfectly safe behind the bolted door of the apartment and refused to accompany them anymore. She took the calls and made excuses, usually that Norah was working. It was when Norah returned the calls that the suspicion set in. It began with the girls teasing her about having a boyfriend while Joe was away, and her laugh not quite matching theirs. It was inevitable that the girls should compare notes. They kept their opinion to themselves, and Norah was reasonably sure that they wouldn't say anything to Joe. Undoubtedly, they thought he was coming back just in time.

Norah sighed. Maybe he was.

Once he was back it would be hard to go on working for Sebastian as though there was nothing between them. All the more reason to get the case solved and go back to her regular job. Norah decided she couldn't afford to work back through Bednarski's book chronologically.

"This one," she said, holding the book so that Gerald Innis could see. "What's this one? Shouldn't it have gone to Public Morals?"

"A series of complaints came in from women who said they'd been forced into sexual relations with this Henry Goberman," Innis explained. "He was a pharmacist and he filled their legitimate prescriptions for stuff like Valium, Seconal, and so on. When the prescriptions ran out and they wanted a refill, he took it out in trade." Innis shrugged. "It could have been handled either by Public Morals or by us, but as Eve had experience in both areas, she was a natural for the assignment."

"With you as her backup?"

"Right. But the case never came to trial. Goberman's lawyer claimed entrapment and the DA bought it."

"How about the other women who brought complaints? You said there were several."

"They disappeared into the woodwork. When it got to the

nitty-gritty, not one of them was willing to appear in court and give evidence. Too ashamed. Didn't want their husbands or boy-friends to know."

Norah sighed. Since even in cases of rape women were often ashamed to give evidence, how much more so in this type of situa-tion in which they had willingly submitted or at least allowed themselves to be seduced? She flipped the pages of Eve's notebook to her second choice and as she did so sensed that Innis was relieved. Abruptly she closed the book. "So we'll waste an hour on Mr. Goberman. I'm kind of curious about this drugstore Casanova."

"What can he tell you? Eve really did a number on him. He fell for her. I mean, he had the hots for her. Who could blame him? And she played him just right. I don't know how he handled the other women, probably he got what he wanted before he delivered the pills, but you can bet Eve wasn't playing it that way. He had to hand over the Seconal before he got his pants off. When we busted in, he was in a bad way, believe me."

"Shamed and humiliated?"

"You can say that again. But, like I told you, the arrest didn't stick."

The Ace Pharmacy was on the dividing line between a slum and a middle-class residential area. The plate-glass window of the store was almost completely covered by paper banners proclaim-ing GOING OUT OF BUSINESS. EVERYTHING MUST GO. SALE. SALE!!!

A look through the glass door showed that there were no cus-tomers fighting over bargains. Long trestle tables had been set down the center of the aisle and on these were piled the small nondrug items that all druggists carried: cosmetics, shower caps, mirrors, brushes, watches, film, hose, and so on. EVERY ITEM $1, the hand-lettered sign read. At some time the $1 had been crossed out and 50¢ scrawled in red ink underneath. Still no takers. Norah and Innis entered. Not a soul, not even the proprietor, was to be seen.

"Hello? Anybody here?" Norah called.

A small man of medium height, paunchy and balding, emerged from what appeared to be a stockroom at the rear and peered over steel-rimmed spectacles. Seeing what he took to a be a cus-tomer, he bustled forward, rubbing his palms together. He was scrupulously clean, his white pharmacist's jacket fresh and starched, but Norah was watching his hands—white, pudgy, almost obscenely well tended, and very nervous.

"Mr. Goberman?"

"Yes, ma'am. What can I do for you?" Catching sight of Innis behind her, Goberman's smile never got beyond his teeth. "*You.* What do you want?"

"We're together," Norah answered, flipping her ID wallet open for the pharmacist to see. Innis almost did a take on that one because it was the first time she'd let a suspect know her rank.

Goberman was not impressed. "Get out of here, both of you," he ordered, the nervous hands clenched at his sides. "Get out. I'm sick of being hassled. I don't have to take this." His milky face curdled. He was breathing unevenly and his breath enveloped Norah in whiskey fumes.

"We just want to ask you a few questions sir," she said.

"I'm not answering. I don't have to. I know my rights."

"I'm glad to hear it, sir. We're asking for your cooperation."

"Really?" He laughed mirthlessly. "You've got real *chutzpah,* miss. I was set up by one of you lady cops. She came on real strong with me, and I fell for it. The next thing I knew, I was under arrest on a morals charge. I was dragged out of here in handcuffs with the whole neighborhood lined up on the sidewalk watching. Then I was mugged, fingerprinted, stripped . . . *stripped.* And searched. I'm not going to forget that in a hurry, believe me."

"You shouldn't," Norah agreed.

"What's that supposed to mean? Listen, I was innocent. Your DA refused to prosecute. Thank God there are some honest officials left."

"I'm not here to argue your case, Mr. Goberman. It's Officer Bednarski's murder I'm concerned with. I suppose you have heard that she was killed?"

"Sure, I heard, but I thought some freak was out killing policewomen that took jobs that should have gone to the men."

"You don't approve of women in police work?"

His face darkened. "I don't think women should be allowed to use sexual enticements as part of police work. I don't think they should be allowed to use sex to hype their arrest record."

"If you thought that Officer Bednarski did that you should have brought charges against her. We have an internal-affairs division to investigate such—"

"Don't make me laugh."

"The department has a strict code of conduct, Mr. Goberman. Your charges would have been thoroughly investigated."

"Sure, sure. Well, all I wanted was to forget the whole thing. I guess I was naive, huh? I should have known I wouldn't be allowed to forget it." Norah frowned and he exploded. "What the hell do you think those signs mean?" He made a sweeping gesture at the banners pasted across his show window and strung on wires across the ceiling. "I've got a ten-year lease here that's got seven years to run. I'm being forced out of business because of that false arrest. I'm running a family business in a family neighborhood. No man is going to allow his wife or daughter or child to come in here anymore and be alone with a sex fiend."

"The charge was dismissed."

"You can see for yourself how much good that did. I'm giving the stuff away and nobody comes in. I had to buy my way out of my lease. I'm selling my house at a loss. Would you believe that? At a *loss*. Everybody else is selling at fifty to a hundred percent profit."

"And it's all Officer Bednarski's fault."

"Who else?"

Norah glanced at Innis. "Just how did Officer Bednarski come to pick on you, Mr. Goberman? What made her select you to, as you say, set up?"

"How should I know?"

"Isn't it a fact, Mr. Goberman, the several of your women customers lodged complaints against you? That they charged that you demanded sexual favors in exchange for selling drugs without a prescription?"

"Lies. The complaints were withdrawn."

"Why were they made in the first place?"

"You want to know why? I'll tell you why. Because I turned those women down, that's why. First they came in here with legitimate doctors' prescriptions, and I filled them. Then they wanted refills, and when I wouldn't give them refills, when I told them to go back to the doctor, they offered me money. Again I refused, because it's against the law. They upped the ante, and I still said no. I explained that I could lose my license and no amount of money would be worth it."

"Very proper."

He nodded with an air of righteousness. "Then *they* offered sex." He jabbed a chubby finger at Norah for emphasis. "*They* suggested it."

"And you declined."

"That's right. And they didn't like that—a woman scorned, you know? So they lodged their complaints."

"To get even. I see."

"Listen, miss, I don't care whether you believe me or not. I don't give a damn. That's how it was."

"They propositioned you. And Officer Bednarski was also the one who made the advances."

"You've got it."

She looked him over, taking her time, letting him know that she didn't consider him exactly prepossessing. "And you resisted."

He squirmed. "Obviously not in Officer Bednarski's case. I'm only human. She was a very exciting woman."

"How late do you stay open, Mr. Goberman?" Norah abruptly changed the subject.

He was startled at first and then relieved. He answered eagerly. "Weekdays till ten, Saturdays till eight, closed Sundays."

"Do you have someone working nights with you or are you here alone?"

"I had two employees. They used to take turns working nights. I had to let them go. I couldn't afford to keep them."

"If you'll just give us their names and addresses."

"What for?"

"We're just interested in knowing whether you were in the store on certain specific occasions."

"What occasions?"

"If I tell you, then you can call them and fix up an alibi, can't you?"

Without a word, Goberman turned to a small file box beside his telephone in back of the cash register, fished out two cards, and hands shaking beyond his control, held them out to Norah.

"Thank you." She took them, copied them out, and handed them back. "One more thing."

"What?" He was warier than ever.

"You did give Officer Bednarski the Seconal she wanted?"

He couldn't deny it. It was on the record, and the pills had been confiscated for evidence. "Only to her. She was the only one. I

swear. I never gave the others anything. I never dispensed one single pill that wasn't covered by prescription."

Innis, jauntily attired in a chocolate-colored silk suit topped like
an ice-cream sundae with a wide-brimmed cream fedora, tilted his
hat rakishly as he and Norah emerged from the dark store into the
bright October sunshine. "You think he did it?"

"I don't think he would have blasted off against Eve and policewomen in general if he were running around killing them."

Innis adjusted his tie, a cherry-striped concoction. "It could be
a kind of reverse defense," he suggested, prancing half a step
ahead of her without waiting for a response. He moved on the
balls of his feet buoyantly, confidently, a lightweight contender
who has just floored the champ.

Norah didn't bother to comment; he was only making conversation. He'd dreaded the interview and he was relieved that it was
over. Why? Suddenly she stopped in the middle of the sidewalk.
"I forgot something."

"What?" He stopped, too, and turned anxiously. "What? I'll get
it for you."

"I forgot to ask him one question. It'll only take a minute. You
go start the car."

"I'm not supposed to let you go anywhere alone."

She shrugged, "Okay, come on if you want to." In the act of
turning toward the pharmacy, Norah gasped. "Look at that. That
kid's got a spray can and he's headed for your car."

"Where? Where? I don't . . ." The dapper detective looked
anxiously to where he'd parked a new sky-blue Mustang II. "Hey,
kid!" Innis yelled, and broke into a run.

The drugstore was empty again when she reentered, but now
Norah knew where to look for Goberman. She reached the threshold of the stockroom just as he was raising the shot glass to his
lips.

"Sorry to intrude." Until that moment she hadn't had a glimmer
of an idea of what to say. The maneuver had been intended to
upset Innis, not the druggist, but suddenly the words were there.
"How much Seconal did you give Eve Bednarski, Mr. Goberman?"

He didn't swallow the drink. "What she asked for."

"And what was that?"

"A hundred. A hundred capsules, a hundred milligrams each."

"Isn't that a lot?"

"Damn right. I told her the regular amount was thirty—one a night for one month—thirty. I explained to her that I have to account for my supplies; my drug book has to balance out. I never know when an inspector might want to look at it. She didn't give a damn."

"You gave her the full hundred?"

He nodded. "She didn't care how many prescriptions I had to kite."

Norah wondered why Eve had made such a point of getting the hundred. Surely thirty would have been as valid for the bust. "Sorry to have troubled you, Mr. Goberman."

Goberman grunted, not waiting for her to leave to knock off his drink. He was pouring out the next before she had even turned around. As she left the store Norah nearly collided with Innis on the run, out of breath, tie askew, and double-breasted jacket hoisted high over his hips. He was so agitated he didn't bother to pull it down into place.

"Say, Norah, that kid didn't have a spray can."

"He didn't?" Her eyebrows went up. "I could have sworn . . . Well, then, nothing happened to your car, right? It's okay?"

"Oh, yeah, sure."

"Good."

His suspicions were only partially allayed. "Did you get what you wanted from Goberman?"

"No, he couldn't remember."

"What? What couldn't he remember?" He blocked her exit from the store.

"I just wondered how many Seconal he had handed over to Bednarski, is all."

"Why? Is it important?"

His concern was all the answer that Norah needed. "Probably not. I had a hunch. It came to nothing. Forget it. Let's grab a bite; I'm starving. You know what I could go for? A stack of pancakes with a double order of bacon. What do you say we find a place?"

FOURTEEN

It was one of those combination luncheonette–coffee shop–ice-cream-parlor places done in pseudo-Victorian style with glass globes simulating gaslight fixtures and plenty of machine scroll fretwork along the walls. It was past the lunch hour, and few customers were left. Two waitresses took their ease near the kitchen door, ignoring the uncleared tables. One of them smoked, surreptitiously cupping the stub inside her palm between drags.

Innis walked past her, automatically heading for a booth.

Norah plumped herself down at one of the littered tables in the center of the room. "We'll get better service out here where they can see us," she said as a waitress glared, sullenly snubbed out the cigarette, and slouched over.

Table cleared, orders given, they waited in silence. The pancakes arrived and were consumed by Norah with gusto while Innis toyed with his corned beef on rye. Evidently his partner's good appetite reassured him, because by the time Norah was finished and signaling for a second cup of coffee the dapper detective had cleaned his plate too.

"Make that two more cups," he told the waitress.

"You know something?" Norah sighed her satisfaction and sat back. "I always think better on a full stomach. So, I was thinking —shouldn't Eve have made a note of the number of Seconal she got from Goberman?"

"I don't see why. Did she cite amounts on any other busts?"

"No, and I think she should have. Anyhow, I'm curious. Let's drive over to the property clerk's office and just check it out."

"Why? Is it important?"

"I told you, I don't know. I just have a hunch."

"Well." His handsome face was contorted with indecision. "I might have it in my notes. Let me take a look."

"That would be great. Save us a trip."

"Yeah. Okay." Innis fished a book out of an inner pocket and fumbled through the pages. "Okay, here it is. August sixth, 10:20 P.M., Henry Goberman. Yeah—Seconal, one hundred milligrams. Thirty capsules."

"Thirty," Norah repeated. "Did you count them?"

"When I turned them in, sure."

"You turned them in, not Eve?"

"I made the collar."

"Right, right. Well, so Eve got them from Goberman and turned them over to you as evidence." He nodded. "Well, she conned you, Gerry, my friend. According to Goberman, there were a hundred."

Innis paled.

"I don't see why Goberman should lie, do you?"

Before Innis could comment the waitress appeared, set the coffee in front of them, and slapped the check down beside Innis' setting. Innis, barely able to contain himself, nearly burst when Norah called the waitress back.

"Miss, we want separate checks, please."

"You didn't tell me that."

"Sorry. We forgot."

"You should have told me when you ordered," the waitress scolded. "Now I've got to void this and write two other—"

"Never mind, never mind, forget it." Innis reached out a hand for the check. "I'll pay it."

Relieved, the woman was about to relinquish the check.

"No, no. Separate checks," Norah insisted. "Thanks anyway, Gerry, but it's a matter of principle."

The waitress looked from one to the other and groaned. "Kooks," she muttered. "All of them, bunch of kooks."

As soon as she was out of earshot Innis leaned across the table. "You said he couldn't remember, that Goberman couldn't remember how many Seconal he gave Eve."

"I wondered if you could remember," she explained. "So now we know what Eve was up to, don't we? She was skimming."

"Skimming?" Gerald Innis repeated stupidly as though he didn't know what it meant.

It was a well-known practice among bagmen, people who delivered illicit merchandise—drugs, payoff money, numbers money—in other words, couriers running between seller and buyer. These people on occasion kept a little something of the merchandise they transferred for themselves. It was a dangerous practice and if caught they could expect no mercy. There were bagmen in the police as well as in the underworld, Norah knew, lower-ranking officers who took the direct payoffs from vice and gambling operations and passed it on to the higher-ups so that sergeants, lieutenants, and captains might keep their hands clean.

"Skimming," Norah repeated, opening her handbag and putting her lipstick out on the table. "I'm amazed you didn't catch on."

"No, no, I didn't. I had no idea. She just . . . when we were getting into the car she just handed me the container with the capsules in it."

"Oh, I wasn't thinking about that. What I had in mind was the other times."

"What other times?"

Carefully Norah now laid her compact on the table beside the lipstick but continued to rummage in the handbag.

"What other times?"

From the handbag Norah now took her service revolver, laying it, apparently negligently, in her lap as though she had merely removed it because she was searching for something else. She didn't think that Innis would draw his own gun, not out in the open—which was why she had chosen that particular table. Just the same, she wanted him to see that she was ready if he should have even a fleeting idea of violence. "I was thinking of when she made her heroin buys."

His eye was on the gun in Norah's lap. "I told you, the captain told you, she was only into small-time stuff—nickel bags. What could she skim off nickel bags?"

"I don't know. I'm not the expert. You tell me."

He only shook his head.

"As I say, I'm not the expert," Norah continued, hand resting casually on the gun. "Couldn't she have adulterated the stuff? If the amounts were so small, maybe the property office didn't bother to have an analysis made. We could ask to have it done now."

"That wouldn't tell us the original strength."

"That's how she could afford to adulterate it in the first place. The point is, Gerry, that I don't see how she could have done any of it without your knowing. I really don't. Norah's grip on the gun tightened. "As soon as Eve made a buy, you moved in. When in the world could she have tampered with the stuff? She couldn't, not without your knowledge and cooperation. Unless, of course, she was honest and you were skimming all by yourself."

"No, not me. I swear, Sergeant. I swear to God. You've got to believe . . ."

"On the other hand," Norah continued as though talking out loud to herself but meanwhile watching Innis' every twitch and quiver. "If you had your own little racket going and she caught you and wanted in . . ."

"No," Innis shouted, but instantly lowered his voice, aware that he'd attracted attention. "No," he repeated softly.

"She wanted a piece of the action or she was going to turn you in. You had to tell her okay, she was in. You had no choice on that. You set up a meet in the ladies' room at Yankee Stadium."

"No, no." He was thinking hard and fast and he came to a decision. "It wasn't like that."

"How was it?"

Gerald Innis poured it out in short bursts as though winded. "She was the one. Eve. She came on like . . . like the Dragon Lady. Not at the start. Oh, no. Not the first couple of weeks. She was a real good kid at the start, anxious to learn, respectful. Then, suddenly, one day, out of the blue, she makes a remark about how dumb those guys were who ripped off the French Connection dope from the property department. She says they made it tough on themselves. How it would have been easier to keep back some of the junk before they turned it in."

"Assuming the people who stole it were the same ones who turned it in," Norah remarked.

"I mentioned that, but she looked at me as though I'd missed the point." Innis seemed to be breathing more easily. "I also told her that had been a real big haul and that a lot of people were involved and it was more or less known how much stuff there was. She let it pass, and I figured the subject was closed, but a couple of days later she brought it up again. She said that if a person wasn't greedy, if he was satisfied to take just a little off the top, he could build himself a nice sideline. She figured that there was only the officer's word for how much he confiscated. The only person

who could contradict him would be the dealer who'd got busted—
if he ever found out. And if he did and talked, who the hell was
going to believe him?"

"But if the amounts were as small as you say?"

"You said it yourself, Norah. She just stretched the stuff a little
more than it was already stretched."

"Does it matter whose idea it was?"

An ugly rash broke out, spoiling his nice complexion. "I guess
not."

That some police officers answered a burglar alarm and then
took for themselves whatever the thieves had left behind, was bad
enough. That there were others who not only skimmed the drugs
they confiscated but became pushers themselves to dispose of what
they'd stolen, made Norah sick. It was unforgivable. Tantamount
to murder. The disgust she felt showed.

"How did you get rid of the stuff?"

"I didn't. She wanted me to push it, but I refused. I couldn't do
it, Sergeant . . . Norah. I swear to God. I couldn't. I turned her
down."

"I would like to believe you."

"It's true. I swear to God, it's true."

"Why didn't you report her?"

"Ah . . ." The groan was long, drawn out. The mottled rash
grew angrier. "I had taken gambling payoffs. She knew it. It was a
standoff."

"So you let her operate. You condoned what she was doing."

He winced as though he'd been struck and waited for the second
hit, but he didn't answer.

"You let her go ahead. You think because you didn't take a
piece of the action that made it all right?"

"No, ma'am," he murmured barely audibly.

"You expect me to believe you?"

"It's the God's truth. I swear."

"You know something, Gerry? You take the name of the Lord
in vain too often. I don't like it."

"I'm sorry."

"And I don't believe you. Don't . . ." She raised a hand to
forestall him. "Don't swear another time, please. Either Eve made
you or you made her—I don't care; I don't think it matters. You
were in it together. You were at Yankee Stadium the night she
was killed. You have no alibi for the time of the murder."

"I never went inside the stadium. I swear to . . ." At Norah's glance, he caught himself. "I'm sorry."

"If you killed Eve then you also killed the others."

Something in her tone was different. Innis caught it and it stopped him just at the edge of panic.

"I couldn't condone that," she told him. Then she raised the gun just to the edge of the table but in such a way that it could not readily be seen by others in restaurant. "If I find out you killed those women, I'll shoot you myself before I let you get away."

Innis' eyes were riveted to Norah's.

"If you didn't commit the murders, if you can come up with an alibi for even one of the crucial times, then . . ." She shrugged. "Whatever you and Eve had going . . . sometimes one has to do things contrary to one's principles." She sighed, lowered the gun, and slipped it back into her purse. "I can understand. Like right now, my father is very sick. He has to have an operation and what with the cost of the surgery and a prolonged stay in the hospital, well, you know what hospital costs are nowadays. I'd say the whole package is going to run close to ten thousand. Naturally, I don't have that kind of money, but maybe you could help me out? I'd certainly appreciate it. So why don't you call me at home? Tonight. No later than midnight."

One by one, Norah picked up the things she'd laid out on the table—lipstick, comb, compact—and returned them to her hand-bag, fastened the clasp, and hoisted the strap over her shoulder. Then she stood up and headed for the door.

"Hey," the waitress yelled, coming toward them. "Hey, here's your check."

Norah jerked her head at Innis. "Give it to him."

"But you wanted . . . you were the one . . ." the waitress stammered in outrage as Norah walked out. The woman turned and slapped the two checks down in front of Innis.

"Looks like you got stuck, mister."

"It wouldn't have had the same impact later on." Norah defended what she'd done in a meeting with both captains. "He would have had time to think. He might have sensed the trap."

"My dear girl, if he didn't sense it then, he senses it now," Sebastian Honn told her. "Your reputation for integrity is just too well established."

Norah thrust out her chin. "I think he bought it."

To avoid any word of the conference leaking out, they were meeting in Norah's apartment—Felix and Honn, Detective Schmidt and Officer Dollinger. Honn, spent cigar clamped between his teeth, paced nervously; Felix sat back in an easy chair, but the ashtray at his side, filled with cigarette butts, betrayed him. Schmidt and Dolly sat apart, as befitted lesser members of the team, and kept their mouths shut.

"And that bit about your father needing an operation." Honn shook his head. "Really, Norah, couldn't you have come up with anything better?"

Felix supported her. "I'm sure Innis took it as intended—a mere convention."

Honn shrugged. "It's immaterial. Nothing's going to happen."

"We can't be sure." Felix was carefully mild.

"What I'm saying, Jim, is that nothing is going to happen *tonight*. What Norah's succeeded in doing is to set herself up, but without any kind of reasonable control over time and place of the attack."

"I don't agree, Sebastian." The courtesy between the two was becoming strained. "Actually, Norah's done very well. She's given Innis a choice: either pay the ten thousand by midnight or get rid of her. Either way, he must act by the deadline."

"Okay. Let's suppose he pays. What guarantee is there that he won't go for her later on?"

"None, I agree."

"Thank you."

"He's got to kill her; there's no doubt about that. The ten thousand would buy him time to plan."

"Great." Honn dripped sarcasm.

"But it's not going to do him any good."

"You can't protect her twenty-four hours a day for an indefinite period. As soon as you take your men off . . ."

"We're going to get him tonight. Either when he hands over the money at the rendezvous or when he tries to break in here."

"Suppose he doesn't do either?"

"He's got to. If he doesn't call Norah on that telephone by midnight, then presumably she informs her superiors of what she's discovered and Detective Innis' conduct is investigated and he ends up under a variety of charges from taking bribes to murder."

The argument back and forth as though she weren't even present was beginning to make Norah nervous.

"I just wish we had more time to organize." Honn sighed and looked at Norah. "I wish you hadn't been so impulsive." He turned back to Felix. "I suppose we have no choice but to go ahead with it. Okay, it's your show; what's the plan?"

"I don't see Innis coming here. What he'll want to do is to lure Norah out. That means he'll call and suggest a place for the payoff to take place. Norah will refuse and insist on her own arrangements. He'll have to go along."

"Okay."

The tension had eased slightly. The conflict between the two commanders was replaced by another kind of stress, that of planning for a situation that could not be reliably forecast.

"Norah will set up the meet at an intimate supper club just a block over, called the Rouge Room," Felix explained. "We'll have the route covered and naturally the club will be staked out. As soon as Innis hands over the money we've got him."

"It sounds all right," Honn allowed grudgingly. "How about wiring her? As long as she's going this far we might as well get something on tape."

Felix licked his lips. "I don't know how much he'd admit. If she asked too many leading questions it might make him suspicious." He gave up. "The equipment wasn't available."

"Damn it to hell." Honn threw a glance at Norah.

That was just after six P.M. Felix made a phone call that set the plan in motion and the long wait began.

The men and women in that room were veterans of that kind of waiting. Tonight they were fortunate—they had light, warmth, all the comforts. There was plenty of coffee, sandwiches, even television to pass the time. By nine o'clock the phone had rung twice —both false alarms. Each time it was Dolly's mother, making sure she was all right.

"Don't call me anymore, will you please, Ma?" Dolly was both embarrassed and exasperated. "We have to keep the line clear, okay? Yes, Ma. I know you love me and I love you . . . No, I can't call you later. I'll call you in the morning." She listened a little more, then broke in. "Good night, Ma," she said firmly, and hung up, her face flaming.

"I'm sorry," she apologized to the room at large.

The response was composed of sympathetic grunts and nods. Everybody had a mother.

By common accord the TV was turned on but the volume kept

low, as though it might interfere with hearing the ring of the telephone. Somehow the low volume, combined with the flickering light from the screen, served to emphasize the silence that had fallen on them.

They watched, or pretended to watch, the hockey game. Norah couldn't help thinking of all the other times she'd sat in that room watching the Rangers with Joe and her father or with Joe alone, sitting, feet up, in companionable comfort. Knowing she was a fan, Sebastian had got tickets for the Sunday-night game. She'd never gone to a hockey game with anyone but Joe and to go with Sebastian seemed oddly disloyal, as the other dates had not. The prospect brought other suppressed guilts to the surface. Silly, of course. Nevertheless, Norah dreaded the date and would have canceled except that Sunday might be the last time she and Sebastian would see each other: Joe was due back on Tuesday afternoon. At this moment, Sunday seemed very far off.

She wasn't particularly nervous over the situation; it would not be the first time that Norah Mulcahaney had offered herself as bait. She had confidence in her backup. She knew that every available precaution for her safety had been taken. But there was always the unexpected, the contingency that could not be foreseen. She would have been less than a realist, if she didn't admit that one couldn't cover all eventualities, less than human if she hadn't had a few qualms.

At 10:10 the hockey game was over and an old Abbott and Costello movie came on. Everybody continued to watch; nobody laughed. The atmosphere was heavy with smoke. Norah's nerves were beginning to tighten.

At eleven o'clock Schmidt thought to switch to the news. That brought a return to alertness and for Norah increased the pricklings of anxiety. Suppose Innis had decided that killing another policewoman might serve as the best way of countering Norah's threat. If he managed somehow to have an alibi at the same time . . . No, no, she was borrowing trouble.

Eleven-thirty. The three men and two women were watching the clock.

"Anybody want coffee?" Dolly asked.

As though in answer, the phone rang. There was a moment of paralysis, then Norah got up. She picked up on the third ring.

"Yes."

"I've got what you want."

"Good." She was brisk and matter-of-fact. "Meet me at the Rouge Room, Sixty-third and Madison. I'll be at the bar. Half an hour."

It had not been possible to trace the call, nor was it particularly important. What mattered was that the street lookouts reported by two-way radio that it had not been made from any booth within the stakeout area. That suggested Norah would be safe en route to the rendezvous. Nevertheless, it was decided she shouldn't wait till just before midnight but leave immediately just in case Innis intended to jump her before she reached the supper club. Felix himself went down in the elevator with Norah and took her as far as the outer lobby. Then she was on her own.

At the intersection of Sixty-fourth Street a Con Ed group in hard hats huddled around an open manhole. Repair crew or detectives? Norah didn't recognize any of them. There was nobody else around that she could see, but they were there—inside that dark store, in the doorway of that apartment house. She willed herself not to look. She was safe, she knew that, yet she walked quickly and kept to the edge of the sidewalk, every sense alert. She felt most vulnerable crossing to the other side of Madison, yet when she made it safely she didn't slacken pace, and she reached the well-lit canopy of the supper club and the reassuring presence of its uniformed doorman with her heart pounding.

Inside, she paused for a moment to absorb the layout and to collect herself.

It was a quiet, decorous place, long and narrow as a corridor. One wall was covered in red damask, hence the name, and the other completely mirrored to give the illusion of width. The reflection of a row of small crystal chandeliers helped. As usual, the bar was at the front and the restaurant section, including a minuscule dance floor, made up the rear area. A pianist positioned in between played soothing late-night melodies. As on the street, Norah could not spot the undercover men that Felix had planted; if she could not spot them, knowing they were there, then Innis would not spot them, either. She felt better. Having located the rear exit and the two rest rooms, Norah approached the bar. She was just climbing up on an empty stool when a voice sounded just behind her.

"Excuse me, miss?"

"Yes?" It was the maître d'.

"I'm sorry. We don't allow unescorted ladies at the bar."

"That's all right. I'm meeting somebody."

"I'm very sorry, miss." The tone belied the words.

Damn, she thought, looking at her watch. Innis wasn't due for another twenty minutes. "I'm a little early," she explained. "All right, all right. I'll take a table."

"There are no tables available."

"What? There certainly are. Right there." She could see three. She pointed at them.

"They are reserved."

Nora bit her lip in exasperation. She'd started out being annoyed, now she was getting anxious. Of all the dumb things to get hung up on. They'd thought of everything, figured every eventuality, except this. To have the whole plan wrecked by this stuffy male-chauvinist regulation . . . No use wishing they'd chosen a less elegant place or that she'd waited to let Innis arrive first. Of course, she could identify herself, show her badge, but that would call attention to herself, which would transfer to Innis when he arrived and might serve to warn him of the trap.

"Look, Captain, I'm meeting a friend and I'm a little early. Now, you're not going to force me to stand outside and wait for him in the street, are you?"

"That's your problem, miss. You'll have to leave." As he sensed victory the maître d's chest swelled and he edged closer to Norah as though intending physically to remove her.

Although she'd started by putting on an act, now her temper flared in earnest. "Don't touch me," she warned. "Don't do it."

And the hitherto-suave flunky turned coarse. "Listen, lady, if you don't leave quietly . . ."

"You allow unescorted men at the bar, don't you?"

The man had actually reached a hand to Norah's elbow, but he now drew it back as though he'd been scorched. One of *those*. His arrogance crumbled. "Lower your voice," he hissed.

Norah raised it. "Answer my question. Do you allow unescorted men in here?" She was beginning to enjoy herself.

"Why pick on me, lady? I only work here. I don't make the rules. I'm on your side, believe me."

"Good. Then you don't mind if I wait for my friend, right here where I am."

"Look, I don't mind. I'm trying to tell you that it's not . . ."

"What's the matter? Something wrong?"

They both jumped. Innis had come up from behind. Instead of the pinch-waisted, broad-shouldered, shiny silk suit that was his working trademark, the detective was eminently respectable-looking in a dark navy business suit.

"Is this man bothering you, Norah?"

She was so delighted to see him and to see him looking as he did that she nearly laughed out loud. "He's trying to throw me out."

"Is that so?" Innis moved in closer to the now definitely cowed headwaiter.

"The lady misunderstood. I never meant that," the unfortunate man protested. "I never did."

"Then you implied it." Innis was smaller and lighter but his look and manner were definitely intimidating.

"No, sir, no, believe me. It's all a musunderstanding. Please, please, sit down." He made a sweeping gesture that included both and then indicated a well-located table.

"Thanks, but we prefer the bar."

"As you wish, sir, of course, of course. Allow me to offer you a drink, on the house."

"Very well, we'll accept the drinks. What'll you have, Norah?"

"Scotch and soda."

"Make that two." As the now obsequious headwaiter signaled to the barman and then made his escape, Innis and Norah moved to the far end of the bar. For a few moments the humor of the encounter carried over and they were easy with each other. With the arrival of the drinks, however, the next phase began. Raising their glasses, they measured each other.

"Well?" Norah raised her eyebrows.

"Oh, I have it," Innis replied, but he made no move to produce the money. "You know, in the short time we've worked together I really got to like you, Sergeant, and what's more, to have a tremendous respect for you. If anybody had told me that you would be doing a thing like this . . . I wouldn't only have refused to believe it, I would have had his hide."

Norah flushed. "Can we get this over with, please?"

"If that's what you want." The detective reached into the inside pocket of his jacket and drew out a white envelope. "You can step into the ladies' room and count it if you want."

"Like Eve Bednarski?"

Innis went purple, and Norah, oddly, was sorry she'd said it. Impatiently she held out her hand for the envelope, and Innis slowly, almost reluctantly, gave it to her. She then put it inside her handbag, twirled around on the stool, intending to slide down and leave. Two very large, very broad-shouldered men in sporty plaid jackets blocked her way. One of them held the familiar wallet open for perusal.

"Internal Affairs, Sergeant. Mind coming with us?"

FIFTEEN

"Internal Affairs," Norah repeated, staring at the men who had closed in on her. They were big, beefy, and pound for pound outmatched her at least four to one. Had she not been so completely flabbergasted, she might have been flattered that she was deemed worthy of such a show of force. "I don't believe this," she murmered. "I just don't believe it."

For answer, the taller of the two—John Ashdown, according to his ID—began reading her her rights.

"I'm sorry, Sergeant Mulcahaney," Innis whispered through the reading. "I didn't want to turn you in. I didn't know what else to do. You left me no choice."

She looked at him in amazement. "Sorry? You're sorry?"

Ashdown put the rights card away. "Okay, knock it off, the both of you. We're not here for a discussion. Sergeant Mulcahaney, my partner and I are witnesses to your taking the payoff from Innis."

"All right, but I can explain."

"You've got the money on you. The bills are marked."

"All right, but—"

"You'll get a chance to tell your version later. Now you're coming with us and it's to your advantage to come quietly."

Norah sighed, cast a quick look around the supper club, and noted that several of the patrons of the Rouge Room had quite suddenly decided to take their leave and were gathering around the coat room. "Whatever you want," she said, and slid off the stool. At a nudge from Ashdown, she started for the door. It had been intended that Innis should leave first and be picked up outside. The operatives planted by Felix, alert to the change in script and seeing Norah headed for the exit with Innis and what looked like a couple of thugs behind her, didn't hesitate to move to bar the way and stop the parade.

"Police," Roy Brennan, in charge of the detail, announced. "You okay, Sergeant?" he asked, keeping his eyes on the men who had been escorting her, hand at the edge of his jacket, ready to draw the gun from his shoulder holster.

"What the hell," Ashdown exclaimed. "What the hell's going on?"

"I was just going to ask you the same thing, buddy," Roy retorted.

And Norah, despite every effort to hold back, began to laugh. She laughed harder and harder, helplessly, till she cried.

Even the next day, sitting in Jim Felix's office and listening as Sebastian vented his frustration, Norah couldn't help but smile as she thought back to the scene at the supper club: the troops confronting one another; the maître d' hovering anxiously in the background; the startled, then titillated patrons.

Sebastian scowled. "It's not funny."

"No. I know it isn't." She bit back the smile. She really didn't know what had got into her lately. She felt lighthearted, laughed so easily, caught herself humming.

"I don't think you realize what's happened here, the seriousness of your situation, Sergeant. It couldn't be worse."

"Oh, I wouldn't say that, Captain."

"It couldn't be worse," Honn repeated.

Norah looked to Felix, but he merely raised an eyebrow.

"What happened is exactly what I predicted," Honn continued. "We've lost control, if we ever had it."

"Innis has been suspended, pending further investigation," Felix reminded his opposite number.

"I don't find that particularly reassuring," Honn countered. "Norah is a walking target; he can pick her off anytime he wants. There's nothing we can do to stop him."

"I take it you don't buy Innis' ploy?"

"Do you?" Honn was scornful.

Felix sighed. "I'm inclined to, yes."

"If he was genuinely disturbed about Norah's blackmail bid,

why didn't he come to me? I'm his commanding officer; I've always stood behind my men. Why didn't he come to me?"

Felix pursed his lips, working them back and forth a couple of times. "You think he should have told you that Sergeant Mulcahaney was demanding ten thousand dollars to cover up a drug operation run by his erstwhile partner and condoned by him, plus gambling and vice payoffs that he received directly? That the cover-up might even extend to evidence of homicide?" Felix asked. Glancing from Honn to Norah and back again, he passed a hand over his mouth. "Possibly he thought you wouldn't believe it."

The color drained out of Sebastian Honn's face and for the first time, at least in Norah's experience, he had nothing to say.

Felix hurried on. "Innis has made a complete confession, naming names, places, dates, and the amounts of the payoffs over the period during which he took bribes. He's involved some middle-echelon drug people, and his testimony is going to disrupt the chain of command of at least two organizations. In my book that makes for a strong assumption of credibility."

"Cheap—if it gets him off a murder charge. I don't buy it." Honn had recovered himself. "As far as I'm concerned, all it proves is that Innis is a lot shrewder than we thought. Bringing in IAD was a bold move. Look what he's accomplished by it: he's effectively got Norah off his back, assuming she was in fact trying to shake him down; if she was merely trying to pin the murders on him, he's strengthened the assumption of his innocence—what killer is going to bring in IAD to assist him? Most important, if Norah should get killed later on—"

"Please." Norah broke in. "I wish you wouldn't keep talking quite so casually about my being killed."

"Who's going to believe Gerald Innis did it?' Honn continued. "Who's going to think he'd be dumb enough?"

"Would you at least not discuss it while I'm around?" Norah asked.

"I'm glad you're beginning to realize your danger."

"You're the one making me nervous, not Innis."

"You believe him. His word is good enough for you." Honn was indignant. "You're willing to accept the word of an admittedly corrupt cop. Okay. Let's go back to the one fact we've got: thirty Seconal were turned over as evidence in the Goberman case. Innis claims that's what Bednarski handed him. How do you know that Bednarski didn't hand him the full hundred?"

"Why shouldn't he admit it, since he's admitted everything else?"

"Because that's a direct link to the murder. You were the one who suggested the real motive was to kill Bednarski and the other homicides were cover-ups," he reminded her. "You want to change your mind?"

"No."

"You tried to set him up and the attempt backfired. He out-smarted you. Admit it. He made fools out of all of us. Does that make you feel any better?"

Norah frowned. "I've been wondering . . . if Innis killed Eve Bednarski, why did he do it in Yankee Stadium?"

"Why not? It was as good a place as any."

"I don't think so. I think it was out of the way and difficult to set up. And how did he get Bednarski to meet him there?" she wanted to know, asking both men. "I mean, if it was ostensibly for a payoff."

Honn shrugged. "Who knows what he told her? Who knows why she went? Maybe she thought she was going to make a big buy, maybe she didn't expect to be meeting Innis."

"Oh, I can think of lots of ways he could have got her to show up," Norah replied. "But why bother? Why go to the trouble of getting into the stadium before the game, putting the 'out-of-order' sign on the ladies' room? They were together all day long; there must have been plenty of opportunities to stick the knife into her."

"Like when they were sitting together in his car?" Honn was heavy on the sarcasm.

"Remember, it had to look like part of the pattern," Felix reminded her. "He had gone to a lot of trouble to set up a pattern of policewomen killed on duty. Now when he got to the murder that really counted, he had to kill her in an atmosphere of such confusion that it would be linked to the earlier crimes and so that suspicion would not be directed as it otherwise would—to the victim's partner."

"I'll tell you what gets me, really gets me," Honn declared in an unexpected outburst. "Its Innis' holier-than-thou attitude. His mealymouthed repentance. Oh, he's so sorry for taking those bribes. He knows he's done wrong and he'll do everything in his power to cooperate to bring the criminals that he once protected to justice. He's sorry that he had to turn Sergeant Mulcahaney in. He hopes she'll forgive him. Bunk. Worse than bunk. It scares me. Forgive me, Norah, it scares the shit out of me."

"What has he got to gain by getting rid of me?" Norah asked. "Everything I know about Innis and about the case is on paper."

"You figured it out. You put the finger on him. He hates you."

She thought back to the encounter at the supper club: Innis' putdown of the maître d', their shared, almost childish glee; his reluctance to turn over the money, knowing she would be taken into custody; later, his red-faced apology.

"He hates you," Honn repeated. "You weren't there during his interrogation; you didn't see his face when he talked about you."

Norah, too, had had her session with Internal Affairs and it had not been pleasant. Even knowing that she must be exonerated, it had not been pleasant. Innis had had no such assurance. In fact, he'd known he was facing the end of his career, if not a jail term. He'd be bound to feel resentment against her, even bitterness, but that he should be thinking of revenge . . . She shook her head.

"You're the most damned stubborn woman I've ever met." Honn spun around to Felix. "It's my opinion that Sergeant Mulcahaney can be of no further use on this case. In fact, she's become a liability."

The breach of departmental etiquette amazed Felix. "I don't share that opinion, Captain."

"Go away, Norah, go away for a couple of weeks." Sebastian Honn's gray eyes were fixed on Norah and urgently pleading. "Take a vacation. Go South. Go join Joe in Italy. That's it. Go to Italy. To Joe."

"Joe's coming home. Next week. Tuesday."

"I didn't know that."

"I've been meaning to tell you."

Both were as aware of Felix's presence as he was of their need to be alone. It was difficult to miss the current between them, but knowing Norah as he did, and accustomed to her cool self-sufficiency and her strict moral standards, Felix was not only surprised but embarrassed by this open flood of feeling and he didn't quite know what to do. He could hardly get up and walk out of his own office. It really wasn't up to him to do anything, he decided, and proceeded to busy himself with whatever papers came to hand.

Honn resolved the situation. "I'm glad Joe's coming home. It's about time. It's the best thing that could happen. Maybe he can talk some sense into you. God knows nobody else can." He got up. "At least until Joe gets back, will you please stay home? Stay home with Dolly and keep your door locked?"

"Yes. Yes, I will."

Honn nodded and turned to Felix. "Thanks, Jim. I'll be in touch."

So it was over, Norah thought as she watched Sebastian, sternly erect, walk out. It was over without anything really having happened. Would it have been better if there had been physical consummation? Would it be easier now to part and forget? She became aware that Felix was talking to her.

"I think Captain Honn is right," he was saying. "I think the smart thing for you to do is to go home, lock the door, and keep it locked till IAD decides one way or another about Innis."

"Yes, sir." She was too dispirited to argue.

"I'll assign somebody to stay with you if you want."

"That's okay, Captain. Dolly and I will make out fine."

The first couple of days passed quickly. Norah spent the time cleaning house, always one of her therapeutic exercises. The trouble was that in Dolly Dollinger she had a helper who was as energetic and efficient as she, and between them the work went fast, too fast. By four-thirty of the second afternoon everything that could be cleaned, scrubbed, polished, and waxed had been. They rewarded themselves with a couple of beers and the evening stretched ahead of them empty.

Dolly looked around the living room, admiring the results of their labor. Her eyes wandered to the two eight-foot-high windows. "Those curtains could use a washing. We can do the curtains tomorrow."

"Great," Norah muttered.

"It's something to do."

"Right. Something to look forward to."

"Come on, Norah."

"Sorry, Dolly. Listen, I appreciate your company, but you don't have to stay in here cooped up with me every minute. You can go out, take a walk, pick up the papers."

"I know."

"I'll be all right. I won't open up the door to anybody. I promise."

"Fine. I'm not going."

Norah sighed. "I think I'll call in and find out if there's any news." She looked to Dolly, wanting her to say "Go ahead."

"The captain will let you know as soon as he knows."

Another sigh. Norah stared at the telephone, wishing it to ring, wishing she would hear, not Captain Felix's voice, but Sebastian's. She didn't really expect Sebastian to call . . . but if only he would.

In her fantasizing of what their last meeting would be like, Norah had never envisioned that they would say good-bye to each other in Felix's office and certainly not in his presence. She could not believe that Sebastian would leave it at that. Maybe she was making more out of the relationship than there had been. Maybe by his silence Sebastian was telling her just that. Forget Sebastian. Think of Joe. In three days Joe would be home.

Would he sense a difference in her? Norah was sure the sisters wouldn't say anything: they didn't know anything. But there was always the so-called friend who felt obliged to speak out. And there was always the chance that someone in all innocence would mention she'd been seeing Honn outside working hours. Don't borrow trouble; think about the case.

"You know what bugs me?" she blurted out without preamble. "That a rookie like Bednarski, still learning the ropes, could have got into skimming and drug distribution and blackmail all on her own."

Dolly looked up from the magazine she'd been reading and in which she wasn't particularly interested. "Innis was in it with her. He provided the contacts."

Once again Norah had a picture of the girlishly handsome detective at the supper club in his conservative, dark blue suit; recalled his reluctance in handing over the marked money, his apology later for turning her over to the IAD.

"Well, who else is there?"

Norah thought of her first meeting with Innis in Sebastian's office, his recounting of the friendship between his partner and Katie Chave that set up the spurious motive, the red herring.

Now that neither woman was watching or waiting for the phone to ring, of course it did. Both jumped and Norah answered. It was Captain Felix.

"Innis has been charged with the murder of Pilar Nieves."

"Nieves?" Norah repeated. "Why Nieves?"

"They found the murder weapon. The gun with which she was shot, complete with silencer, was in Innis' locker."

"At the precinct? They found the gun in his locker at the precinct?" Norah was stunned.

"His apartment was searched without result. It was Captain Honn's idea to try his locker."

Norah's heart started to pound.

"He's being arraigned right now, and the case will go to the grand jury on Tuesday. There's no doubt that they'll bring in an indictment. So you're no longer under house arrest. Norah. You can consider yourself released. Norah?"

"Yes. I'm sorry. Yes, Captain. I'm just so amazed that he kept the gun."

"It's been known to happen."

"But in his locker at the precinct!"

"I suppose he thought nobody would look there."

There was a pause. Felix spoke again. "Norah? If you want some time off . . ."

"Oh no, no thanks, Captain. I've had too much time off already. I'll be in tomorrow. Thanks for calling and letting us know." She hung up. Barely had she done so, before she could even pass the news on to Dolly, when the phone rang again and before answering she knew for sure who it would be this time. She was right.

"Have you heard?" he asked.

"Just this minute. Captain Felix called."

"Good. Well, good." Robbed of his opening gambit, Sebastian Honn didn't know how to proceed. "I wanted to make sure somebody told you."

She could only follow his lead. "That was thoughtful of you. Thank you."

"Well . . ."

They'd never been at a loss for words before; on the contrary, the words had spilled out, one interrupting the other, talking at the same time, anticipating. She thought of something to keep him on the phone. "Captain Felix said it was your idea to look in the locker."

"Yes. I don't know what made me think of it, but thank God I did. The truth is that I finally faced up to the possibility that somebody on my squad could be corrupt. I was so sure that every man and woman in my command was pure. I was so smug. God forgive me, if I'd kept my eyes open . . ."

"Don't think like that."

"I guess that's a form of self-indulgence, too. So, I guess we won't be seeing each other anymore. I'm taking some time off. I'm going to go away, do a little hunting and fishing, and thinking. When I get back I may put in for retirement. I don't know. I haven't decided."

He'd survived the addiction and death of his son, the death of his wife, but this last blow could finally break him. "I hope not, Sebastian. I hope not. Good luck."

"You, too."

Neither wanted to be the first to hang up.

"Norah?"

"Yes?"

"Those tickets . . . those tickets for the hockey game tonight . . . I can't make it, but you might as well have them. Please. I'd like it if you'd use them. Why don't you go with Dolly? I never was that crazy about the game; I got them for you. They're good seats. I'll send them over."

Then he hung up.

The atmosphere was supercharged, crackling with suppressed energy as the crowd converged on Madison Square Garden for the game.

Everybody was out to have a good time, Norah thought as she and Dolly Dollinger were swept into the human stream flowing from the Eighth Avenue entrance, along the enclosed plaza, and to the lobby of the sports arena. If she could just let go and enjoy herself as Dolly was so obviously doing. The case was closed, the perpetrator caught. Those policewomen who wished to rescind their resignations would be welcomed back. Policewomen all over the city would breathe more easily and return to their regular duties and their normal lives. She'd be back at her regular job and her regular life. It was all neat and tidy.

Norah handed over her tickets to one of the ticket takers and received back the torn stubs: tower A, gate 18, section 233, row A, seats 1 and 2.

They rode the escalator two flights up, turned right along a tunnel corridor to gate 18, handed the stubs to an usher, and were shown down a flight of concrete steps to their places.

"Gee, these are great," Dolly said enthusiastically as she took off her coat and draped it over the metal pipe that acted as handrail and separation between their row and the more expensive section of seats directly below. "Just great," Dolly repeated, and joined in the burst of applause that greeted the emergence of the home team in their white and blue uniforms as they came out on the ice. Good-naturedly, she also joined in the scattered boos that greeted the opposing team, clad in dark uniforms as befitted the villains. Each side went to its own end of the rink, skating in serpentine formation till the announcement over the loudspeaker.

"Ladies and gentlemen, our national anthem."

The teams lined up facing each other at center ice; the lights dimmed; the crowd rose to its feet and joined together in the singing as the organ blared. Before the last notes were played they broke off into cheers and applause for the start of the game.

After everyone had sat down again Norah was still standing. "I have to make a phone call."

"What's up? Norah . . . Norah!"

She was gone, running up the stairs, and a thunderous cheer from the crowd turned Dolly's attention back to the ice. The Rangers had won their first face-off and were storming into the opposition's blue zone, swarming around the net. A promising start.

Two players scuffled; a stick was raised; the crowd yelled. The referee's arm shot up and he blew the whistle. Penalty. The crowd applauded, for the referee's decision penalized the opposing player and gave the home team its first power-play opportunity. Quickly the classic formation was established, the puck passed back and forth, and, faster than most eyes could follow, it slipped behind the goaltender and came to rest in the net. The red light went on. There was a second's stunned silence, then bedlam. Seventeen thousand five hundred people got to their feet with a roar of approval, raising clenched fists high in delight; lights flashed, horns blared, the organ pumped out chords. Score! Score!

"Ranger goal by number 77, Phil Esposito, with an assist by number 8, Don Vickers. Time, 3:51 of the first period." The announcement was greeted with another roar.

Norah slipped back into the seat beside Dolly.

"You missed a great play."

"I called the lab. It seems there were no fingerprints on the gun."

It took a couple of seconds for Dolly to shift from one world into the other and to realize Norah was referring to the gun found in Innis' locker. "When are there ever? The stock doesn't take prints. Everybody knows that."

"The barrel was wiped clean. Completely. Why should Innis do that? Why should Innis have kept the gun?"

"Are we back to that? So he made a mistake. Forget it, will you? Let's enjoy ourselves."

"I can see him keeping the gun up to the time I confronted him, but after that . . . no, I can't buy it. To keep the murder weapon after he decided to call in Internal Affairs . . . it was just plain suicide."

Dolly sighed. She had to agree.

"That gun was the only direct piece of hard evidence in the entire series of homicides. No other evidence existed. Why should a perpetrator as shrewd and cool as this one hang on to it? There's only one reason: he kept it in reserve so in case things got hot he could plant it on somebody else."

The two women looked at each other.

"And then he made a mistake," Norah continued. "In the process of planting the gun in Innis' locker he got his own fingerprints on it—on the barrel. So he had to wipe it clean."

SIXTEEN

The initial excitement of the game had subsided; the two teams reverted to their usual, less inspired level of play, and the crowd seemed almost relieved to be released from the high pitch of excitement of the early minutes. As far as Norah and Dolly were concerned, they were oblivious of what was happening down on the ice, the reaction of the crowd, or even of where they were.

"Who could have planted the gun?" Dolly wondered. "Who had access to Innis' locker?"

Anyone on the force could walk in without being challenged, so that didn't help, although it was more likely to be someone at the precinct. Who at the Four-two was so closely linked to the undercover policewoman that he was willing to kill her and at least two other innocent women to hide that link? Norah asked herself. Who besides Gerald Innis knew that Bednarksi and Chave were friends and part of that small group of women who had brought suit to recover their jobs? Innis might have mentioned it to any number of people, but as far as Norah was aware, only one had made the connection between Bednarski and Chave and the other victims. That one had passed the information on to her while making a great show of confidentiality. By demanding that she keep the information to herself for even a short time, he had succeeded in intensifying Norah's reaction. She had passed her feelings on to her sister officers, and certainly that had been a factor in diverting the course of the investigation. He had even given her the credit for breaking the case.

Norah stopped, appalled. Had she really let herself be gulled, or was she now jumping to conclusions?

Dolly Dollinger saw her friend's anguish and knew there was only one reason for it. "Honn?" she whispered.

"*No*," Norah instantly responded. "*No*." How could she have thought it even for a second? He was as beyond suspicion as any man could be. He had been cleared of all implications of corruption by the Knapp Commission; he was largely resonsible for the restructuring and operation of the new Narcotics Squad, which was recognized as clean. His own son had OD'd on heroin. How could such a man be involved in pushing drugs or taking bribes from essentially the same people who were reponsible for killing his son? Unless . . . Maybe his wife's long and expensive illness had driven him to it. Might he not have seen a kind of bitter justice in using money from the drugs that had killed his son to save his wife?

He had a lot more to lose than Innis. If Bednarski had stumbled onto *his* corruption and threatened *him* with blackmail, *he* could not risk being seen with her on the outside, as Innis might, so the meet at Yankee Stadium made a lot more sense. For all his charm and humor there was a cold streak of pragmatism in the man. Having lost both wife and son, he had only his reputation left. He would protect it at all costs.

The crowd was on its feet again, but neither Dolly nor Norah moved. *He* knew that Mrs. Rogoff lived directly below Norah, that she was old, alone, crippled, that if she called for help, Norah would respond without question. He knew because Norah had told him while making small talk at dinner the very night of the attack. From the start he'd tried to get Norah off the case. When he couldn't, he'd wined and dined and romanced her and subtly made her think along the lines that suited him; while seeming to oppose her, he'd actually led her. Bits of joyous memories were twisted into sinister and incriminating signs. Norah broke out into a cold sweat.

The crowd groaned. The red light was on—at the wrong end of the ice.

"Boston goal scored by number 10, Jean Ratelle. Unassisted. Time of the goal, 8:58 of the first period." The announcer's statement was accompanied by a few scattered cheers for an ex-Ranger who had been traded.

The two policewomen remained seated and locked in their own private worlds. While Norah struggled with herself Dolly Dollinger was inclined to accept Honn's guilt. She'd always had reservations about him but had supposed it was because he was cutting in on Joe. She had to remind herself that they were not dealing here with just another case of police corruption, to which they'd all unfortunately grown accustomed, but of murder. Multiple murder. And Dolly Dollinger was aghast to discover she'd grown so callous that she accepted murder as simply the next and logical step.

"What are you going to do?" she asked, her voice trembling.

"I don't know," Norah answered. What could she do? What real evidence did she have? None. If she'd had any, he would hardly have let her live.

"Norah? Now what's the matter?"

Hadn't he been constantly warning her that she was in danger? All that talk about staying home, locking the door—she'd bought it, and so undoubtedly had Captain Felix. Be rational, she cautioned herself. How could he afford to have anything happen to her? He would not want anything to happen that could be remotely connected to the case, not now, when Gerald Innis was about to be indicted. He wouldn't dare touch her now. Unless it could be made to appear an accident. Her mind and her emotions struggled with the monstrous. A traffic accident?

No, she had no car. A pedestrian accident in traffic? It might arouse suspicion.

Then Norah thought of Katie Chave.

Katie Chave's death had been an accident and readily accepted as such because there'd been no way for anyone to know that Katie would be in the lingerie department of Gimbels at the precise moment a bomb went off. Norah hadn't mentioned to anyone where she was going tonight and she was certain Dolly hadn't, either. Would it be accepted that nobody knew? One person did know, of course. He knew very well that Norah Mulcahaney and Dolly Dollinger would be at Madison Square Garden tonight for the big game against Boston; he knew in what location they would be sitting, the exact seats, in fact, because he had provided them. Up to now Norah hadn't been able to utter the name even silently to herself. Now it slipped from her on a suspiration of regret. *Sebastian.*

She squared her shoulders and thrust out her chin. If he thought that she would be so lost in mid-Victorian vapors that she couldn't see how he'd manipulated her, then he didn't know Norah Mulcahaney. He didn't begin to know her. But he'd find out. She felt dizzy. The lights flickered in front of her eyes. She grabbed the pipe rail in front of her to steady herself.

"Are you all right?" Dolly asked.

Norah squeezed her eyes shut, then opened them. Everything was back in focus. She bent down to look under the seats. Nothing. Of course not, it wouldn't be there: too obvious. Where, then? Somewhere near . . . Oh, blessed Lord, where?

"What are you looking for? Are you sick? Norah? Maybe we ought to get out of here."

"I think . . . I'm not sure." Once again Norah had to use the rail to steady herself. Then suddenly she pulled her hand back from the cold metal as though it were fiery hot and she'd been singed. She stared at it. She contemplated the length of pipe, reached out and pushed Dolly's coat farther along. There, where the section was joined, were the telltale marks of an inexpert soldering job.

"Call the Bomb Squad, Dolly," Norah whispered. "Get to a phone and call the Bomb Squad right away." It was Dolly's turn to gape and turn pale. "After that get hold of Captain Felix. I'll contact security here and get the evacuation started."

They raced up the stairs, out gate 18, and to the curving inner corridor. The few stragglers out in the hall ignored them. Dolly headed for the nearest bank of phones, and Norah found an usher. She showed her ID.

"Where will I find your security chief?"

At age forty-seven Stan Haugevik could still strong-arm a drunk out of the building and have few, if any, people around realize what was going on. He could sweet-talk an obstreperous celebrity into the custody of his companion, nurse, or chauffeur without arousing resentment. Stanislaus Haugevik had been in security and dealing with the public for twenty-six years. He'd started as a department-store guard—not exactly work, but steady. To relieve the boredom and augment his income because he had a wife and two children one of whom was retarded and required specialized care, Haugevik began to moonlight weekends and nights as a guard at sporting events. Somehow he found the time to attend the John Jay College of Criminal Justice and even got himself admitted to the course run by the FBI in Washington. He became an expert in security. Haugevik had talked a would-be jumper down from the top row of the stadium at Forest Hills during the U.S. Open. He had disarmed a man who had invaded an Olympic star's dressing room during the Ice-Capades. Only recently he had been of considerable help to the police brass in maintaining order during demonstrations by the police rank and file in front of the Garden. The security chief, wearing a bold plaid sports jacket and snappy alpine-style fedora complete with speckled feather in the headband, was on the main level of the arena just behind the Ranger bench when Norah located him. He was a stolid, stoic man, but what Sergeant Mulcahaney now confronted him with sent cold fear coursing through his veins.

"We can't stop the game and announce there's a bomb in the building," he protested. "It would start a panic for sure."

"Why don't you just quietly send some of your men up to section 233 and get that cleared?"

"Once those people start leaving, assuming we can get them to leave without telling them why, the rest of the house is going to notice."

"So then you make your announcement."

In frustration and uncertainty he puffed out his lean cheeks. "You say there's a bomb in the handrail. I've got to have more than just your say-so to stop the game, evacuate the building."

"You'll have it, all right, if the bomb goes off while we're standing here talking. You'll also have the panic you're so afraid of. And quite a few dead bodies."

Haugevik mopped his brow.

"There just no way he could have got in. No way. We maintain a tight security system."

"How about your work crew? Could he have got hold of a uniform somehow?"

Haugevik shook his head. "Every man on that crew is a veteran of fifteen or twenty years and is personally known to us. No stranger could substitute without being immediately spotted."

"So maybe he slipped in with the vendors and concessionaires?"

"Every person that walks into this building has to show ID."

"So he borrowed somebody's." Norah was getting more and more anxious. "Do you personally know every kid that hawks beer and ice cream during a game? No security system in the world is foolproof." The sick feeling at the pit of her stomach was getting worse. "Please, this is no time to argue. Why don't you do as we discussed? Send your men up to section 233 and get the evacuation started. By the time announcement becomes necessary a big part of the vulnerable area will have been cleared. Maybe all of it. People are so wrapped up in the game it will take a while before they realize anything unusual is going on."

Haugevik had not reached his present positon by being afraid to make a decision or by being slow about it. Once he accepted the necessity, Haugevik wasted no time. He deployed his force expertly. As Norah had predicted, at least one segment of the threatened area was well on its way to being cleared before the worried buzz spread through the vast crowd. The referee then stopped the game and the players filed off the ice, and still the crowd remained no more than bewildered. Then the announcement: "Ladies and gentlemen, your attention, please. We have been asked by the police to evacuate the building. There is no danger. There is no danger. Please walk, do not run, to the nearest exit. The evacuation is merely a precaution. There is no danger."

Stunned silence. After a couple of seconds and still in relative quiet, the seventeen thousand five hundred got to their feet and started edging into the aisles, uncertain, slightly dazed, but in good order. Of course it didn't last. It couldn't.

"Fire? It could be a fire."

The whisper originated high up, way up in the highest gallery just under the rafters. It was transmitted from person to person, spreading as though it were itself the flickering flame of a wind-borne holocaust. It grew into a cry. The cry became a shriek, a ululation from thousands of throats. People began to push and shove, to jump over seats and fight to get ahead, screaming till that first whisper sinking down from the top of the building became a blanket of sound that settled over the empty ice rink like a malevolent cloud. It reached Haugevik, who now gave further instructions to the announcer.

"There is no fire, ladies and gentlemen. Please be calm. I repeat: there is no fire. No fire. You are safe. The threatened area has already been cleared. The rest of the building is being vacated purely as a precaution." The announcer's voice was professionally even, but the man himself was shaking.

The security chief now signaled the organist, who responded with a mighty chord and then went into the first tune that came into his head: "The Surrey with the Fringe on Top."

Norah, in the outer corridor of the second promenade helping to direct the evacuation, was startled. Then she grinned. It might not be appropriate, but it was doing the job. People hadn't perceptibly slackened pace, but they didn't seem to be quite so frantic, shoving a bit less. The music did help, she thought.

As the very last spectator, a booze-flushed, lurching, two-hundred-pounder, made his way out of the corridor to the escalator, all the while muttering darkly about getting his money back, rain checks, rescheduling, Norah breathed a sigh of relief and took a moment to relish the silence of the empty building. Then she heard steps coming up the fire stairs. Could that be the Bomb Squad already? She went around just as the door opened and the first of the squad, wearing wellpadded jacket, baggy pants, and what looked like a deep-sea diver's helmet, lumbered toward her, kit in hand.

"Am I glad to see you," she exclaimed. "Come on. I think I know exactly where it is. I'll show you."

Without waiting, Norah started back to gate 18. She turned right, ran quickly down the steps to row A, where she and Dolly had been sitting. "There." She pointed to the pipe rail and the lumpy join. "It's got to be in there. There's nowhere else it could be."

She turned expectantly, but there was no one behind her. She was alone in the vast and empty arena. Where was he? Why hadn't he followed her? What was he waiting for? There wasn't any time to waste; the bomb might go off at any moment. She opened her mouth to call and in that instant knew the answer. He had not followed her because the bomb was due to go off and he knew it. He knew, because he had put it there.

The man in the protective suit and helmet was the killer.

Norah ran, ran as far and as fast she she could from seats 1 and 2, row A. section 233, but not out through gate 18 and the false safety of the corridor on the other side of that concrete wall. He would be there. Surely he would be there waiting. She reasoned that he would prefer not to kill her by any direct action, not to shoot or knife or strangle her—not out of sentiment, but simply to avoid the appearance of murder. Of course, he would if he had to. She ran past gate 18, staying inside the arena and hoping that she could get far enough from the source of . . .

The explosion.

Instinctively Norah threw herself down on the floor.

The noise was like nothing she had ever heard before. The

ground under her shook, the whole building seemed to quiver on
its foundations. She clasped her arms over her head and closed
her eyes and waited for the rubble to fall and bury her.

Actually, it wasn't as terrible as she'd expected. The echo was
almost worse than the original detonation. It seemed as though it
would go on reverberating forever under the vaulted ceiling into
infinity. But finally it lessened, faded, and died. In its place came
something that started as a soft sibilance like the rush of summer
rain, then turned into a cloudburst of falling debris– Again Norah
hunched in on herself to wait until it, too, subsided and was followed by a thick mist of choking dust.

Still on the floor, she dared to open her eyes and look out from
beneath her arms like a child awakening in the night. It was almost dark. A heavy pall of smoke hung over the entire building,
so thick that at first Norah thought the power had been cut off.
Then she made out shafts of light aimed down on the ice—
spotlights cutting through the acrid smog. Structurally, as far as
she could tell, the building appeared intact. In fact, the damage
appeared to be limited to the immediate area in which she and
Dolly had been sitting. That was a shambles. Entire sections of
seats were ripped loose, their metal supporters contorted into
hallucinogenic sculptures. The seats were hurled in all directions,
and one unit of orange-upholstered chairs had been set down on
center ice, as though put there for the use of very special specta-
tors.

Trying to get up, Norah became aware of a heavy weight on her
back. Panic seized her. She was pinned, pinned under God knew
how many pounds of what? Was her back injured? She felt no
pain. Cautiously she tried to move her legs. They responded.
Thank God. She calmed considerably. Not able to turn and look
to see what had fallen on her, she squirmed to test its weight and
bulk and decided that whatever it was was not resting completely
on her but was supported at one end. She managed to turn her
head. It was the mangled undercarriage of a seat section and the
end of it rested on the flight of stairs going up. She could, she
thought, if she were careful, wriggle free without causing the
burden to shift.

Concentrating on the maneuver, Norah didn't hear the footsteps. Using the shaft under the seats as the hypotenuse, she had
just moved inward toward the right angle where she was free of
the weight and was resting before crawling out when the hackles of

danger warned her. Squinting, she could barely make him out as he moved toward her through the settling black grit, picking his steps as deliberately as the first astronaut on the moon.

The scream never rose from her thoat. It would have been useless: the scream would float up above the spotlights and the silent loudspeakers and lose itself as the explosion and its echo had done. There was nobody near enough to hear. Not yet. But there would be. Soon.

If she could hold out . . . just a little while. Cringing, Norah watched the camouflaged figure coming closer at the same unvarying, inexorable pace. And then, instead of screaming, she gave a great sigh and started to laugh—oh, weakly, but laugh—till the tears came and turned to sobs. That weird, alien figure coming at her was not Sebastian. It wasn't tall enough or thin enough. It moved differently: Sebastian walked with a slight list to the right; she knew Sebastian's walk; he could not disguise it from her even if he tried. The sob of relief was tinged with shame. She told herself that she had never really believed him guilty, but, of course, she had. Then she asked herself, would she so readily have accepted Joe's guilt? She knew she would not. She thought that she would have had to see Joe actually commit the murder with her own eyes, and even then she would have searched for a reason to justify it.

So if the killer wasn't Sebastian, who was it?

If she lay there long enough she was bound to find out, Norah thought ruefully—much good it would do her. Somehow she had to get on her feet and move and keep moving till somebody—police, fire department, or the real Bomb Squad—showed up. She had dragged herself far enough to clear the beam, but as she started to get up the ragged metal edge tore her slacks and ripped into the flesh of her thigh. Instinctively she screamed, then clenched her teeth on the pain as she felt the blood spurt. Back down on her knees, she crawled a little farther till she was sure that she was clear. Getting up, she almost screamed again as her right leg crumpled under her weight. She must have twisted it, perhaps when she fell. She tried a second time to put weight on it. Waves of pain assaulted her. One after the other she fought them off, blinding flashes of color separated by brief periods of easeful blackness. It would have been so simple just to close her eyes, slip to the floor, and let unconsciousness bring relief. Her leg would not support her. There was nothing she could do to save herself. . . Even as she registered the hopelessness of her situation, Norah clung to the concrete ledge of the upper section of seats and pulled herself along, putting her weight on the other leg with its bleeding thigh.

And he kept coming at the same, steady pace.

He made an easy target, Norah thought. If she shot him, she could hardly miss. But by the time she got her weapon out of her purse he would have finished her. She wasn't anxious to precipitate the showdown. He could in fact move in and finish her at any time. They both knew it. She was content to let him draw it out as much as he wanted.

Yet he must know that he didn't have a limitless amount of time, Norah thought as she continued doggedly to pull herself along. He must realize that a full contingent of emergency forces was on the way, that at any moment police, firemen, and the real Bomb Squad would be swarming all over the arena, up the aisles, along the rows.

Why did he persist? Why didn't he leave well enough alone? The case was closed. Though Innis would be charged only with the murder of Pilar Nieves, once he was convicted, the other murders would be considered solved as well.

Would it do any good to talk to him, to point that out? Surely he knew it. Shrewd as he'd shown himself, he must realize that killing Norah would reopen the case. Obviously he didn't care. He must be obsessed with hatred to stalk her like this, Norah thought, shuddering; obsessed, to risk being caught almost in the act of murder. What had she ever done to him? she wondered as she continued her slow and painful progress. She tried to fix on the answer, which lay just at the edge of her subconscious.

If she asked him would he tell her? Before he killed her?

Norah didn't need to look down to know that she was losing a lot of blood. She could feel the fabric of her slacks, wet and warm, clinging to her useless leg. Her strength was failing. If she could just manage to reach the ramp of exit 19, just ahead, and to turn the corner . . . With an effort of will, forgetting all else, concentrating only on moving, she hauled herself the last couple of feet. Once around the corner and out of his sight momentarily, she sprawled on the cold floor. Surging pain brought her back to consciousness. Delving into her handbag, Norah now got her gun.

It wasn't a bad place to make a stand, she thought. It gave her one big advantage—she would see him before he saw her. When he came around the corner he would be instinctively looking straight ahead rather than down and to one side, where she lay crouched. In that brief second's hesitation before he shifted his gaze she would have the first shot.

She heard the faint beeping of patrol cars and the wailing of fire sirens. They're here, she thought. Thank God. She imagined the vehicles screeching to a halt, the men pouring out and bursting into the building. Relief brought cold sweat and her grip on the gun relaxed—then tightened again. It wouldn't happen that fast. There were procedures to be followed in this kind of situation.

She slipped off the safety.

On her knees, side supported by the wall, gun in both hands and arms extended as close to the combat position advocated by the NYPD as she could manage, Norah waited.

Don't shoot unless you have to, then shoot to kill.

Norah had always had considerable mental reservation about that tenet. Now, in this situation, she must follow it. She would have the first shot, but she would not have the second. Her arms trembled; she could not hold the position much longer, but she didn't dare shift.

He appeared at the corner, peering straight up the ramp, exactly as she'd anticipated. She fired instantly. Whether out of instinct, or because her arms had grown weary, she lowered her aim just a fraction—it seemed a fraction, but it was enough so that the bullet hit well below the heart. The man in the padded coat and helmet jerked at the impact, then, clutching at his wound, sank in an eerie kind of slow motion till he lay on the floor beside Norah.

She reached for the gun he'd dropped.

"Damn you." The voice was muffled inside the helmet. "Damn . . ."

Not the voice but the tone, its bitter resentment, jogged her memory. The first time she'd heard it she'd ignored it, attributing it to the antifeminine bias that some men in the department still nurtured. She should not have ignored it the second time; she should have sensed that it was personal that second time, when he'd come to ask her help. But she hadn't got the message, so he'd firebombed her car.

All just to get his sister off the force?

He was breathing in heavy, irregular gasps, sucking at the air. Norah crawled closer and raised the visor. The hate she saw in that moment as she leaned over Francis Xavier Quinn and looked into his glittering amber eyes made her pull back quickly.

Norah had gone to see Mairead but had not said what Francis Quinn had wanted her to say. On the contrary, she had gone to check him out; she had implied to his sister that he was under suspicion. Had Mairead somehow let that slip? Francis Quinn idolized his sister; if he thought Norah had denigrated him in her eyes in any way he would want revenge.

He would make Norah pay, no matter what the cost.

That explained this last heedlessly desperate attempt to kill her, but what about the actual murders? According to Mairead, her twin brother had scarcely known Eve Bednarski, might have given her a lift once or twice, but even that was a long time ago. Could Mairead have been wrong? Eve was a sexy number. Why shouldn't Francis have been as susceptible as everybody else? Could Mairead have suspected? Was that the reason for her sudden urge to cooperate? Was that why she'd presented herself to Norah with her opportune recollections about her classmate—to divert attention from Francis? If so, how much of what she'd told Norah was true and how much fabrication?

Though Mairead didn't talk about the bond between them as openly and compulsively as her brother did, there was no doubt she felt very close to him. It was evident in the way she'd rushed to his defense—instantly, hotly, and convincingly providing him with an alibi for the night on which Norah had been attacked. Was it then that Mairead had first begun to suspect what her twin had done?

At last Norah heard the sounds she'd been straining to hear—voices, footsteps, the drag of equipment. At last firemen and police were inside—cautiously making their way, wary of fallen timbers and weakened supports, and of the possible presence of a killer. She could hear them down on the main floor. From there they could not see her and Quinn even if they should look up. She could call out, of course. She looked at the wounded man. How bad was he? He seemed to be breathing normally; his eyes were open; he was conscious, but if he, too, heard the sounds below he gave no indication. She would not call to her rescuers, Norah decided, not yet. They would be there soon enough. She hoped they would not arrive too soon.

"Want to tell me about it, Frank? Want to tell me why you killed Eve and the other women?"

No answer.

If it was a crime of passion, if he killed Big Red because she betrayed him with other men, then why Pilar Nieves and Audrey
Ochs? "Mairead said you dated Eve," Norah lied. "Were you in
love with her?"

"In love? With her? She was scum. *Scum.*"

The virulence was startling and shocking. "Then why did you
kill her?"

He turned his head away.

"Were you involved in the drug operation with her? You, not
Innis?"

He remained obdurately silent. Having provoked one outbrust,
Norah groped for a way to provoke another. "Your sister says—"

"You leave Mairead out of this. She had nothing to do with it.
Nothing. Leave her out."

"I can't."

"I tell you she had nothing to do with it. She's not involved."

The facts were beginning to fall into a logical sequence. Instinctively Norah knew that this time she had it right. "Mairead knew
you were going with Eve, that you were crazy about her. She also
knew, from way back, that Eve was out to make a big score any
way she could. She also must have known what Eve was turning
in from her buys; after all, Mairead was working in the property
clerks office, wasn't she?"

Quinn groaned.

"Mairead knew what was going on. That would make her an
accessory after the fact, at the very least."

"No, no, she didn't know. She didn't know. I swear. I made
sure she didn't know. It was just Eve and me, the two of us.
That's the truth. I was crazy about Eve, but she wanted more out
of life than being a policeman's wife or his widow. I couldn't
blame her." He gasped. "She could have had . . . any man . . .
she wanted." He gasped again. Evidently talking, especially from
a prone position, was becoming difficult. He turned on his side
and raised himself partially on one arm. "The operation was her
idea; I couldn't say no. Eve skimmed the junk and I got rid of it.
Mairead didn't know. The amounts were so small that we never
turned any of it in directly. It was always picked up from the precinct by somebody from the lab and delivered to the property
clerk. Mairead never signed any of the receipts, never."

There were other ways for her to have found out, Norah thought, but said nothing.

"We set ourselves a certain goal, a certain amount, and after that we were going to quit, go away somewhere, and lead a normal life. But when the time came, Eve didn't want to quit. She wanted more. It was easy, so easy. She said if I wanted out, okay, she'd find somebody to replace me—no sweat. It wasn't the money she was after, because we didn't spend a cent of it; we didn't want to attract attention; it wasn't the money but the excitement she was hooked on, the thrills, the danger . . ."

So there it was, Norah thought, in all its simplicity and primeval ugliness: the pattern for murder—jealousy combined with greed.

"How did you know I'd be here?" she asked. "How did you know Dolly and I would be at the game and where we'd be sitting?"

Now the footsteps and voices came from the outer corridor and Quinn heard them, too. He slumped back to the floor and closed his eyes.

"Frank, how did you know where I'd be tonight? Who told you?"

"Norah? Where are you? Norah . . ."

Sebastian, that was Sebastian calling. She didn't try to guess how he'd come to be there, she was only glad that she'd have this one more chance to see him now that she understood her own feeling toward him. He'd sense the difference and she hoped that he could accept the friendship she'd offer. Of course, she could never tell him how she'd made the adjustment; she could never let him know that she'd actually suspected him . . . even for a moment.

When Norah awoke she discovered that she was lying on a stretcher in the corridor. Her first sensation was the thobbing in her thigh and, glancing down, she saw that it was swaddled in bandages. An IV bottle dangled overhead. Strange faces passed in and out of focus as she drifted in and out of consciousness. One of the faces was Sebastian's. She fixed on it. He was gray as though he, too, had lost blood, but he smiled when he saw that she was conscious.

"You're going to be all right," he murmured. "It's only a flesh wound. You'e going to be all right."

"Quinn?" she asked, because she couldn't see him anywhere.

"He'll live," Honn replied shortly. "He'll live and he'll stand trial. Don't talk. Save your strength."

Dolly appeared at Honn's shoulder. "Oh, Norah . . ."

Norah managed a smile for her friend but stuck to what was uppermost in her mind. "How did he know . . . Quinn? How did he know I'd be here?"

"It was my fault," Dolly wailed.

"My fault," Sebastian grunted.

They looked at each other.

"There was nothing wrong with your telling your family you and Norah were coming to the hockey game," Honn said.

"But I shouldn't have mentioned your name, Captain. I never should have done that."

"Will one of you please explain what you're talking about?" Norah broke in.

Dolly swallowed. "My mom got a call this afternoon from somebody at the precinct trying to locate me. The caller said it was urgent, and my mother had no reason to doubt it. She said that if I wasn't at your place then she didn't know where I was right that minute but that she did know you and I were coming to the hockey game tonight. The caller then asked if she knew where we'd be sitting. She didn't know, of course, but she understood we'd got the tickets from a friend, a Captain Honn." Dolly groaned. "She was trying to be helpful."

"And I was just as anxious to be helpful," Sebastian admitted ruefully. "The con was that the call was for Dolly. If it had been for you I would have checked it out. But she said Dolly's mother had had a heart attack, that she was okay, in the hospital and resting comfortably, but that naturally the family was anxious to contact Dolly."

"She?" Norah whispered.

"From then on, it was a repeat. I asked her if she'd tried your place and she said she had but there was no answer. So then I told her I had no idea where Dolly might be at the moment but I happened to know the two of you would be at the hockey game tonight."

"A woman . . . it was a woman."

"Right. I figure Quinn got his sister to make the call for him. Mairead . . . isn't that her name?"

Mairead, Norah thought. It always came back to sweet, innocent, fragile Mairead Quinn.

"I gave her the seat location. I volunteered it. Couldn't wait," Sebastian Honn exclaimed bitterly.

But Norah had stopped listening. *Leave Mairead out of it. She's not involved. She didn't know what was going on.* Quinn had been determined to protect his twin sister. Would he have asked her, even allowed her to make the calls for him? Norah didn't think so. Quinn had sworn that Mairead never received any of the junk that Bednarski and her partner turned in, not even secondhanded through the lab messenger. She never signed for it. She made damn sure not to, Norah thought. But she was in it, in it right up to her lovely, graceful neck. She directed Norah's attention away from Francis by implicating Innis, but not to save her brother—to save herself. Did she regret having gone to Norah? Was she afraid she'd said too much? What had she said exactly? Norah strained to remember.

Of course, yes. Mairead had reluctantly agreed that Francis had indeed given Eve Bednarski a lift now and then after class. The occasions must have been frequent enough so that Mairead though Norah would find out on her own if she bothered to ask around. Having admitted it, Mairead hastened to cover up by adding that, of course, Francis had given them all lifts at one time or another. Norah had taken it to mean all the women in Mairead's class, but she realized now that that was not what Mairead had been thinking. How often, she wondered, had she and Captain Felix and the rest of the team speculated on just what basis, beyond their all having got their jobs back through the court order, the killer had made his selections? Now she knew. Those particular victims had been chosen because they had been Mairead Quinn's special friends and because her brother was acquainted with them through having once or twice given them a ride home.

Fearing that Norah might interpret the subconscious import of what she'd said, Mairead had sent Francis out to hunt her.

Quinn could have had leftover explosives from the firebombing of her car. It would have been no trick to assemble another device.

"When did your mother get that call?" she asked.

"Early afternoon."

"Around three," Honn specified.

Plenty of time to organize everything, Norah thought. The plot was the same, but the characters were reversed. It was Mairead who had been in the drug deal with Eve, and Frank who had found out and determined to cut his sister loose. He killed the other women to cover up the drug angle and then he killed Eve Bednarski to rid his sister of her accomplice. But as long as she remained on the force he couldn't deprive Mairead of the means and opportunity to set up again. So he had appealed to Norah.

Frank Quinn was indeed obsessed, but not with hatred for Norah or Eve or policewomen in general. He was obsessed with love—for his sister.

"Mairead," Norah murmured. "Mairead is responsible."

"Sh." Sebastian bent over her. "Never mind. Rest."

She was being wheeled along the corridor with Sebastian walking alongside.

There was no way that Mairead could be made to pay, Norah thought—not on the drug charge or on the murder charge. She might conceivably even turn states evidence against her brother just to make sure. And he would not utter a word against her. Norah closed her eyes.

"Hold it. Wait a minute."

The stretcher stopped. Her eyes flew open. Her heart accelerated its beat.

"Wait a minute. Let me through, please. Excuse me, Captain. If you don't mind, I'll take over now."

Norah smiled up at her husband. "You weren't supposed to get here till Tuesday."

Joe Capretto grinned. "I got lonesome. I couldn't wait any longer—not two days, not two hours. I got on the first available plane out of Fiumicino and here I am."

He'd put on weight, got himself a terrific tan, and was handsomer than ever. "Nobody called or wrote you to tell you to come?" Norah asked.

"Nobody."

"Not Dad or any of the girls or anybody else? Nobody told you anything?"

"What's to tell?"

"Nothing."

"Good."

It didn't matter whether he'd been sent for or had come on his own, Norah decided. It didn't matter at all.